Raven's Feast

Raven's Feast

Hakon's Saga Book II

Eric Schumacher

To Marie, Aidan, Lily, and the rest of my family, for your love, patience and support

Acknowledgements

This book may never have come to be without the advise, support and help of a handful of individuals. First and foremost, I need to thank Marg Gilks and Lori Weathers, whose keen eyes helped shape the story for public consumption. I am indebted to Gordon Monks, chief marshal of "The Vikings" re-enactment group, and the rest of the early readers, who served as an invaluable source of insight and feedback during the final days of writing. I want to thank Creativia for taking a chance on not just one of my stories but two. And last but certainly not least, I want to thank my readers, who have asked for this sequel and who have waited patiently for me to finish it. It is to you all, and to the countless others who have gladly accompanied me on this journey, that I owe a huge debt of gratitude.

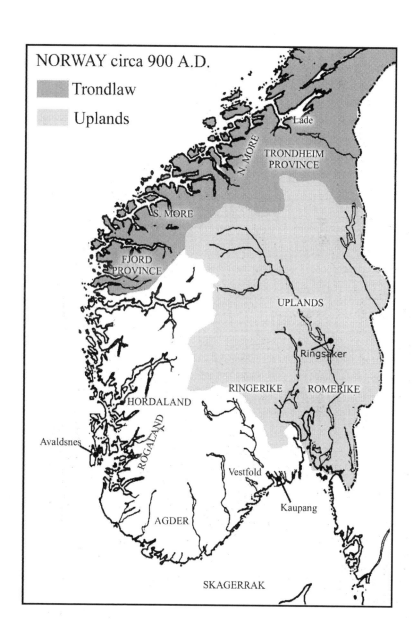

NORWAY circa 900 A.D.

Trondlaw

Uplands

Lade

N. MORE

TRONDHEIM
PROVINCE

S. MORE

FJORD
PROVINCE

UPLANDS

Ringsaker

RINGERIKE   ROMERIKE

HORDALAND

ROGALAND

Avaldsnes

Vestfold

Kaupang

AGDER

SKAGERRAK

Glossary

Aesir – One of the main tribes of deities venerated by the pre-Christian Norse. Old Norse: Æsir.

Balder – One of the Aesir gods. He is often associated with love, peace, justice, purity, and poetry. Old Norse: Baldr (pronounced "BALD-er").

Balder's Eyelash – A chamomile substitute also known as sea mayweed. It is found in many coastal areas of Northern Europe, including Scandinavia and Iceland, often growing in sand or amongst beach pebbles.

bonder – Free men (farmers, craftsmen) who enjoyed rights such as the use of weapons and the right to attend law-things. They constituted the middle class. Old Norse: baendr.

byrnie – A (usually short sleeved) chain mail shirt that hung to the upper thigh. Old Norse: brynja.

Dominica – Day of God. Sunday.

Dreki – Old Norse for "dragon" or "serpent."

Frey – Brother to the goddess Freya. He is often associated with virility and prosperity, with sunshine and fair weather. Old Norse: Freyr.

Freya – Sister to god Frey. She is often associated with love, sex, beauty, fertility, gold, magic, war, and death. Old Norse: Freyja.

Frigga – The wife of the god Odin and the highest ranking of the Aesir goddesses. She is often associated with love, marriage, and destiny. Old Norse: Frigg.

fylke (pl. **fylker**) – Old Norse for "folkland," which has come to mean "county" in modern use.

fyrd – An Old English army made up of citizens of a shire that was mobilized for short periods of time, e.g. to defend against a particular threat.

godi – A heathen priest or chieftain. Old Norse: goði.

Hel – A giantess and/or goddess who rules over Niflheim, the underworld where the dead dwell. Old Norse: Hel.

hird – a personal retinue of armed companions who formed the nucleus of a household guard. Hird means "household." Old Norse hirð.

hirdman (pl. **hirdmen**) – A member or members of the hird. Old Norse: hirðman.

hlaut – The blood of sacrificed animals.

jarl – Old Norse for "earl."

jarldom – The area of land that a jarl ruled.

kaupang – Old Norse for "marketplace." It is also the name of the main market town in Norway that existed around AD 800–950.

knarr – A type of merchant ship. Old Norse: knǫrr.

Nidhogg – The name of the dragon that gnaws at a root of the world tree, Yggdrasil. Old Norse: Níðhǫggr.

Niflheim – The mist-filled afterlife for those who did not die a heroic or notable death. It is ruled by Hel. Old Norse: Niflheimr.

Night Mare – The Night Mare is an evil spirit that rides on people's chests while they sleep, bringing bad dreams. Old Norse: Mara.

nithing – A person without honor. Old Norse: níðingr.

Njord – A god associated with sea, seafaring, wind, fishing, wealth, and crop fertility. Old Norse: Njörðr.

Odal rights – The ownership rights of inheritable land held by a family or kinsmen.

Odin – Husband to Frigga. The god associated with healing, death, royalty, knowledge, battle, and sorcery. He oversees Valhall, the Hall of the Slain. Old Norse: Óðinn.

Ostara – The celebration of the goddess of spring that bears that goddess's name.

seax – A knife or short sword. Also known as scramaseax, or wounding knife.

skald – A poet. Old Norse: skald or skáld.

shield wall – A shield wall was a "wall of shields" formed by warriors standing in formation shoulder to shoulder, holding their shields so that they abut or overlap. Old Norse: skjaldborg.

steer board – A rudder affixed to the right stern of a ship. The origin of the word "starboard." Old Norse: stýri (rudder) and borð (side of the ship).

skol – A toast to others when drinking. Old Norse: skál.

thing – The governing assembly of a Viking society or region, made up of the free people of the community and presided over by lawspeakers. Old Norse: þing.

Thor – A hammer-wielding god associated with thunder, lightning, storms, oak trees, strength, the protection of mankind. Old Norse: Þórr.

thrall – A slave.

Valhall (also **Valhalla**) – The hall of the slain presided over by Odin. It is where brave warriors chosen by valkyries go when they die. Old Norse: Valhöll.

Well of Urd – A well or lake that lies beneath the world tree, Yggdrasil. It is also from this well that the Fates (or Norns) come. Old Norse: Urðarbrunnr.

wergeld – Also known as "man price," it was the value placed on every being and piece of property.

Yggdrasil – An immense mythical tree that connects the nine worlds in Norse cosmology. Old Norse: Askr Yggdrasils.

Yngling – Refers to the Fairhair dynasty, which descended from the kings of Uplands, Norway.

Part I

Odin's sated birds
Afterwards clawed the fliers;
The ravens sought their food,
And glutted their lust.
Hakon's *drapa*

Chapter 1

The Vik, Summer, AD 935

Hakon sank to his knees before the broad trunk of a maple tree and clutched the cross that hung from his neck.

Closing eyes that stung from lack of sleep, he tried to recall a prayer he had learned in the Christian court of his foster father, King Athelstan, but it would not come. Instead, images invaded his thoughts that were neither wanted nor welcome. Images of Erik and his bloodied battle-axe. A crimson-faced Gunnar roaring as he beheaded the youth who had speared him. The glint of Ivar's blade as it slashed Aelfwin's neck and her life poured forth, dark and horrid, onto her killer's hands. Quickly they came, one after the other, uninhibited; and just as quickly, Hakon's bloodshot eyes opened to erase them.

For three days now — ever since the battle against Erik — the visions had accosted his young mind. They came in the quiet moments to torment his thoughts and steal his peace. When he rested. When he slept. When he prayed. Chilling images that varied in their horror, yet whose vividness never faltered. Fighting them was like fighting the mist.

"You curse your luck, boy."

Hakon flinched at the sudden voice beside him, and his hand instinctively reached for the grip of his seax, but it was only Egil Woolsark, the aging leader of his household guard. He had once been a renowned warrior in the army of Hakon's father, Harald. Now he served Hakon and was the only man in Hakon's employ allowed to call his teenage king "boy." He usually used the term affectionately, unless it involved the Christian God, as it did now.

Egil nodded at the cross in Hakon's hand, the movement shifting his white strands of hair to briefly reveal his bald scalp. "The battlefield belongs to Odin, not your White Christ."

Hakon glowered. It was a common rift between them, and he was tiring of Egil's derision. "Save your words for the afterlife, Egil."

Egil snorted and changed the subject. "The enemy moves."

Hakon pushed himself to his feet. Though he'd seen only fourteen or fifteen winters — he had lost count of which — his body felt far older. The battle with his brother Erik had battered and bruised him, and the subsequent march to the coast had taxed his limbs, a reality that became even more apparent as he followed Egil through the woods toward the enemy camp.

Egil knelt at the edge of the woods and Hakon dropped down beside him. The camp lay but an arrow's flight away, a few paces inland from a small beach. It was a crude base, home to a motley rearguard whose mission it was to protect the ships that rocked in the nearby surf. Within the camp's protective fencing, warriors scrambled to dismantle their tents and pack their sea chests. Camp women helped gather their supplies.

Hakon eyed the enemy coldly. He felt no remorse for their impending doom. The crushing loss of Aelfwin had frozen him to such feelings. Besides, he had pushed his army hard to get to this place; he could not deny them the weapons and armor and arm-rings of the enemy warriors, for they were the spoils of victory. Nor would he let these nameless men take the ships beached on the shore, especially the one that used to belong to his father. *Dreki*, or *Dragon*, was her name. Even from this distance, Hakon could see her tall sides and sweeping prow towering over the other ships resting beside her.

"We should attack now, while all is still chaos," growled Egil.

"Aye. Bring them forward," Hakon responded.

Egil flashed a grin full of rotten teeth and moved off to ready the men, including Hakon's allies, Jarls Sigurd and Tore.

Little by little, his warriors crept through the forest and fanned out on either side of Hakon, their weapons drawn but held low. No one wore helmets or metal armor for fear the sound and sheen would alert the enemy. Within the camp, the warriors were oblivious to their peril, for all were intent on leaving.

Hakon pulled his seax from its sheath and squeezed its leather grip. It had a shorter blade than his long sword, which he had named Quern-biter, and was a better weapon for the close-quarters fighting of the shield wall. Slowly he slipped his arm into the straps of his shield, wincing as his bruised forearm slid across the wood. He exhaled slowly, steeling himself for the coming bloodshed.

"Loose!" came Egil's command from somewhere back in the trees.

Arrows arced through the morning air, seeking their prey with a wicked hiss. In the camp, three warriors crumpled to the ground. Another two grabbed at the missiles now protruding from their limbs. Screams shattered the morning calm. Seagulls scattered with angry cries.

Hakon charged from the underbrush as a second volley of arrows sent even more men to their death. Shield up and short sword ready, he sprinted, his aching body now alive with adrenaline, his battle cry joining the yells of his sword-brothers who charged beside him. Ahead of him, Hakon's friend Toralv hacked with his axe at the twine holding the gate shut. Hakon kicked the gate open and charged into the camp, shield high, ready for the missiles he knew would come. And come they did. An arrow ricocheted off his shield rim and lodged in the turf by his feet. A spear followed, slamming into the center of his shield and sending a stab of pain across his forearm. He yanked it free and moved on.

"Shield wall!" Hakon yelled at his men.

With practiced skill, his front rank came together beside him, overlapping their shields with his. To his right stood Egil. To his left, the young giant Toralv. Behind them, the second rank brought its shields up and readied itself. Jarl Sigurd's men fanned out to his right. Tore's line moved left. Before them, the enemy rallied around their leader, a brute of a man who carried only a sword and shield and wore neither armor nor helm. They too formed a shield wall, though in the face of Hakon's army, it looked pathetically small. Still, they did not lack in courage. They pounded their weapons on the shield rims and urged the attackers to come and die on their blades.

"Forward!" Hakon yelled.

His men advanced, their shields locked and weapons ready to strike. The enemy took a step backward, retreating with surprising order. The camp women scattered like rats in a burning hall. Some made for the ships. Others for the safety of the trees. Hakon's army ignored them, concentrating instead on the threat aligned before them.

"Faster!" implored Hakon. He could not let them reach their ships. His ships.

Hakon's warriors began to jog, doing their best to keep their shields even. The enemy continued their retreat. A few of their less seasoned warriors broke ranks and ran for the ships. The leader bellowed for the others to hold the line. He was not a man afraid to die, for despite the overwhelming numbers coming at him, he kept his men focused and ready.

The lines met with a thunderous clash that echoed across the beach. Hakon stared at the youthful face of the warrior before him. After the battle, he would remember that there had been fear in the boy's eyes, but in the heat of battle such things didn't register — all that mattered was surviving. And so Hakon stabbed over his shield rim at that face. His blade struck something, though just what he could not tell, for all was chaos and jostling. He pulled his seax back just as a spear point slid past his shoulder. An axe blade followed, hooking the top of his shield. Hakon pulled back sharply, yanking the axe-wielder forward and off balance. Egil sliced his blade across the warrior's thigh. As the man faltered, Toralv hacked into his neck and the warrior dropped dead at Hakon's feet.

Hakon stepped over the body, locked his shield with Toralv's again, and continued pressing forward. Beside him, Egil roared as he brought his sword down on a man's exposed head, splitting his skull.

A cheer rose suddenly, and Hakon ventured a glance about. The enemy leader had fallen, and so too had his standard. The enemy shield wall crumbled and men broke ranks and ran. Hakon's army pursued them, slicing the hapless cowards in the back as they reached the shore or tried to climb aboard the ships. Around the standard a pocket of warriors fought on, but they too soon fell under the relentless blades of their assailants. Hakon's army swarmed the ships, attacking the women and the few men who tried to protect them, for the battle frenzy was upon them now and nothing would stop them until their anger and lust were slaked.

Hakon watched for a moment, then turned his back to the scene. Behind him rose the screams of the dying and the molested. He closed his mind to it, wanting only to cleanse himself of the blood that clung to his skin and breathe deeply of air not fouled by death.

Tossing his battered shield aside, he knelt on the pebbled strand beside the sea and dipped his hands into the cold water. He scrubbed the dirt and gore from his face and the youthful whiskers that now grew from his jaw, realizing distantly that for the first time, he hadn't vomited after a battle. Though whether that counted as maturity or callousness, he couldn't tell, nor did he wish to know.

Washed and refreshed, he stared at his reflection rippling on the ocean's surface, at the icy eyes, long nose, and wheat-colored tresses. Men said he carried the looks of his late father, King Harald. Whether there was any truth in that, Hakon didn't know, for he had only known his father as an old man, long after his signature "fairhair" had gone white and his eyes rheumy with age.

Calmer now, Hakon gazed at the ships. When he found the one he sought, he approached her reverently, ignoring the corpses draped over her gunwales and floating in the surf beside her hull. *Dragon* was named for the serpent head that adorned the bow-post in battle and for the long, sloping lines of her oaken hull. She could seat thirty-four oarsmen per side, with room for more in the fore and aft decks. It was one of the greatest ships the North had ever seen, and now it was his. Hakon waded into the surf and ran his hand over the carvings that decorated her lines — serpentine designs that depicted the life and adventures of Hakon's celebrated father.

"It is good to see you again, my old friend," Hakon whispered, remembering with a pang of nostalgia all the times his father had sailed off in her to some distant land or battle, leaving Hakon alone with the hope that one day he too might follow his father's path. And now she was his. He smiled at that thought, but his gladness was short-lived, for someone coughed behind him. Hakon turned to see Egil standing on the strand, the crimson feculence of battle spattering his white beard and namesake woolen shirt, or woolsark.

"It is done," Egil said simply. Behind him, the warriors were beginning to strip the enemy dead of their weapons and possessions.

Hakon nodded. "See that the booty is shared equally, and our dead and wounded cared for," he said. "Then fetch the jarls. We have much to discuss." Egil nodded and turned to leave. "And Egil," Hakon called, "wash yourself."

Later that morning, Hakon sat with his war leaders, Jarls Sigurd and Tore, his nephews Gudrod and Trygvi, and Egil. Before them crackled a small fire, for though daylight now brightened the beach, the sun had failed to break through the clouds.

"Today was a great victory!" Sigurd began in his usual boisterous manner. His thick build and auburn mane reminded Hakon of a bear. He ruled a land far to the north called Trondelag, a land Hakon's father had given to Sigurd's father. He was also one of Hakon's closest advisors and the man responsible for bringing Hakon back to the North from Engla-lond to fight Erik. "We should give a sacrifice of thanks to the gods, eh, Hakon?" He winked at his Christian gibe, but Hakon was in no mood for such jests and did not rise to the goading. Nearby, the gulls had gathered their own army and meticulously pecked and tore their way through the corpses. The sight and sound of it sickened Hakon.

Trygvi scratched at the lice in the depths of his unruly brown hair. "That was no great victory, Sigurd. That was but a skirmish in comparison to the battle with Erik." He studied his nails for a moment, then flicked something into the fire.

"It was merely a joke," Sigurd explained, shaking his head at Trygvi's thick-headedness.

Trygvi was the son of Hakon's older half-brother Olav, a brash man who had died for underestimating Erik. Sadly, Trygvi had inherited Olav's propensity to act before thinking, a trait that made him a formidable fighter in the shield wall but not very sensible. What Trygvi said, however, was true: the battle with Hakon's brother, Erik Bloodaxe, and his army of Westerners and Danes had been bitter. Erik's larger force had fought uphill and had eventually broken the shield wall of Hakon's smaller army. Only the late arrival of Jarl Tore and his men had changed the momentum of the fight and crushed the enemy's will.

Hakon looked in Jarl Tore's direction. He, like Sigurd, Gudrod, and Trygvi, was kin. His wife was Hakon's older half-sister Alov, making him Hakon's brother-in-law, which was a strange thing to contemplate, given their difference in age. The past week had been hard on everyone, but especially on Tore, who was no longer a young man and whose tangled gray hair, slumped shoulders, and red-rimmed eyes revealed the strain of two battles in so short a time. Tore caught Hakon's eye and smiled tiredly, stretching the thick scar on his neck, a wound he'd received winters ago that still kept him from speaking, save for well-chosen words, and had earned him the byname "the Silent."

"Battle or skirmish, it doesn't matter," Hakon interjected. "What matters is that we did well today. But there is still much to do. Today we have taken my brother's ships. Now we take his wealth."

Those in the group looked at each other. "What do you propose?" Egil asked as he studied a silver bracelet that had been part of the plunder.

"I propose that we take back Kaupang at Skiringssal." The comment drew all eyes to Hakon.

Long ago Hakon's grandfather, Halfdan the Black, had erected a massive hall in the Vestfold, close to the burial mounds of his forefathers. He called the structure Skiringssal, or the "Shining Hall." At some point a marketplace, or kaupang, had sprung up on the shore of an inlet near the hall. It was the closest thing the North had to a trading town, though it was far smaller than Hedeby in the land of the Danes, or Birka to the east. Bjorn the Chapman, another of Hakon's half-brothers and the father of Gudrod, eventually inherited the land and the hall and built the marketplace into a small town.

Ever jealous of the town's wealth, Erik Bloodaxe killed Bjorn when he came to power and placed a Dane named Ragnvald over the land. Ragnvald's father was a Dane of some import in Jutland, with ties to the Danish king, Gorm. Men had questioned the appointment at first, but it had proven to be one of Erik's wisest moves. It repaired relations with the Danes and brought more Danish traders to the town, which in turn put more gold in Erik's coffers.

Hakon looked at Gudrod and Trygvi. "It is time to retake the land your fathers ruled."

"Nothing would make me happier," Gudrod said, speaking for both of them. Of Hakon's two nephews, he was the slighter man, with a long, thin frame and straight blond hair he often wore in a ponytail. Now it hung straight about his face, covering the wound on his forehead he'd received in the battle with Erik. Like Trygvi, he was older than Hakon, but unlike Trygvi, he was far more clever and industrious.

Sigurd adjusted his hulking frame on the log where he sat and stroked his auburn beard. "Killing Ragnvald could bring the Danes against us."

"I would rather take that risk than let Ragnvald rule," Trygvi said forcefully. "It is our land. Our town."

"I agree that it may cause problems with the Danes, and I also agree that we can't let one of Erik's men rule there. We should attack quickly, before Ragnvald has a chance to prepare." Hakon's icy eyes scanned the faces around him. "I have asked much of you these past days, but I will need your support in one more fight. What say you?"

"Aye," said Gudrod and Trygvi in unison.

Sigurd nodded. "I suppose I have one more fight in me."

Egil shrugged. "I am your man, Hakon. I go where you go."

All eyes turned to Jarl Tore, who kept his gaze on the flames before him. "I will put the question to my men," he responded in his rattling voice. With his damaged neck, every word was a struggle for the graying man. "Those who wish to fight can do so. I will not join them. It's time to let some of the younger whelps earn their fame. I have earned mine already."

Hakon grinned at the boast and patted Tore's shoulder. "I understand, my friend."

He turned back to the others. "We sail on the morrow. Egil, take Trygvi and Gudrod to inspect the ships. We have men enough to sail ten of them, I think, so choose the best and see that they are seaworthy."

"What of the others?" asked Egil. "There are another ten good ships there. It seems a waste to leave them for some no-name to find." Which was true. A good ship could take years and plenty of silver to build. Plus, as Hakon's army grew, the ships would be needed, or so he hoped. But transporting them would take more time and men than he had, especially if he wished to sail on Kaupang quickly.

"Leave that to me," Tore interjected. "We still have our ships moored to the east of here. I will take the remaining ships to my fleet and bring them to Kaupang." He swallowed several times to clear his damaged throat. "Just have the ale ready for me. Getting all of these ships down there will be thirsty work."

"So it is settled," said Hakon. "We will divide the ships equally between us when Jarl Tore brings them." The men grinned at their leader's generosity. He dismissed their grins with a wave. "Now away with you."

Tore and Sigurd remained with Hakon after the others left. They sat silently for a time, each lost in his thoughts. Tore held his hands to the

flames as Sigurd prodded the embers with a stick. Hakon scratched at
the blond stubble on his chin, waiting for them to speak. He knew them
well enough to know that something was on their minds. Finally, he
could bear their silence no longer. "You have something more to say?"

Sigurd's eyes peered out from under his chestnut-colored brows.
"Your victory over Erik is just the beginning, Hakon. When men get
word of his defeat, there will be upstarts ready to take his place. You
must make your victory known and show your strength. Since he
prefers not to fight, let Jarl Tore sail to the west in strength to spread
the word of Erik's defeat."

Tore grunted. "That I will gladly do."

"Is it not strange to send the man we call 'the Silent' to share the
story of my victory with others?" Hakon winked at his kinsman to
show him he meant no offense.

"Before this," he pointed to the scar, "my voice boomed like Thor's
own thunder."

Sigurd rolled his eyes. "That was your farting, old man. Not your
voice."

Hakon laughed. "Then it is done. After you bring the ships to Kaupang, you shall carry my victory message west."

A silence settled back over the group like a winter's snow. Sigurd
poked at the fire again. "There is more, Hakon," he said after a time.
The mirth that moments before had danced in his eyes was now gone.
"You must also consolidate your power. Quickly. The sooner you marry
Groa, the better."

Sigurd had arranged the marriage to guarantee the support of an
area known as the Uplands in the battle against Erik. But the princess
Groa had proven to be ill mannered and repugnant. Worse, she was
the daughter of Ivar, the self-styled king of the Uplands, and the man
who had murdered Hakon's childhood love, Aelfwin, on the eve of the
battle with Erik as a sacrifice to the war gods. The very mention of
Groa and her father stoked a black fury Hakon had been struggling to
suppress — a fury that now began to boil over.

Sigurd must have seen it, for he held up his hands to calm his king. "I see in your face the pain it brings you. Nevertheless, this is your oath and the price of your kingship."

"You know nothing of the pain I feel, Sigurd," Hakon spat, then looked away until he could control his rising ire. When he was calmer, he turned back to the jarls. "Besides, I cannot marry her until I have priests here to baptize her. That was the bargain."

"We may not have the time for that," rasped Tore. "You must see the marriage through soon. For the sake of us all."

Hakon rose, his icy eyes skewering one man, then the other. "The marriage will happen, Tore. Never fear." He strode from the fire, lest he say something he might regret.

As Hakon stormed through the camp's gates, he caught sight of the prisoners from his battle with Erik. They had captured some fifty men in total, including his brother. Four days prior, Erik had sat on his horse, resplendent in his helm and battle armor at the head of an army that numbered more than a thousand men. Now, under the watchful eyes of Hakon's warriors, Erik shuffled among the survivors, bruised and bloodied, his shirt and trousers torn, his armor and weapons stripped from him, his army crushed. Hakon approached him.

"You should have killed me when you had the chance, brother," Erik said when Hakon drew near. "For now I will haunt you until I've had my revenge."

Hakon looked up into his gray-green eyes. "I will rest well, knowing I spared your life, Erik. But I do so only once. If you return, I will not be so charitable."

Erik thrust out his chin with its dirt-matted red beard. "I will return, Hakon. This realm belongs to me!"

"Our father gave you the land to rule, not to plunder and use like a whore. You abused your right, and so now you stand here before me, a prisoner."

Erik spat in his younger brother's face. It was a snap reaction to Hakon's harsh words, but it was the wrong thing to do, for Hakon still burned with the rage caused by the words of Sigurd and Tore. Hakon turned from his brother, wiping away the saliva with his sleeve.

"Walk away, brother," mocked Erik. "You have not the courage to —"

Hakon spun and slammed his fist into Erik's stomach with all his might. The air shot from Erik's body and he dropped to his knees, his head bowed as he struggled for breath. Before he could recover, Hakon smashed his fist into Erik's face. His brother's head jerked back and he crumpled unconscious to the ground. Blood poured from his crushed nose. Shaking with rage, Hakon spat upon him as the other prisoners looked on despondently.

Chapter 2

"This is like sailing into Niflheim," grumbled Egil as the ship crept forward.

Niflheim was the world of mist and darkness, where the goddess Hel ruled the corpses of dishonorable men and the serpent Nidhogg gnawed at the roots of the World Tree, Yggdrasil. Hakon crossed himself at its mention and stared into the grayness ahead. Dense billows pregnant with moisture swirled around *Dragon*, slickening the decks and shrouding the land they now approached. Gathering moisture dripped from the hair and faces of the warriors at oar and the fangs of the prow beast. The lack of wind left room for a maddening chorus of directionless sounds that tormented Hakon's nerves: the soft slap of oars against water, the creak of the ship's strakes, the shrill cry of unseen gulls. It was cold, but Hakon's apprehension warmed him. A bead of sweat trickled down his armored back.

The fog had rolled in the night before as they camped, cold and fireless, on their ships in a cove on the south side of a nearby island, away from the roving eyes of Ragnvald's scouts. Hakon's councilors had cautioned him to wait for the fog to lift. It was a bad omen and a danger, they warned. Bad things lurked in the fog, like evil spirits and unseen rocks and trolls hiding below the water's surface. Hakon feared the fog too, but he had seen scouts during their southward journey and sensed Ragnvald would be waiting. To tarry now was to give the enemy more time to prepare. However frightful, the fog would shield their movements from watchful eyes, and so he had decided to come.

Now, as his eyes peered into the billowing whiteness, he hoped he had been right. The ships traveled in single file with *Dragon* in the lead, Hakon's nephew Gudrod at the bow-post, listening and watching and guiding with hand signals, for he had grown up with Trygvi in this area and knew it well. The other ships followed closely behind, though Hakon could barely see them. In each rowed a skeleton crew encumbered by wounded and the remnants of Erik's army.

Gudrod lifted both arms. Oars up. He was looking to his right, where every so often the fog would reveal a stretch of rocky coastline. Then, suddenly, he pointed. Egil pulled hard on the steer board. In unison, the left side of the ship pulled while the right back rowed. *Dragon* turned her head and glided toward land. Behind them, the other ships followed.

Hakon walked to the prow, peering into the grayness ahead. His sword, Quern-biter, was in his hand. A span of beach peeked through the fog, then emerged from the shrouding mist as *Dragon* slipped nearer. They were in a bay formed by rocky, tree-topped fingers of land on either side. There was no sign of movement.

Dragon bit into the sand and came to rest. Quickly, Hakon and most of his crew disembarked and ran up the beach to form a protective shield wall. Egil came with them.

"Which way, Gudrod?" Hakon whispered.

He pointed with his drawn sword into the grayness as crewmembers from the other ships joined them. "North. There is a track we can follow. It leads through the woods in front of us and will take us to Kaupang from the inland side."

Hakon saw no trees, only thick, shifting fog. He crossed himself and pulled his cloak tightly over his armored shoulders.

When all the ships had landed, the army moved inland. Fifty men stayed behind to guard the ships and prisoners. About two hundred paces in, they found the tree line. Hakon halted his men and took a knee behind his shield. He waited, half expecting spears and arrows to shoot from the shadow of the forest. Nothing happened. He motioned the column forward.

If they had landed unnoticed, that cover was soon lost within the trees. An army of warriors made noise. Too much noise. Though wet pine needles carpeted the ground, branches still snapped, belts creaked and metal grated – it was inevitable, and nerve-wracking. With each step, Hakon expected Ragnvald's army to materialize before him or to strike from some unseen location, but the only army they encountered was the shadows and tree limbs and the forest animals that scurried in the underbrush.

They walked on, angling inland. Here, the fog thinned and the land funneled into a gap between two tree-studded hills. Hakon surveyed the landscape. If Ragnvald wished to defend himself, this was the perfect spot.

Gudrod motioned him forward and pointed to his right. "Kaupang is over that hill. Mayhap two flights of an arrow from here."

"And Skiringssal?"

"Ahead. A thousand paces or so."

"Be alert!" Hakon whispered to his giant friend Toralv, who walked nearest him. "Spread the word." Toralv moved off to do Hakon's bidding.

In the end, an attack never came. Rather, the landscape opened and dipped into a basin through which a fog-shrouded stream meandered toward the bay off to Hakon's right. On the opposite side of the stream, nestled on a rocky rise of land, was Skiringssal...or what was left of it.

The hall and the structures surrounding it had been set ablaze. Hakon cursed under this breath as he gazed upon the destruction. Though he had never spent time here, he still felt the sting of its loss. The hall had been built by his grandfather and inhabited by his half-brothers Olav and Bjorn. It was here that his father and his nephews had been raised. And now it was gone, reduced to a pile of ash and clusters of blackened beams that reached like broken fingers for the indifferent sky.

"The wood no longer smolders," Egil commented, suggesting it had been burned days before. Which meant Ragnvald and his warriors were gone.

A sudden chill crept up Hakon's spine. "Gudrod, take us to Kaupang. Use a route not many would travel."

Gudrod took them along a path that angled up over the tree-lined hill so that they came on Kaupang from the inland side. They approached cautiously, though they need not have, for the town had been reduced to nothing. All that remained was smoldering wood, dead bodies, and swarming flies.

Hakon motioned his army forward and entered the smoking maze of homes and pens and shelters with his arm across his nose to mask the stench. Amid the destruction lay the bloated and beast-torn bodies of gray-haired men and women, young children, and animals, their blood forming dark, coagulated rivulets on the muddy ground. Ragnvald had taken the town by surprise, for most of the people had been sliced in the back while attempting to escape. There were no warriors among the dead and no organized defense that Hakon could see.

"Ragnvald has taken everything of value," Egil noted sourly, "and destroyed the rest. The bastard probably took it all to Hedeby to sell." He spat to punctuate his disgust.

Hakon wove his way through the destruction to the shoreline and gazed out at Kaupangskilen, the inlet on which Kaupang lay. Flying gulls protested the interruption of their feasting, casting shrill curses down upon him as rage and heart-sickening sadness wrestled for equal purchase of Hakon's soul. His destruction of Erik's army had prompted this carnage, yet there could be no other way. He could not turn back time, nor would he have wished for any other outcome against his brother. Erik had placed Ragnvald over these people. The blood of these people was on his hands, yet it hurt nonetheless.

Gudrod joined Hakon at the waterfront.

"I'm sorry, Gudrod," Hakon said after a time. "This is not the inheritance I wished for you, or your cousin."

"It is not your fault, lord."

"Oh, this is definitely my fault. If Erik had had the victory against us, do you think any of this would have happened?"

"So you wish you had been defeated by Erik, eh?"

"No. That is not what I meant."

"That is what it sounded like. Put your guilt aside. Someone else destroyed this place." Gudrod remained silent for a time, and then suddenly snorted.

"What?"

"The gods love their mischief, eh?" He cursed then and cast his eyes to the sky. "Ragnvald will come again," he said. "We would do well to plan for that day."

"You will stay?"

"Where else would I go? I belong here. It is my home."

Hakon smiled weakly. Unlike his cousin Trygvi, who acted on emotion, Gudrod was far more practical. "You will need men to rebuild this place."

"We have some. I could use the prisoners though."

"You can have all of them save Erik. He is mine."

Gudrod nodded, satisfied.

Hakon sent a party of men to retrieve the ships and sail them up the Viksfjord to Kaupangskilen, though he left ten men to watch from the headland at the fjord's entrance with instructions to light a beacon fire should Ragnvald unexpectedly reappear. He also sent a scouting party north and west. There was a chance that the destruction of Skiringssal was a ruse, and that Ragnvald was still near.

The scouts did not find Ragnvald, but they did find thralls — a group of them — and brought them before Hakon. Blood and mud and soot caked their skin and torn clothing, giving them the appearance of people risen from the grave. They walked together under the watchful eyes of the scouts, unarmed and miserable. There were roughly twenty of them, mostly men and women of middling age, wearing the cropped hair and leather collars of thralldom. They stared at Hakon and he stared back, unsure of what to make of the thralls or why they, and not any townsfolk, had survived. After a time, Hakon broke the uneasy silence, calling to his men for water and food.

"Who are you?" Hakon called to a young man who stood at the head of the group.

The man bowed his head. "They call me Theuderic," he croaked.

It was a Frankish name, though he spoke the Norse tongue well enough. "Who did this, Theuderic?" asked Hakon.

The young man's eyes turned to the dead. "A lord. He and his men. Two days ago." He spoke haltingly.

"Why? Did he say anything before he did this?"

The man shrugged. "I don't know. He just came. He and his men. In the early morning. We were asleep...there." He pointed to a pen closest to the woods. It was a holding pen, the kind where slaves were often kept before going to the trading blocks. Guarded, the pens offered little escape, but in the chaos of battle, it would have been easy to dig beneath the lowest beams and disappear.

"And then they left?"

"Yes, lord. In their ships."

"How many ships?"

The man shrugged. "I don't know. We were hiding. I don't know the lord who attacked and I ran when he came. I didn't see his ships. I am not from this place."

Hakon stopped his questioning then, for the food and water had arrived, and the slaves grabbed greedily at it. Many looked as if they had not eaten for days, and they grunted over their meager fare like pigs at feeding time. Hakon felt a pang of pity for them. They had survived one trial only to be cast into the next. Why had they not run away? The answer, Hakon realized, was as sad as their presence on this beach — they had nowhere else to go. Their leather collars marked them as escaped slaves who could be killed or recaptured without penalty. Even if they cut the collars, the scars of their wearing would reveal the truth.

It was then that Hakon caught sight of a young man at the back of the group. He had his head down, revealing what looked to be the remnants of a tonsure in his black hair. He wore a rough woolen robe that fell to his ankles. It was tied together at the waist with a thin rope in the fashion of a monk.

Hakon approached the man. "You are a monk?" he whispered in Latin when he reached the man.

The man looked up at Hakon with eyes as green as spring grass. He nodded.

"From where?" Hakon asked.

"Northumbria...lord," the monk whispered, bowing his head as he did so.

"What is your name?"

"Egfrid, lord."

"From what monastery?"

"Chester-le-Street."

"The monastery where Saint Cuthbert's bones lie."

The monk did not try to hide his astonishment. "The very same, lord."

It was said to be a place of great solitude, where monks painstakingly translated Latin gospels into the tongue of the Anglisc, though Hakon had never seen such books. Hakon guessed that the Danes and Northmen had raided it as they raided every other holy place in Englalond, for they cared little about the venerable history of a place or for the treasure of words — they wanted only the coins and booty that bought them ale and whores and more men.

"Eat. We will talk more later." Hakon stepped away and left the monk to his food and to his shock at being questioned by a young lord of the Northmen who spoke Latin and knew of his monastery and his saints.

That afternoon, as the funeral pyres burned along the shore and blackened the summer sky with the smoke of corpses, Hakon climbed to a rocky perch on the hillside behind the town and sat. He needed time to think, to be away, to settle himself and his mind.

The past week had been a storm of action and trial, of victory and heartache, but the storm was now at an end, at least for now. There would be more storms to come; Hakon was not so naïve to think that the realm would come together so easily. The North was still a fractious land divided by fjords and mountains and islands that bred differences in language, customs, and desires. Men would fight as they always had, to impress the gods and increase their wealth and their fame, or to protect their belongings, their beliefs, and their ways of life. Mayhap they would fight more so, now that Erik was gone and his untried brother ruled. The Danes would also come again, as would the Swedes in the east. But for now there was peace. It was time to offer up a prayer of thanks for the storm's conclusion and for the gifts that the storm had left in its wake.

The thought of prayer turned Hakon's mind to the church and to his foster father, King Athelstan, who had once told him that everything happens for a reason. So far his people had shown little interest in his faith, yet God had presented him with the High Seat of the North and the chance to fulfill his dream of becoming the first Christian king of the Northmen. If Athelstan was right, then Hakon had been given this gift for a reason, and now it was for him to pursue it. But to do so, he needed support. He was no priest, nor could he alone complete the task. His mind wandered to Egfrid. Surely he could preach to the people or baptize Groa, but could one man really affect change across the realm? Hakon didn't know, and frankly, he was too tired to answer the question. He needed rest, and he needed to rebuild Kaupang. Of those two things Hakon was certain. The rest, he decided, God would answer in time.

Chapter 3

The following day, Hakon and his army began the long process of re-building Kaupang at Skiringssal. It was arduous work, made harder by the summer heat and the fact that Ragnvald had been so thorough in his destruction. Yet Hakon refused to leave his nephews with nothing, and so the men pulled damaged wood from the wreckage and salvaged what they could.

As his men repaired the town, Erik and the other prisoners cleared some land on the hillside overlooking Kaupang for Gudrod's new hall. Skiringssal's luck, he argued, was now gone, and to rebuild it in its original location would only invite more trouble. After a thorough survey of the entire area, they decided on a boulder-strewn spot on the hill just inland from Kaupang. Once cleared and leveled, it would make for a far more defensible place, with a view of the bay and easier access to the market.

The first task was clearing the hillside of boulders and trees. Not only would their removal make it possible to level the land, once rolled down the hill, the boulders would form a natural defensive barrier at the base of the slope. Some of the stones were so large, their momen-tum felled trees that could be used in the rebuilding process. It was backbreaking and dangerous work that took the lives of two of Erik's men and injured a handful of others. Fitting punishment, Hakon rea-soned, for all that Erik had destroyed.

❦

As the army worked, Gudrod sent some of his warriors to meet the local landholders. Upon hearing the name of their new overlord, the men came gladly, for most of the locals remembered Gudrod and his cousin Trygvi. With them, they brought what food and provisions they could spare. It was a kindness Hakon did not expect, but one that set his mind at ease — he had made the right choice in giving this place back to his kin.

Though the work was hard, the time in Kaupang for many was healing — it was a time to mend wounds, celebrate fallen comrades, drink, and eat. Hakon healed too, though his healing took an entirely different form. During the days, he worked alongside his men, reveling in the camaraderie of shared tasks. But at night, the Night Mare came as she had every night since Aelfwin's death, planting in his young mind images that were both strange and horrid. One night she brought a smiling Aelfwin to him, with her endearing, split-toothed grin and captivating green eyes. But as Hakon reached for her, her head fell back to reveal the giant gash at her neck where Ivar had sliced with his blade. Aelfwin laughed at his horror while her blood soaked her chest.

Men too came to Hakon's dreams. He recognized most. Udd, Finn, Heidar, Brand, Gunnar — men who had died under Hakon's blade or as a result of his actions. They approached and knelt before him, swearing oaths to stay with him always — oaths that Hakon did not want.

Each morning, Hakon awoke drained. On the third such morning, his throat burned and his teeth chattered despite the fire that crackled nearby. His body ached too much to rise.

Toralv nudged him with his foot. "Time to get up, lord."

Hakon peered up at his good friend, whose huge frame blocked the morning sun. "I cannot, Toralv."

"You cannot? Are you ill?" Toralv knelt and placed his calloused hand on Hakon's forehead. "Lie still. I will be back."

Toralv returned with a cold cloth that smelled of the sea, which he placed upon Hakon's forehead. He then set about preparing an infusion of herbs and sea salt that, when finished, he dribbled into Hakon's mouth. It tasted terrible and stung his throat, but Hakon was too sick to protest. Hakon slept then, though he did not remember falling asleep, or the sleep itself. It was the sleep of the dead, mercifully sealed from the Night Mare's assaults.

When he did finally awaken, it was dusk. He lay on the ground beneath two furs, feeling stiff and achy and perplexed. He knew not whether it was night or early morning. His head hurt but no longer burned. Toralv sat nearby, tending the fire and scratching at the black hair that was growing awkwardly on his teenage face. He handed Hakon a wooden cup when he noticed Hakon was awake. "Drink this."

Hakon sipped the warm, bitter fluid. "What is it?"

"It is a mixture made from a plant my mother called Balder's Eyelash. She used to make it for us when we were ill. It helps you sleep."

"It tastes like piss."

Toralv's dark brow cocked above his right eye. "And you would know what piss tastes like?"

Hakon smiled weakly. "Does it help with visions?"

Toralv's big hand moved to the charm at his neck. Like many men, talk of visions and supernatural events made him uneasy. "What sort of visions?"

"Of Aelfwin. And men I've killed. They haunt me in my sleep."

Toralv seemed relieved. "I know not whether this drink can cure that, lord. That seems like something only time can cure."

Hakon's head was throbbing again, so he closed his eyes. "Do you not see things like that?"

"No, lord."

That figured. Toralv's easy temperament shielded him from most things that bothered other men. In fact, Hakon had rarely seen him sad. He wondered briefly what Toralv had done when Erik's men had killed his family. Had he cried? Did he ever think about them?

Sigurd's voice broke Hakon's train of thought. "How does he fare?"

"He is healing, lord."

"Will he be ready to move soon?"

"You may speak to me, Sigurd," Hakon said without opening his eyes. "I am not dead yet."

Sigurd grunted, although Hakon knew there was a smile there. "You sleep like you are. I suppose you are just relaxing by the fire then, letting everyone else do your work?"

"That's exactly what I am doing. Is it not obvious?"

Sigurd's belly laugh brought a smile to Hakon's face. "Aye, lad. I'm afraid it is."

"I will be on my feet soon enough. How goes the work?"

"Well. We have a new foundation for the marketplace already laid, and a spot on the hillside has been leveled for the hall. They have a good start to things. The locals are helping, which is what we wanted. Jarl Tore arrived today as you slept and brought the ships with him, but he left before you awoke. He will take your story to the western chieftains. It is time for us to leave."

Hakon pictured all of this in his mind as Sigurd spoke. "Very well. Start preparing the ships and informing the men."

That night, as the fires dwindled and the men began to snore, Hakon lay awake. His eyes stared up at the dusk of the summer night, though his mind wandered through images and ideas and plans. He thought of his men and his kingship and his future, of Athelstan and Aelfwin and Groa. But mostly he thought of the monk whom he had discovered his first day in Kaupang. Egfrid.

"Toralv," he whispered.

His friend stirred, then rolled over.

Hakon reached over and shook him, which set his head to throbbing. "Toralv," he said a little louder. "Wake up."

"Huh?"

"Are you awake?"

"I am now," he mumbled. "What is the matter?"

"I need a favor."

"Can it not wait for morning?"

"No."

Toralv sat up and rubbed his face. He had been sleeping on his left side, and his dark hair curled in that direction like a wave. "What then?"

"Do you know the slave who dresses himself in a robe with a rope at his waist? Dark hair?"

"Aye."

"Find him and bring him here."

The big man scratched his head. "Now?"

"Now."

Toralv rolled from beneath his blanket with a grunt, grabbed his sword, and trudged into the night. He returned moments later with the monk, who looked mightily uncertain.

Hakon sat up and tried to ignore the throbbing in his temples. He patted the ground beside him. "Sit, Egfrid," he commanded in Latin.

The monk knelt beside Hakon as if he were about to pray and rested his thin hands in his lap. Toralv peered at his king and the monk dubiously, then reclaimed his sleeping spot and disappeared under his blanket. Hakon watched his friend for a time before turning back to Egfrid. The crackling fire illuminated the monk's young face and worried eyes. He would be handsome, Hakon decided, were it not for the dirt that clung to his face and the twigs in his hair.

"Chester-le-Street is famous for the texts it produces, is that not right?" Hakon asked after a time.

"They are called gospels, lord. But yes, that is correct. Your knowledge of our monasteries is impressive."

Hakon ignored the compliment. "So, do you write?"

Egfrid nodded hesitantly.

"Good. Find something to write on and something to write with. I have a message that I need you to take to King Athelstan."

Egfrid's mouth dropped open. "I don't understand."

"There is nothing to understand. I am freeing you," Hakon continued. "But in exchange, I need you to deliver a message for me. Find writing utensils and come to me again tomorrow."

"My lord," he stuttered. "That is not enough time to prepare writing instruments properly. Such things take time."

Beside them, Toralv began to snore. "I know, Egfrid. But I don't have more time. You will need to do your best."

"But how am I to find King Athelstan? How am I to get to him?"

The desperation in his voice grated on Hakon and his aching head. "That is for me to worry about. Toralv." Hakon kicked his friend.

Toralv grumbled, "What now?"

"Take Egfrid back to his pen, then return to me. I have one more task for you."

With a muffled curse, Toralv threw off his blanket and rose. Egfrid's eyes went wide as Toralv yanked him to his feet and pushed him away. When Toralv returned, he was still scowling. "May I lie down, or will you have me wandering off again into the night?"

Hakon rubbed his temples. "I need you to find a crew for a knarr that can sail to Engla-lond with the priest."

Toralv tensed. "Why?"

"I need the monk to deliver a message to King Athelstan."

He snorted. "What you ask is not so easily done. You need a crew that knows how to get to Engla-lond and has a ship to make that journey. And men who know how to find the king once they arrive. Should I just wander up the coast and start asking people?"

Hakon was in no mood for sarcasm. "Just do as I ask."

"Why must the monk go?"

"King Athelstan must hear of our success," he said as he laid his head on a rolled up cloak. "The monk will be trusted. More than any warrior we send." It was a half truth but enough to convince his friend.

Toralv cursed. "I will find a crew."

Hakon closed his eyes. "You have a day."

"A day?"

"You heard Sigurd. We leave soon. We have no more time."

Toralv cursed again.

The next afternoon, Hakon's army gathered to sacrifice to their gods for safety and fair weather in their upcoming journey. Hakon watched from his perch on the hillside, clutching a wooden cup of Toralv's concoction in one hand, his cross pendant in his other. After a year among the Northmen, he no longer fought against their religious practices, but neither could he watch them indifferently.

The monk, Egfrid, sat at his side, watching the sacrifice in slack-jawed silence with a sharpened stick in his hand, its tip blackened by flame. He crossed himself when Sigurd drew the blade across a horse's neck.

"Read to me what you have so far," commanded Hakon.

The monk pulled his eyes away from the ceremony and bent over a tablet made of bark that had been thinned and softened with a knife blade. It was the only writing surface Egfrid could manufacture at such short notice. Later he would commit the missive to memory as well as transfer it to vellum; for now, the bark would have to do.

"*To King Athelstan, the glorious and generous servant of God, King of the Anglisc. I, King Hakon, brother in Christ and former fosterling in your charitable household, send greetings.*

"*It is with joyous heart and humble thanks to our most Holy Master that I send you these good tidings. Erik Bloodaxe, son of Harald Fairhair, has been defeated by the forces of righteousness and will be expelled from this land. I know not where he will fare, but have a suspicion, owing to his relationship with Jarl Einar of the Orkneyjar, that he might soon be seen in your kingdom. I pray that this will not come to pass, but I must warn you nevertheless to keep vigilant watch for him. He is a cunning fellow and I would not doubt that he will continue to be dangerous until the day he dies, and probably thereafter.*

"*Concerning my forthcoming state of affairs, there is much to be done. Erik has torn asunder many of the right and proper structures of this realm and I fear my work to rebuild this land will be ceaseless. To that end, I would ask you to send me a force of fearless brothers in Christ, monks all, to assist in bringing the light of our faithful Lord to this dark place. The task will not be without its perils, as the Northerners do not know, and therefore do not understand, that this world is ruled only by God. Yet I know that the good brothers do not lack for courage or zeal and, therefore, your task of finding such men should not be too troublesome."*

Below them, the gathered army cheered as Sigurd splashed the horse's blood on the prows of the ships. The monk paused.

"Continue," Hakon commanded.

"As...As for my own personal affairs, there will soon be some changes (although I freely admit, these are born of necessity and not choice). In a month's time, at the honey moon, I am to marry the daughter of a powerful jarl named Ivar, one of the men who helped me win this kingdom. I accept this responsibility as due payment for the assistance this same jarl afforded me, yet my heart is heavy. The weight comes as a result of cruel misfortune and, even now, I find it hard to describe. I will spare you the details and come straight to the point. Aelfwin is dead. I found her here among the Northerners, a slave to Jarl Ivar, lost in her hope and used beyond description. I tried my best to restore her dignity and spare her life but, in the end, lost the struggle."

The monk paused and looked at Hakon.

"Keep reading, Egfrid."

"Please convey my profound and heartfelt condolences to her parents. She will be remembered always in my prayers and, I hope, in yours as well.

"I pray that this letter finds you in good health and spirits. Please convey to Louis, Byrnstan, Father Otker, and the others that I think of them often and pray that God keeps them well. May God protect you all and keep you always in His embrace. Your friend and fellow king, Hakon Haraldsson."

When Egfrid stopped reading, Hakon looked over at the bark. "Read it back to me again. In full."

Hakon listened as Egfrid spoke the Latin words one more time. When he finished, Hakon nodded. "Good."

Below them, another cheer rose into the air as Sigurd sacrificed a goat and collected its sacrificial blood — the hlaut — in a wooden vessel.

"We are organizing a ship. I will send for you when it is time to leave."

Egfrid nodded and left Hakon on his perch.

That night, under a cloud-scattered sky that shone gold and blue with the evening sun, the army celebrated, enjoying each other's company for the last time with songs and poems and brotherly oaths sworn over too many cups of ale. Given the destruction of Kaupang, there were no lordly halls in which to dine or eating boards at which to sit, but no one seemed to mind. Men simply cut slabs of steaming meat directly from turning spits and lounged on the beach as they tore the meat from their knives. Though they were effectively three armies — Sigurd's, Hakon's, and those of Tore's men who had remained behind — the last few months had woven them into one group with a common memory of victories gained and lives lost. The fight against Erik was an adventure that had forged brotherhoods and allegiances stronger than the best Rhein steel — an adventure that would live on in tales told this very evening and carried down through the ages.

"Life is good, eh, Hakon?"

Hakon had been quietly watching the feast from a fire he shared with Sigurd. "Aye. Life is good. We have much to be thankful for."

"Skol to that," Sigurd concurred, hefting his cup and spilling some ale down his wrist in the process. "The gods have rewarded us nicely."

Hakon, who had not fully recovered from his illness, stuck to his warm drink of Balder's Eyelash and sea salt. "How long will it take to sail to Avaldsnes?" he asked after a slurp from his cup.

Sigurd shrugged. "Seven days. Mayhap less if the gods smile on us."

"I would hope they will, after all you've sacrificed to them," Hakon commented. "If the gods don't bring fair wind and weather, you may want to consider following my god." He winked at his friend, who laughed, then rose to get more meat.

As Sigurd stepped from the circle, Toralv knelt beside Hakon. "It is done," he said under his breath. "I have found a ship and a crew. They will meet you south of the other ships tomorrow. They are locals, but have traveled to Engla-lond before."

"Warriors?" Hakon asked.

Toralv shrugged. "They are traders mostly. But the captain, Halldor, and some of his crew look capable enough."

Toralv's words did not comfort Hakon. The men did not sound like they could protect Egfrid if it came to a serious fight; but then, it was too late to worry about such things. The plan was in God's hands now. "Did they name a price?"

"Two pounds of hack silver. Half now, and half upon their successful return."

It was a fair price. Hakon clasped his friend's shoulder. "Thank you, my friend. You have done well."

"And yet I feel as if I've done something wrong."

His words caught Hakon off guard, and for a moment Hakon didn't speak. "You have done the right thing, Toralv," he finally said. "You will see."

The following morning dawned windy, though not entirely unpleasant. Patches of blue dotted the sky like shifting islands in a sea of gray. In another cycle of the moon, that gray would begin to blot out the blue, carrying with it rain, then eventually, snow.

Hakon stood beside *Dragon*, watching the inlet churn in the dim light. The wind swept southward, its soft howl calling the men to sea. Hakon ran his finger mindlessly along the post of his ship's prow as she danced on the water. Like all of the ships, she was laden with coiled ropes, oars, and other supplies, and smelled of fresh caulking. Flies buzzed where Sigurd had splashed the hlaut upon her strakes. It was time to head west, to their homes. And time for Hakon to rid himself of Erik forever.

"We have come to say goodbye, lord. And to thank you."

Hakon glanced over his shoulder to find Gudrod standing behind him. Trygvi was with him. Their cloaks and hair tossed in the wind.

"Thank me? For what? I leave you with little."

"You leave us with everything," Gudrod said. Of the two, he was normally the one who spoke. "The inland fields are intact and will be ready to harvest. The hall and marketplace are under construction. The locals are happy. There is still much to do, clearly, but with the help of the gods, we will make it happen."

"I trust that you will," Hakon replied. It was more of a command than a comment, for Hakon needed the income from Kaupang. The cousins understood the not-so-subtle meaning and nodded solemnly. Hakon smiled and grabbed Gudrod's wrist. "Until we meet again."

Hakon turned to Trygvi. "Protect Gudrod, Trygvi. He may be older and wiser, but you are stronger."

Trygvi's smile was more like a sneer. "We will not disappoint you, lord. Fare well."

Back on the beach, the men packed their sea chests and said their final goodbyes. Hakon left his nephews and went in search of the thralls, whom he found in the same pen from which they had originally escaped. It had been repaired but still smelled of burnt wood and mud. Egfrid knelt with his elbows resting on the crossbeams, his hands together before his mud-streaked face. Hakon reached through the gate and tapped his shoulder. The monk ended his prayer and looked at Hakon with his green eyes.

"It is time. Grab your things."

The monk crossed himself, grabbed a small leather bag that held his measly belongings, and rose.

Together they walked farther down the beach, away from the main army, where a small group of men hefted their sea chests onto a small sea vessel known as a knarr, or trading ship. It was deeper in draft and thicker around the midsection, but it would mark them as traders instead of warriors and keep them safer in the long journey to Athelstan's hall. Or at least that's what Hakon hoped.

Toralv was there, towering above the others and looking anxious. Beside him was an older man with sun-browned skin and graying hair. His eyes were blue and friendly. The man bowed when Hakon approached, revealing a silver necklace from which various charms hung, including a hammer of Thor and a Christian cross. "Lord."

"You are Halldor?"

"Aye, lord."

"You wear a Christian cross," Hakon remarked. "How is that?"

"Aye, and Thor's hammer, and a charm to invoke Odin's powers. One can't have enough gods to protect him, especially at sea."

"I see. Well then, let us be on with this." He motioned to Egfrid. "This monk's name is Egfrid. He is your charge now, Halldor. Bring him to King Athelstan safely. I trust you know how to find the king?"

"I have been to Engla-lond before. We will find him, lord."

"It is imperative that Egfrid and his message get to the king. Do you understand?"

"Message?" The creases in his face stretched as his brows arched.

"Egfrid carries a written message from me to King Athelstan. It must remain dry."

Halldor's mouth twisted into a wry smile. "Dry? On a ship? In the ocean?"

Hakon did not smile, for if water reached the bark, it would smear the charcoal. "You think I jest, but I don't."

Halldor looked from Egfrid to Hakon, and his smile vanished. "We will find a way, lord."

"Good." Hakon handed a small sack of silver to the sea captain, which Halldor then handed to one of his men to weigh on a scale. "You will receive the rest upon your successful return. As promised."

"And where will I find you when I return?"

It was a question to which Hakon had no answer. "I don't know. Come here first. They will know where to find me."

"A pound, Halldor," his man called from the scale.

Halldor spit in his palm and extended it to Hakon, who took it in his own calloused grip to seal the bargain.

Hakon pulled his seax from his belt and cut the leather neckband that marked Egfrid as a thrall. He then gestured to Egfrid to approach the ship. "Keep the bark dry, Egfrid."

The monk unconsciously rubbed his neck and nodded, then walked toward the knarr. After five paces he turned. "I am not certain why the Lord has delivered me from thralldom, but from now to the end of my days I will be thankful to you and to Him. And I will do everything in my power to see your message delivered safely."

"Go with God, but do what Halldor asks of you. Understand?"

The monk nodded and turned.

As Hakon and Toralv walked back to the army, Sigurd approached, his eyes on the knarr. "A trader and a Christian," he said to no one in particular. "I do not like the looks of that."

"Then do not ask questions," Hakon replied, grabbing Sigurd by the shoulder and turning him back toward the army. "We have more important things to attend to, like putting out to sea. Come, Sigurd — it is time to head west."

Sigurd grunted, his eyes still on the knarr, though there was nothing more he could say.

Chapter 4

Avaldsnes, Rogaland, Early Summer, AD 935

Sunny, cloud-filled skies graced their journey south around Agder, then north along the western coast. Though the constantly shifting wind forced the men to row and a light rain fell on their fourth day, the trip was uneventful. The men used the time to rest their weary bodies, mend clothing and weapons, and give the gods thanks for their lives. Hakon basked in the sun's warmth and the easy banter of his men, and did his best to avoid the malignant stares of Erik, who was tied to the aft-deck upright that they used to hold the sail when it was furled.

On the seventh day, Hakon's army reached the Karmsund Strait, a narrow waterway formed by the island of Karmoy on the west and the mainland of Rogaland to the east. They had come here because it was in that strait, on the northern end of Karmoy, that his family's estate at Avaldsnes sat. It was a strange feeling, being back in these waters. The last time Hakon had seen these shores, he had been a small boy, peering out at the low green land with tearing eyes as his ship took him away to Engla-lond. Now he was returning to claim all he had left behind and all that had previously been his brother's and his father's before him, a thought that filled him with equal measures of elation and uncertainty.

"Ottar!" barked Egil, tearing Hakon from his thoughts. "Take watch." Ottar was Egil's nephew, who hailed from the far north, where the trees grew thick. He was not only the best climber, but he also had the eyes of a keen hunter. If anyone could spot trouble, it would be him. For despite his defeat, this was still Erik's land, and there was no telling what dangers lurked. Hakon gazed behind him at his fleet. It would take a mighty king, or a mighty fool, to attack them, but it did not hurt to be cautious.

"We're being watched!" called Ottar as the ships made their way into the strait. "There."

Two horsemen watched them from a copse of trees on the south-eastern edge of Karmoy. How Ottar had seen them in the shade of those branches was beyond Hakon.

"Erik's?" Egil wondered aloud.

Hakon glanced at his brother, who sat upright, his sunburned neck craning for a better view. "We'll find out soon enough," Hakon said. "Ottar — anything to the east?"

"Nothing," he called from his perch.

The men pulled steadily at their oars and the ships glided up the strait. The horsemen kept pace, weaving their way along the track that followed Karmoy's eastern shore. Hakon guessed they belonged to Erik, but whether they belonged to a force large enough to challenge Hakon and his army was anyone's guess.

By mid-afternoon, Hakon and his fleet had reached the narrowest section of the waterway. To the west lay a hilled island that constricted the channel. Hakon remembered it well from his youth, for it was said that long ago a sea king named Augvald had built a hall there and stretched a thick chain across the waterway to stop ships laden with goods. Hakon had often sought that chain as a young boy, but had never found anything. Across the strait, to the east, were the low-lying shores of Rogaland.

If arrows were to fly, this was where they'd come. The men loosened their shields in their racks along the gunwale and sank lower at their oars. Hakon guided his ship into the center of the strait to distance himself from the shorelines and any possible bowmen. But the precautions were for naught. The ships sailed through the waterway unmolested and just past the western island, hove into a broad bay on the western shore. Farther into that bay, off to their left, was another smaller bay, and it was into this that the ships now turned. And there, before them, was Avaldsnes.

The estate truly was magnificent. On either side of the bay, grassy hills sloped gradually to flat hilltops. On the hill to the west was a copse of trees and an ancient burial mound around which sheep grazed. A low wooden palisade ringed the hill to the east, protecting the hall and structures that comprised the estate. Hakon's eyes took in the scene, then came to rest on the narrow pebbled beach before him, where a wall of warriors stood.

"Fools!" Egil spat. "Do they think they can stop us?"

Egil had the right of it, for there were mayhap twenty men in all, some with armor, all with shields. Hakon's crew alone could slaughter them.

Sigurd glided his ship up next to Hakon's. "Well?" called the jarl from his ship. He looked amused. "What say you?"

"Stay here," Hakon ordered. He then called to his own crew to row ahead slowly.

Dragon slithered forward.

"I am Hakon Haraldsson," he called to the men as they neared the beach, "and I come in peace!"

"We know who you are, you snot-nosed lout!" called a burly, gray-haired man from the center of the shield wall. Years before, that same man had commanded the ship that had taken Hakon to Engla-lond. His name was Hauk Hobrok, and he had once been Harald's champion. Now he was old. "And we know that you have come to take what is ours."

"I come to take what is mine by rights, Hauk." Hakon motioned to his hirdman, Didrik, who stood near Erik. Like his twin brother Gunnar, who had died in the battle with Erik, Didrik was short and stocky, with shoulder-length blond curls and large round eyes the color of polished oak. The only difference between he and his brother was the scar that wound from Didrik's bottom lip to his chin — a scar that now danced as he commanded Erik to rise.

"Bring him here."

Didrik cut Erik from the upright and pulled him roughly to the bow. The warriors on the strand shifted uneasily when they saw their leader.

"So it is true," Hauk called. "Erik is alive. But it changes nothing. We have sworn an oath to protect his family."

"Don't be fools!" Hakon called. "You cannot protect them from an army. You will be butchered."

Hakon turned to Erik, who lifted his chin and gazed proudly at his men. "Stop this fight," he said to his brother.

Erik gazed at Hakon with disdain in his gray-green eyes. "No. They will die facing their enemy, and the gods will see their courage."

"You mistake my words, brother. I don't care about your men; I care about your family."

Erik's brows narrowed.

"You know the truth of it, Erik. Once the blood madness is upon my men, they won't stop. They will rape your wife and slit her throat. They will slaughter your sons like sheep. And you will watch it all."

Fury smoldered in Erik's eyes. He knew the truth as well as any man and could do nothing to change it. "May the gods damn you, Hakon," he hissed.

Hakon's hirdman Didrik jabbed his spear butt into Erik's back in response to his curse. He crumpled to the deck and knelt there until the pain subsided. When he had recovered, he rose and called to his men, "Lay down your weapons! There will be no bloodshed this day."

The men looked at each other but did not release their weapons.

"Drop your weapons. All of you!"

The men dropped their weapons onto the strand, and Hakon's army landed its ships. Once they were on the beach, Hakon approached Hauk. The last time they had met, Hauk had towered over Hakon. Now Hakon looked his father's champion square in his hate-filled eyes.

"You always were a thorn in my ass, Hakon."

Hakon smashed his forearm into Hauk's nose, knocking the older man to the sand. A line of dark blood rolled from his nostrils and into his gray mustache. "You will address me as King Hakon, Hauk, and remember always that I spared you from certain death this day."

Hakon called to Erik's household guards, "You men have until tomorrow to leave this place. You may go with Erik or you may go elsewhere, but you cannot remain here. Come," he called to Egil. "Let us greet my kin."

Hakon ascended the path to the main hall, ringed by his core hirdmen: Egil, Toralv, Ottar, and the stocky Didrik. He passed through the palisade gate and into a courtyard in which thralls stood silently, watching him. A few chickens clucked around their feet. Hakon's eyes scanned the servants in their threadbare clothing. Some Hakon recognized from his youth. Others were new to him. They all looked miserable.

It was in the hall that they found Erik's wife, Gunnhild, and her seven children. With them were Gunnhild's maidservants and two gray-haired guards. They must have seen what had happened on the beach, for they held no weapons.

Hakon had never seen his sister-in-law, but he had heard stories about her beauty. She was indeed stunning, but in the way that a hanging icicle is stunning: captivating, yet cold and dangerous. Long, raven-black hair framed her thin face and pronounced cheekbones. Her ice-blue eyes studied Hakon as a wolf studies its prey before pouncing.

Four boys and three girls of varying ages stood around her — presumably Hakon's nieces and nephews. The oldest child, Gamle, was roughly Hakon's age and stood closest to his mother, ready to protect her, but Hakon was in no mood to fight.

"Gather your things," he commanded. "You will depart tomorrow."

"Is my husband here?"

"Aye."

"Bring me to him."

Hakon stepped forward and stared into her fierce eyes. He could feel his own anger rising and struggled to quell it. "My men," Hakon motioned vaguely to his hirdmen, "wish me to kill you and your family and be rid of the entire poisoned line of Erik. The only reason you are still alive, standing before me, is that I have chosen to spare you all. But my charity only goes so far. Best you remember that, Gunnhild, the next time you presume to command me."

Her icy gaze never faltered.

"Pack your things. You may see Erik when I say so."

Gunnhild stormed into her sleeping chamber with her children and maidservants in tow. Her guards looked about helplessly. "Leave," Hakon told them.

Hakon gazed at the silent hall and the long empty platforms that lined its interior. This was the heart of the estate, its lifeblood. It was here that Harald had held his elaborate feasts, entertained family and guests, ruled his kingdom and his household. His hospitality and generosity were renowned, and drew family and visitors from far and wide. Traders, jarls, neighbors, and strangers — all were welcome in Harald's hall and many were the nights that Hakon sat in silence by the great hearth, listening to their tales and learning of life beyond this strategic plot of land. Now the hall stood silent save for the crunch of dry rushes beneath his feet and the squeak of rats in the thatch above.

A massive oak chair stood in the shadows at the far end of the hall. The High Seat of the realm. Polished to a dark sheen, it was as close to a throne as the North had. According to the skalds, dwarves had carved it from the limbs of Yggdrasil and woven hidden runes into the serpentine designs on its legs and arms that proclaimed its storied history and protected the line of Yngling kings — Hakon's forebears — from the blades of men. Hakon approached it and ran his fingers along the intertwined snakes that formed its arms. To Hakon, who had seen his father's frame fill the High Seat many times, it was a symbol of absolute authority and dark pagan tradition. And now it was his, a thought that filled him with equal measures of awe and trepidation.

Hakon stepped back into the sunlight and took stock of the structures that surrounded the hall. While their number befit a king of Harald's stature, their condition did not. Broken gates hung awkwardly. Here and there, the daub had chipped from walls, revealing the wattle within. Most of the thatched roofs were old and in need of repair, and were no doubt infested with vermin. Entire sections of the wooden palisade were broken or caving in. It struck Hakon then that the estate was nothing more than a microcosm of the crumbling realm he had inherited from his brother.

Hakon's eyes shifted to the beach and the boathouse that stood just inland. As a child that house had been his refuge, a place for him to disappear into the boyhood fantasies of adventure. How many times had he snuck away from the hall to run his small hands along the gunwales of *Dragon* and the other ships that lay within the shadows of that shed? Or stood on the ship's aft deck pretending to sail the whale road to far-off battles like his father and older half-brothers?

The memories brought a smile to his face that quickly disappeared, for there was still much to do before Erik's departure. Chief among them was telling Toralv of his cruel, but necessary, plan.

"It is time."

Hakon blinked and sat up slowly, tired and sore. He had spent a cold night with his army, sleeping on the ground beside a fire that had long since succumbed to the night winds. His men had urged him to rest in the sleeping chamber of the main hall, but Hakon had refused. Until the entire hall had been scoured of Erik's memory, he would sleep with his men.

"Is everything set?"

"Aye," responded Toralv. He looked as tired as Hakon felt, with dark rings beneath his eyes that told of a sleepless night keeping watch on Erik and his men, as well as seeing to Hakon's plan.

Hakon wiped his face to remove the vestiges of sleep that clung to him, then rose and followed Toralv to the rise overlooking the beach. Beneath a steely gray sky, his army formed a silent, watchful shield wall that stretched from one hilltop to the next, their cloaks and hair blowing in the salty sea breeze. Below them, Erik's people grunted and cursed as they dragged overloaded chests, sacks, barrels and other personal effects to the waiting knarrs. Women — thralls and free alike — hauled pots, cooking implements, tools, food, and stacks of furs under the watchful eye of their dour mistress, Gunnhild, who was quick to remonstrate but unwilling to help. Children darted through the crowd, oblivious to what this exodus meant for them, while sheep bleated and chickens clucked in their wattle cages. In the midst of it all towered Erik Bloodaxe, his fiery tangle of hair standing out like a beacon.

"They will soon be done." The remark came from Egil, who had come to stand beside his king.

"Come, let us bid my brother and his family farewell."

Hakon picked his way down the winding path toward the mass of people below. His army followed. Erik's household stopped their work and eyed the approaching warriors. Hakon ignored their malignant stares and strode to Erik.

"Brother," Hakon greeted him when they stood facing each other.

Erik's face pinched into a scowl. He said not a word.

Hakon sighed and walked back to the slope, then turned to face Erik and his people. "At our battle," he called to the group, "I banned Erik from this land, never to return. But I did not extract an oath as I should have. Now I shall have it. Erik, swear before your gods and your people that you shall never return."

Erik laughed loudly. Like fire, it spread to his followers. Hakon did not smile. Instead, he signaled toward the boathouse and waited until Toralv appeared with Erik's eldest son, Gamle, in his grasp. The youth's face was bloody, his body bent from the beating Hakon had ordered. Toralv held a seax close to the teenager's throat.

"No!" Erik roared and pushed toward Toralv. Toralv pressed his blade's point into Gamle's neck until blood trickled from the wound. Erik stopped cold and turned to Hakon.

"I cannot give you what you seek," bellowed Erik.

"That is bad luck, Erik," responded Hakon.

Toralv wrestled his prisoner to his hands and knees, then stabbed the blade into the back of Gamle's right hand. Gamle screamed and collapsed, cradling his shattered paw. Tears streamed from the boy's eyes.

Hakon glared at Erik. "Do not test me, Erik, or I will kill your boy slowly before your eyes. And then I will post his head on a stake for the birds to eat."

Erik's fists coiled, turning the flesh white across his knuckles. Hakon turned to the boy's mother, Gunnhild, hoping to find some mercy there. She stood rod straight with her jaw set hard. The ire in her eyes was icier than Erik's. Her fingers bit into the shoulders of Guthorm, her second oldest, as she held him back. The rest of her children, who ringed her, looked on helplessly.

Toralv grabbed Gamle's hair, pulled his head back, and brought the knife down to his throat again. Hakon raised his hand again and the blade began to bite. Gamle tried to yell, but his neck was too taut.

"Stop!" Erik finally yelled. "Stop. I will swear."

"Husband, no!"

"Silence, woman. This is not your decision to make."

Hakon turned quickly to Didrik, lest Erik change his mind. "Bring a cup of ale. Make haste!"

Didrik returned moments later with a full cup, which he passed to Erik. Erik took it roughly in his hand, spilling half its contents as he did. Toralv kept his knife on Gamle's neck as the crowd looked on expectantly.

"Ale-pledge before your gods and your people, Erik, that you shall never return to his realm."

Erik made the pledge, then dripped a portion of ale onto the pebbles at his feet to seal the bargain.

Hakon nodded in acceptance. "May the winds take you and your family far from this land, brother, never to return."

Toralv kicked Gamle away.

"May the gods curse you," growled Erik in impotent fury.

"Your gods hold no sway over me, Erik." Hakon turned his back to his brother and walked up the path so that everyone on the beach could see him. "If you are a thrall, you shall remain here. The rest of you must go." He then turned and hiked up to the burial mound where he could oversee Erik's departure.

Erik's two ships left later that morning with his family, his small army, and those of his personal effects he could fit in the holds. Hakon and Sigurd sat together near the burial mound, watching them sail from the bay.

"Where will they go?" asked Hakon as the ships disappeared from the bay.

Sigurd pulled a blade of grass from his mouth and flicked it away. "If I were him, I'd go to the Danes."

Hakon nodded. It made sense. The Danes were friends to Erik and could give him refuge for a time. "Ragnvald?"

"Or Gorm. Though I doubt he'll stay there long. That kingdom isn't big enough for the two of them."

Hakon nodded. According to the reports, Gorm had just become the sole ruler of Jutland and the islands to the east of it. Erik might be welcome for a time in his court, but eventually he would have to earn his keep, which was a position that would be as welcome to Erik as a punch to the gut. He was not accustomed to servitude, which meant he would eventually look for opportunity elsewhere. "Engla-lond, then?"

"Aye."

Hakon nodded. It was as he thought. "It is strange to watch him go," Hakon said. "For the past year he has been the focus all of my energy and attention. His presence overshadowed everything, even my dreams. Now he's gone."

Sigurd snorted. "Erik has been a problem since the first pimple sprouted on his ugly face." Which may have been an exaggeration, but Hakon felt no need to argue. "Oh, it's good to see him go and know that we don't have to live with that red-haired bastard fouling up this kingdom any longer. I just wish a storm would come and take him to the bottom of the sea for the crabs to feast on. Not that the crabs would enjoy him, mind you." He chortled at his own joke. "Anyway, it is time we shift our attention to other things, for there will be other challenges. And they will come sooner than you think."

"His sons, for one."

Sigurd picked another blade of grass. "Aye. His sons will come in time. But that is not what worries me now. It is the unseen challenges lurking somewhere out there," he waved his paw in the direction of Rogaland, "that have my thought cage spinning. That is why it is so important to consolidate your power now. You must strengthen your hold on the realm before the next fool with a sword comes to claim it for himself."

Hakon sighed. He knew Sigurd had the right of it; but at that moment, he had not the energy to dwell on more challenges or on his marriage to Groa. "Come," he said, shifting his thoughts away from his counselor's heavy words. "Let us break open Erik's stores and feast on the wealth of my departed brother. It is time to prepare for the future."

Chapter 5

The families and their retinues began to arrive just days after Erik's departure. They came at the behest of Jarl Tore, who had spread the word of Hakon's victory through the western fylker and invited men to feast the Midsummer solstice with their new king. By foot and on horseback, in fishing boats and warships, they arrived, some from as far south as Agder and others from as far north as the Trondelag. Jarl Tore the Silent came with them, looking far more fit than he had the last time Hakon had seen him.

"Egil has been sneaking sips of the feast mead, by the looks of him." It was Ottar who said this. He sat with Didrik and Hakon on the path leading up to Hakon's hall, watching the newcomers arrive. Down on the beach, Egil worked his way through the crowd, exchanging hearty hugs and laughter with a fair amount of the men, and even some of the women. "I've never seen him laugh so much."

Didrik chuckled. "Give him some time. Right now his poor friends are ale-starved. Just wait until the drinks flow and mens' tongues loosen and we hear the truth of their histories together. Egil's surliness will return soon enough when the boasting and teasing start, I'd wager."

"Aye," Ottar agreed as he scratched his wiry bicep. "You may have the right of it, but it will be fun to hear their tales nonetheless."

"Remind me to take the men's weapons before the feasting begins," Hakon put in, not liking the prospect of drunken men, loose tongues, and weapons.

"That I will gladly do," responded Didrik.

"Who's that?" Hakon asked, pointing at a knarr that had just appeared in the bay.

The men followed Hakon's finger and studied the ship for a while. They shrugged. "Some trader, I'd imagine," said Ottar. "No one of import anyway."

Which didn't seem right, because Sigurd and Tore had met on the beach, and were watching the ship approach. Hakon said as much to his comrades. "Come. Let us learn who this newcomer is," he said, rising.

They walked down the path to the shingle and joined Sigurd's group. "I've never seen such interest in a knarr. What's in it that has you and Tore standing here waiting?" Hakon asked his jarls.

Sigurd glanced at his king, his face alight. "What's in it is my wife," he said, punching Hakon on the shoulder. It felt like a hammer blow.

"Your wife?" Hakon asked as he rubbed his shoulder. "I thought she was in Is-land." Sigurd had sent his wife and daughter away to protect them from Erik. That had been more than a winter ago, and he had not seen or heard from them since.

"She was," he said with a growing grin. "But that's the ship she took to Is-land, so it must be that she's returned." Jarl Tore patted Sigurd on the shoulder, obviously pleased, for Sigurd's wife, Bergliot, also happened to be Tore's daughter.

Hakon looked back at the ship. "How can you tell it's her? The ship has no markings."

"I can tell."

And just then, a woman stood up beside the prow and waved. She was a tall woman, with hair so blond it was almost white. She wore it braided and pulled back from her angular face in a coiled bun, as was the fashion for a married woman. About her shoulders rested a rich cloak lined with polar bear fur.

As the ship drew closer, another woman appeared beside the prow. This woman was taller than Sigurd's wife, and thinner, with auburn hair that danced about her face in tight ringlets.

"Astrid has grown, eh, Tore! She is a young woman now. She will need a husband soon."

Sigurd grunted. "We will need to find a man to match her spirit-edness."

The knarr glided onto the sand and the crew dropped the gangplank. As soon as it hit the beach, Sigurd bounded up to the ship's deck and crushed his family in a bear hug. Hakon smiled at his friend's joy.

Jarl Tore met his daughter on the beach and held her before him. There was a tear in his eye. He wiped it away, unashamed.

"Father," she said through her smile.

"My heart is full at the sight of you," he rasped. "And this beautiful girl!" He grabbed his granddaughter's hands. "Look how you've grown." Astrid's cheeks blushed under the happy gaze of her grandfather.

"I forget myself," Tore finally said. "Come! You must meet your new king." He guided his family to Hakon. "King Hakon. Allow me to introduce you to my daughter, Bergliot, and granddaughter, Astrid." Each in turn bowed respectfully.

"It is an honor to meet you, King Hakon. I have much to thank you for," Bergliot said. She was mayhap in her late twenties, with keen blue eyes and ruddy cheeks that lent some color to her fair skin. She met Hakon's gaze evenly, obviously used to being in the presence of powerful men.

"I look forward to getting to know you. And you as well, Astrid," said Hakon. The girl smiled, more with her eyes, which were the color of pine needles, than with her lips. She looked amused, Hakon decided, though just at what was hard to tell. Hakon returned her smile, though in his stomach something fluttered.

The Midsummer feast began the following evening. The guests gathered weaponless in the golden dusk to watch Sigurd sacrifice a pair of fat lambs and horses in honor of the gods of the summer, and to pray for a bountiful harvest. He then lit the pile of wood stacked on the beach. As the flames climbed into the clear sky, the crowd encircled the growing bonfire and cast their own prayers at the flames in the hope that the smoke would carry their supplications to the gods in the sky.

Hakon watched from the doorway of his hall, content to let his people hold their ceremony and equally content to abstain from it. For it was also the Feast of St. John, or at least some time close to it. He had spent his morning quietly praying to Christ and felt bolstered in his faith despite the pagan ceremony.

The people soon grew tired of the heat and found their places at the eating boards, which Hakon's thralls had placed along the shingle. Hakon strode down the path to the feasting ground, dressed in his finest garb and ringed by his hirdmen. For he was the new king and it was important that his guests saw him for what he now was: a giver of rings and the vanquisher of his brother Erik. When he reached the beach, he made a show of sitting in the High Seat that had been his father's and brother's and was now his. The display was not lost on his guests, who stared in silence as he slid onto the seat. That is, until the ale arrived and their attention shifted to their cups.

"Look at all of these people who have come to celebrate you," Sigurd said to him, waving his arm expansively. He sat to Hakon's right — the seat of honor. "Does it not feel good to finally be king, Hakon?"

A grin stretched across Hakon's face. He grabbed Sigurd's shoulder and shook it. "It was hard to envision a few short moons ago, but it has truly come to pass. And I owe much of it to you, Sigurd."

Sigurd's laugh was deep and hearty. "That's true. You do! But don't worry — I won't let you forget it." He stood then and bellowed to the crowd with his cup raised high. "To Hakon! May he enjoy a long and successful reign!"

"To Hakon!" came the response of hundreds.

That night they ate simply but well: cuts of lamb, stew with horse-meat, slices of fresh dark bread, soft cheese, and strawberries. It was basic fare for the new king of a realm, but it was all Hakon's household could muster at such short notice. Hakon abstained from the sacrificed meat but gorged on the bread and cheese and berries.

As he ate, he settled deeper into the oaken chair of his forebears and felt the stress slide from him. For the first time in weeks, he allowed himself to relax and simply enjoy the chatter and laughter of his guests, the pale summer night, the crackle of the bonfire, and the warmth of the food in his belly. At one of the closer tables, his hirdman Didrik and Toralv were engaged in a drinking bout. Each had four cups lined up before him and when Ottar said "Go!" they guzzled one after the other in a race to empty them all. It was close, but Didrik won out, and stood with his hands held high as the rest of the tables cheered his prowess.

"Again!" slurred Toralv. "I'm just warming up."

Didrik, who was built like a small boulder, belched at him. "You might be twice as tall as me, Toralv, but you're still no match for me at the table. Ottar, show this young man how it's done. Thrall! Bring us more ale!"

"Such ale isn't meant to be guzzled," grumbled Jarl Tore who, like Hakon, had been watching the competition from the head table. "It's too good for the likes of those scoundrels. Almost as good as the ale I have in More," he boasted. "Two rings of silver says we swap their ale for piss in the next round and they won't even notice."

Hakon laughed. "I'll take that wager. The more for us!"

Tore grinned, stretching the scar on his neck. "The more for us," he repeated drunkenly. "Such ale shouldn't be wasted."

"It is Erik's," Hakon said. "He was kind enough to leave us some."

"Ah," said Tore as he took another swig, "that is even better. To the victor go the spoils, eh? Did he leave his brewer too?"

"Sadly, no."

Sigurd snorted. "Enough of Erik and his ale. Let us enjoy happier things, eh? I have a surprise." Sigurd clapped his hands twice. "Astrid!" he called.

All eyes turned to Sigurd's daughter, who rose from her bench near the crackling fire and walked to the center of the feasting field. In appearance she was indeed a bit awkward, with long, gangly limbs and a shock of wild auburn curls that shot in all directions. But there was something about the peace that graced her face and the way she held her eyes half closed and head tilted, that was utterly captivating. It was as if she listened to some unheard voice that no one save her could hear.

She bowed slightly to Hakon, closed her eyes, and then lifted her chin, ignoring the chatter about her. A soft voice rose from her swan-like throat. One by one, the guests took note and silenced their talk. Astrid's voice filled the silence with a fluidity and depth that belied her gangly looks. She sang of a young wood nymph whose forbidden love for a human boy forced her to choose between mortal love and immortal life. She held her eyes closed, as if singing to a vision in her mind that could only be shared through the mellifluousness of her voice. When the song ended, no one spoke. No one dared shatter the moment.

Astrid did not wait for recognition, nor open her eyes to see if the audience approved. Instead, she launched into the next song, one that betold the passionate, reckless love shared between King Harald and his third wife, Swanhild. If the first song shackled Hakon, this new song filled him with awe. Though he had heard the tale many times from his father's skalds, he had never heard a woman sing it. In fact, save for his mother in the darkness of his father's hall when his youthful energy robbed him of sleep, he had never heard a woman sing, for such things were forbidden in the Christian halls of Engla-lond.

When the song ended, the audience sat rapt. Even the young children and the hunting dogs lay still. It was Sigurd's thunderous clapping that broke the spell. Those around him quickly followed suit, including Hakon.

Sigurd elbowed his king again. "My daughter leaves for Is-land a little girl, barely able to squeak, and returns a young woman with the voice of an enchantress, eh?"

Hakon blushed. He could only nod at Sigurd's words.

"Thank you, Astrid," Jarl Sigurd called to the girl. "That will be all." She bowed again in Hakon's direction and took her seat beside her mother.

The following morning, his head thick from the previous night's festivities, Hakon summoned the noblemen to his hall. The chieftains and jarls, bonders, and warriors entered in groups according to their loyalties and sat on the platforms that lined the walls. As the hall filled, thralls moved silently among the guests, passing out cups of ale and pieces of hard bread. Hakon sat silently before them on the High Seat with Egil and Sigurd standing by his side.

When they were settled, Hakon began. He thanked his supporters and welcomed those who had stayed neutral in the fight against Erik. He then reminded all of his promise — that from this day forward, all men would be odal born to their property as they had been in the time before Harald. The men cheered Hakon's words, for his promise would ensure that once again, land could pass from father to son without dispute.

But owning land came with obligations, and this too Hakon impressed upon them. The men would be required to attend the law assemblies, or things, to settle disputes peacefully and to pay their taxes. If the war arrow came to their homes, they needed to heed the call with sons, or weapons, or both. Those who did not accept the obligations would have their odal rights revoked. Some of the nobles argued the practicalities, insisting that the North was not yet a unified kingdom, and each district, or fylke, came with deep histories and individual needs. Meeting those obligations, they insisted, might be difficult given long-standing grievances between neighbors or hard weather or poor harvests.

Hakon rebutted the argument flatly. "I have put before you a simple proposition. We will reinstate the regional things next summer and the law shall rule all men once more. If you cannot find a way to set your differences aside and meet your obligations, you may have your odal rights taken away. Remember that. All who accept these terms, stand."

To a man, they stood.

Hakon smiled. "Thank you. Now, go back to your families and friends. We will feast again tonight."

When the assembly adjourned, Hakon headed down a trail that led to the south side of the hill on which the estate sat. It was a trail he had taken many times as a young boy when something troubled him, or when he saw his father mistreat his mother. Now he walked those very same steps again, his feet picking their way from memory past a copse of pines to a boulder that stuck out from the southern slope like a pimple. He climbed the boulder and sat with his legs hanging off the edge. Before him, the strait stretched southward. To the east lay the crisscrossing patchwork of Rogaland with its sun-sparkled waterways. Hakon turned his face to the blue sky and let the sun warm his fair skin.

"I see we had the same idea."

Hakon spun. Astrid stood in the shade of one of the pines behind him with that same amused look on her freckled face. It was as if she knew of a comical secret to which no one else was privy.

"Am I disturbing you?" she asked politely.

"No," answered Hakon a bit too hastily. He motioned to a spot next to him. "Please."

Astrid sat beside Hakon, smoothing her overdress over her long legs as she did so. She was certainly not shy.

"I used to come here when I was little," Hakon explained. It was small talk, but he wanted to avoid an awkward silence. "When I was trying to escape work."

Astrid grinned. "I cannot picture you hiding."

Hakon smiled back, remembering how his mother would always find him. "I was not very good at it."

Astrid hugged her knees up to her chest. Hakon watched her from the corner of his eye, suddenly aware that he knew very little about this girl other than the fact that she could sing and her ease in his presence made him uncomfortable.

"Why did you let Erik go?"

The question took Hakon by surprise. He was expecting something simple, something innocuous to start the conversation. Hakon thought to rebuke her for her directness, but stopped himself. Her question, he realized, was not meant to harm — it was merely asked out of curiosity. "Why do you ask?"

"People say that you let him go because of your religion. Is that true?"

"You are bold to ask such questions. You barely know me."

She turned to meet his gaze and for the first time, Hakon realized just how green her eyes truly were. They were more like emeralds than pine needles. "My father taught me to be direct," she said without malice. "I am sorry if it offends you."

"Then you have learned your lesson well."

She grinned at Hakon's subtle jest but did not let up on her interrogation. "So it is true?"

He scratched at the whiskers on his chin, trying to come up with an explanation Astrid might understand. "Aye. To a certain extent it is." Hakon's mind turned to Father Otker and the words he had spoken to Hakon not long before Hakon had come to the North. "A teacher once told me that it is easy to kill, but it takes courage to forgive. Those words kept me from killing a man named Udd in a duel. Admittedly, that was a mistake. But they also kept me from killing my brother, and that was no mistake. I suppose deep down I didn't want to kill him. He is family. Besides, all of my other half-brothers are dead. The killing had to stop, and I am glad stopped it with Erik." He shrugged and glanced at her. "I guess that's the best explanation I have for letting my brother go."

"Your teacher does not sound like a warrior." She brushed a curl from her freckled cheek. It was a mindless gesture, but it ignited Hakon.

It took him a moment to respond. "You are right. He is a priest."

"A Christian priest?"

"Aye, a Christian priest," he said guardedly.

"Why do you follow the words of a priest when you are a king?"

Again, a frank question born from curiosity but delivered with surprising boldness. Hakon turned his face away lest she see the growing annoyance in his eyes. He didn't like her questions, but he didn't want her to leave. "It is difficult to explain. My father ruled not with wisdom, but with violence. My brother ruled with greed, anger, and suspicion. I want to rebuild this realm, make it safer, make it more lawful. Men cannot be ruled with fear alone."

"And the words of a monk can help you do this?"

"The words of the monk are my sun stone. They guide me, and they help me show people a different way."

"Can you not show people a different way without using a religion that few people here accept?"

Hakon looked sidelong at her. "You think me foolish," he said, no longer able to contain his anger. "The gods here teach men to fight, to deceive, to fornicate, to take. Just look at the stories we've been told since we were children. Odin, the shape-shifter god of war. Thor, the fiery god of storms and weather. Loki, the trickster. They are unruly, unpredictable. We sacrifice to appease them, and yet they never are. They teach us that violence and warfare are the natural way of things. They teach us that cunning and deceit are welcome. How can such gods provide guidance for a lawful, united realm?"

"You think the followers of the Christ-god are any different?" The edge in her voice matched Hakon's. "Your Christian kings and warriors kill each other as liberally as our kings, only in the name of a different god. I have heard the stories of Mercia and Wessex and Northumbria and the rest. I have heard of the slaughter Charlemagne brought to the people of his lands. Don't think I don't know about their wars and their deceit and their bloodshed. The rule of law existed because of the sword, not because of some god-man who died on a cross." She stopped herself and looked away, and for a long moment they held their lips tight and their thoughts to themselves.

It was Astrid who broke the uneasy silence. "Your words are dangerous, Hakon. Especially here."

"I know," he acquiesced, hoping to calm the situation before she stormed off in anger. "They are not words I usually speak to others. But then, others do not usually ask me questions like yours. The point is: whether I rule in the name of my god or yours, it'll take courage. So I'd rather put my trust in my God."

She turned her head away. He looked at his feet. The silence stretched.

"Your singing last night," Hakon finally said when the silence grew unbearable. "It was beautiful."

"Thank you." She must have heard compliments before, for his produced only the faintest of smiles. Or perchance her anger still smoldered inside of her and she was reluctant to let it go.

"Where did you learn to sing like that?"

"One of my maids taught me. She used to sing to me at night before bed. Her voice was beautiful, and growing up, I sought to mimic it. When Erik took over and we had to leave, I started singing some of her songs to calm myself. That was a frightening time." Astrid paused before switching the subject. "Father tells me you will be married soon?"

Hakon frowned. "Aye."

"I am sorry. Did I displease you again? I —"

Hakon waved the apology aside. "No, it was a fair question."

"You do not wish to marry?"

"Not this girl."

"Why not?"

Hakon sighed, then told her the story of Aelfwin. "Groa and our marriage opens my wound anew, and Ivar knows it," Hakon concluded. He left out how unattractive Groa truly was and how he despised her looks almost as much as he despised her and her family. "The only reason I marry Groa is because of my oath to Ivar. But it will never remove the hate I have for them." He looked off at the horizon lest Astrid see the anger and pain in his eyes.

It was then that he saw the large warship headed up the strait toward the estate. He rose.

"I am sorry," she said, also standing. "I did not mean to drive you away."

Hakon grunted a response as his mind tried to work out who the new visitor might be. The ship was too large to be a local chieftain.

Astrid followed his gaze to the ship. "Oh," she said.

"Come." He grabbed her arm, and together they headed back to the estate.

Sigurd stood at the door of Hakon's hall with Egil, studying the approaching ship. When Hakon arrived, the jarl regarded first Hakon, then his daughter. Astrid bowed her head without word and entered the hall.

"You look like a fox who's been caught stealing eggs," growled Sigurd. Egil chuckled.

Hakon ignored the jibe. "Who are they?"

"I don't know," Sigurd said. "But let us go find out."

The ship rounded the peninsula and rowed slowly into the bay below Avaldsnes. Hakon and his jarls gathered on the beach along with a number of curious guests. The ship stopped an arrow's flight from the beach, and a man appeared beside the dragon-headed prow. He was a big man with raven-black hair and an equally black beard that covered a large portion of his shining byrnie.

"I seek King Hakon, son of Harald Fairhair, and the boy who defeated my friend Erik?"

"I am here," answered Hakon, stepping forward from the group. "And who are you?"

"My name is Ragnvald. Some call me the Dane. My king, Gorm, bids you greeting," he called across the water, "and congratulates you on your victory against your brother."

The words hit Hakon like a slap to the face. Around him, his people stirred, for the slaughter in Kaupang was now common knowledge. "The same Ragnvald who murdered women and children in Kaupang?"

"Some may see it that way."

Hakon saw again the bloating dead, the flies, the charred remains of the marketplace. "Is there another way to see it? You have a lot of courage to come here after what you did."

"I am not here to talk about Kaupang. I come here at the request of King Gorm. May I come ashore?"

"If you wish to die, you can come ashore. Otherwise, you may speak from there so all might hear your king's message."

Ragnvald shrugged his big shoulders, indifferent to Hakon's threats. "As you wish. My king seeks a friendship between our people."

"And what price does your king ascribe to friendship?"

"Ah. That is a fine question. Your brother profited much from our relationship. You could enjoy the same."

"You speak of trade with Kaupang?"

"Aye. That and other dealings."

The smirk on Ragnvald's face set Hakon's nerves on edge. "My brother profited, you say? You mean he whored himself for gain. And in the end, where were you and your Danes in his final struggle?"

Ragnvald hesitated.

"I will tell you where. You were killing innocent merchants, trades-men, and families in the town my brother let you control. Then you ran like children when the fight turned against you. Here is a question for you, Ragnvald the Runner: Are you prepared to give me control of Hedeby so I can return the kindness you showed my people in Kau-pang?" Hakon turned to his men and shouted, "Who here would like to control Hedeby and all of the trade within it?"

The warriors cheered.

"Well, Dane?"

Ragnvald kept his lips tight.

"Or here's another question for your king to consider — if Gorm is not willing to protect the towns I let him control, is he willing to come to my aid when I need it most? Based on what I've seen, I'd say the answer to that is 'no.' What say you, Ragnvald?"

As Hakon spoke, the warriors aboard Ragnvald's ship grew more and more agitated and began casting curses in Hakon's direction. Ragnvald silenced them with a chop of this hand. "See how your words upset my men, Hakon? Remember those words when we burn your kingdom, enslave your people, and rape your women. And remember too that things could have gone differently for you."

"You would lay waste to my kingdom regardless of my words, Ragnvald. The only thing to prevent it would be to whore myself to your king as my brother did, and that I will not do. Tell your King Gorm that he can show his friendship by halting Danish incursions into our lands, and discussing fair, open, and safe trade among our people. He can also send wergeld to the people of Kaupang to help them rebuild what you so ruthlessly destroyed. Let us start there, and we'll see if we can build a lasting friendship thereafter."

The jarl spat over the gunwale. "I will tell my king of this exchange."

"Do so," said Hakon.

The man motioned for his crew to back row from the bay. Hakon watched them until they disappeared beyond the peninsula.

"The wolves smell prey," remarked Sigurd. "The challenges to your throne have come quicker than even I imagined."

Hakon ignored the jarl and motioned Egil to his side. "Watch Ragnvald until he's left the area. Make sure he means no malice."

Egil nodded.

"Bastard," Hakon cursed to himself and turned from the beach. He should have known the Danes would waste no time.

Chapter 6

"Damn it!" Hakon dropped his blade and clutched his wrist where Egil's blade had sliced the skin. Blood ran crimson between his fingers. It was a superficial wound, but it throbbed nevertheless.

"I have warned you to be patient, Hakon." Egil's cheeks glowed red from exertion and adrenaline, and he smiled wolfishly. "You saw my shield drop and in your haste to finish me, you let your own guard down. You assumed that because my hair is now white with age, I can no longer bear a shield in single combat for as long as you." Egil pointed his practice blade at Hakon's wrist. "Have that tended to quickly. It's unseemly for kings to faint."

Hakon stalked to his hall, ignoring the eyes of his feast-guests who had been watching the sword practice with interest. As he entered, Astrid turned from the loom at which she worked with her mother, Bergliot. Seeing his wound, she hastened to him. Bergliot stood back, her brows raised as she looked at her husband.

"May I?"

Hakon held out his wrist for Astrid to examine. "You'll need a bandage. Wait here."

Sigurd, who had been sitting at a table, shook his head. "You call that a wound? I've seen little boys with worse cuts than that."

"Nevertheless," said Astrid as she returned, "it needs a bandage."

Hakon smiled sheepishly, trying his best to avoid the parental gazes of Sigurd and Bergliot.

"Hold this hard on the wound," she said, handing Hakon a clean cloth. "Now sit." She pointed to the bench beside the hearth, where logs smoldered. "When I tell you, remove the cloth."

"Most people would not order a king so," Hakon chided as he sat on the bench.

"I am not most people," countered Astrid.

"That is true," responded Hakon.

"I am afraid I have not taught her well," confided Sigurd as he watched his daughter work.

"You have raised her to be confident. There is no wrong in that."

"Remove the cloth," she ordered even as her cheeks flushed with Hakon's comment. Hakon complied and let her tightly wrap the wound with a second cloth that she had smeared with some sort of poultice. "Keep it clean and bandaged until it starts to scab, then remove the bandages during the day. Try not to use it too much until the scab is half gone."

Hakon smiled politely despite the ridiculous notion. Of course he would use it.

Sigurd called to Hakon's thralls for ale. "Thank you, Astrid," he said to his daughter as the thralls re-entered the room and placed cups before the two men. "That will be all."

Understanding immediately, she bowed slightly to them and left the hall with her mother.

"A singer and a healer. You have quite a daughter, Sigurd. She will make a fine wife for someone."

Sigurd took a sip of ale and burped. "Don't get any ideas, Hakon."

Hakon switched the subject before the conversation turned awkward. "So?"

Sigurd eyed his young charge earnestly. It was a look that rarely graced his face, and Hakon felt his stomach turn.

"It is time for my men to return to their homes." Sigurd studied his ale cup as he spoke.

Hakon's stomach twisted tighter. He had known this day was nigh, but to finally hear the words was more difficult than he imagined. Since his arrival in the North, Sigurd had been his guide, his advisor, and his friend. As contentious as their relationship had been at points, Sigurd was the reason he was sitting in Avaldsnes today. Now the decisions would be his to make. Alone.

"We shall leave with the next good wind...with your blessing, of course."

Sigurd's words made Hakon laugh despite his misgivings. "My blessing? Since when have you asked for that in anything you've done?"

Sigurd grinned mildly at the jest. "You know me too well. As for you —"

Hakon held up his hand, masking his unease with a brave face. "Spare me, Sigurd. I know what comes next."

Sigurd nodded. "Ivar waits. If you leave before the next full moon, you will be there in time. Do not tarry, for the Danes lurk." Sigurd sipped at his ale as Hakon swallowed the bitter message in his words — the marriage to Groa would need to happen soon. "You will need men," Sigurd went on. "Tore and I have spoken, and we think some of our own men — the younger ones — will stay with you, as is their right. I am sure some of your younger guests will stay too." It had been a week since the Midsummer feast, and some of the guests had started to leave. As if in answer to that thought, Sigurd said, "Have Egil find them before too many more head for home."

Hakon stretched his good arm across the table and grabbed Sigurd's wrist. "You have been a good friend and a wise counselor, and I thank you for it. On the next fair wind, you shall sail home."

The winds came two days later, late in the afternoon. Sigurd, Tore, and their men spent the waning daylight hours loading the ships and preparing them for the long northward journey.

Hakon opened barrels of Erik's good ale, and let the men feast together one last time. He celebrated alongside them, though his mood was heavy. He would miss them, Sigurd most of all. The auburn-haired bear of a man was more than a counselor and friend — he was Hakon's compass. With little in the way of thanks, he had helped Hakon navigate the North, its people and its politics. Though Hakon had not always welcomed his decisions, he could not argue with the results. Now the decisions would be Hakon's own, and the consequences his to bear. The realization had been eating at Hakon for days, but this night, as they feasted for the last time together, the thought hit home.

Hakon polished off his cup of ale, then stood and exited the hall. His belly hurt from too much food, and his eyes burned from the smoke of the hearth. He needed some air and a place to empty his bladder. At a dark spot along the palisade, he unlaced his trousers and let his piss pool before his feet. Nearby, a half-naked couple groped each other behind the smithy.

"Are you done?"

Hakon glanced over his shoulder and found Astrid standing behind him, a grin on her face and a heavy cloak draped over her slight shoulders. Hakon laced his trousers, straightened himself, and mindlessly wiped the crumbs from his tunic. "I was...I was just —"

"I know what you were doing." She presented him with a cloak. "I saw you leave the hall. Would you like to go for a walk?"

Hakon grabbed the rough cloak and smiled. "A walk would be good."

She started down the track that led out of the palisade then veered right along the hilltop. Hakon donned the cloak, which hung almost to his ankles, and followed.

"Where did you get this cloak?" he asked as they made their way to the eastern side of the grassy hill. "It's huge, and smells like a dead boar."

"It's my father's," she said without looking back. "I've never heard him referred to as a dead boar."

Just then, Astrid tripped. Hakon grabbed her arm before she hit the ground. "Careful. Here — follow me. Step where I do."

He took the lead and slowed his pace to allow her to follow in his footsteps. She was agile for such a gangly girl and picked her way along the dark path without further incident. When they got to Hakon's rock, they sat and gazed out at the Karmsund Strait.

"It is wondrous," Astrid remarked, giving voice to his own thoughts. Before them, the light of the low northern sun stretched its scarlet glow across the waters of the channel, while far above, stars twinkled in the rich blue of the summer night.

"You must be looking forward to getting back to your home," Hakon offered after a time.

"Home," she repeated. "It is strange, but I do not think of Lade as home. Is-land is more home than Lade." She shrugged in her cloak. "I suppose that will change in time."

Though he didn't say it, Hakon didn't think Astrid would be in Lade for long. Knowing her father, he was already scheming to marry her off to someone who could increase his area of influence. Mayhap a Halogalander or a More-man. That place, wherever it turned out to be, would be home.

A wolf howled in the distance, interrupting his thoughts. It was far off, across the channel. Astrid looked in the direction of the sound as a second howl followed the first, then another. "The pack is hunting," Hakon observed.

"Aye," she agreed as she pulled a dagger from beneath her cloak and held it before her, letting the red light dance along its blade. It was a fine dagger, with a patterned blade and a handle of polished bone. Hakon tensed, but quickly realized the blade's appearance was not malicious.

Calming, he said, "That is a nice blade, but will do little to protect us from a pack of hungry wolves."

She laughed and handed him the weapon. "It is not meant to protect us from wolves."

Hakon moved the blade in his hands, appreciating its balance and the worn smoothness of its handle. "Did your father give it to you?"

"Aye. He did. Although its original owner was another. See here." She pointed to a runic etching on the blade.

Hakon twisted it until he could read the runes. "Thora. That was my mother's name."

Astrid smiled.

"This is my mother's?"

Astrid's smile broadened at Hakon's surprise.

"Truly?" He studied the blade again with undisguised delight, for it was the only piece of his mother he'd seen here at Avaldsnes — Erik had effectively wiped her existence from this place. The handle and outer sheath were of antler, most likely caribou. The inside of the sheath was wool, which was meant to keep the blade from rusting. Besides the runic inscription, the smith had etched a tiny, amazingly intricate snake pattern into both sides of the metal.

"Why do you have this?" he asked.

"My father told me it was a gift of thanks. Your mother was round with child, and knew you were coming soon. My father, who was here on this estate at the time, agreed to help her find your father, who was away. She gave birth en route, on a beach. Luckily my father had had the foresight to bring along maidservants in case you decided to come early, which you did." She rocked sideways into Hakon to chide him. "As the leading man in her presence, she let my father name you. He gave you the name of my grandfather on my father's side. And as thanks, she gave him the blade, which was the only valuable possession she had with her that would be suitable for a man. My father kept it, and gave it to me when he sent me off to Is-land. And now I give it back to you as thanks for defeating Erik and allowing me to return home. The circle is complete."

Hakon marveled at the dagger. It represented so much more than a token of appreciation shared between Hakon's mother and Astrid's father. It was a symbol of the connection Hakon and Sigurd had to each other. He had been there from Hakon's beginning. More father than his own father. More friend than loyal subject. No wonder he had shepherded Hakon so unflinchingly to the High Seat. Most others would have balked at Hakon's faith and age and inexperience. Sigurd had not. That blade, and the story surrounding it, cut to the very core of Sigurd's loyalty.

"Hakon?"

Hakon shook himself free of his thoughts and focused once again on the blade. "I know not what to say."

"A simple thank you would do." She smiled.

He grinned. "I thank you then."

Astrid's smile faded. "Just remember me when you hold it. That is all I ask."

A long time ago, in Engla-lond, sitting by the River Itchen, Aelfwin had sat by his side. Then, as now, the girl was leaving for a different life. Would that he could have that time with Aelfwin back now; he would have tried to force her to stay. But she, like Astrid, would have refused. He looked at Astrid now, wondering what fate awaited her, and prayed it would be good. She stared down at the water, her face hidden in her curls.

He swallowed and answered lamely, "I will." It was all he could think to say.

The following morning, the respective households collected on the strand below Avaldsnes. Hakon watched from the door of his hall as Sigurd sacrificed a chicken and spread its blood across the sloping prows of each departing ship. Sigurd then poured mead into the surf and raised his hands to the heavens. He spoke to those gathered about him, though from this distance, Hakon could not discern his words.

Before the previous night's feast, Sigurd had given all of his men the choice to stay at Avaldsnes if they so wished. Tore and the remaining locals did the same. In all, nearly one hundred men voted in favor of remaining, many of them young, single, with little to return to. These now said their goodbyes to comrades and family.

Hakon joined them in their farewells and found it far more difficult than he imagined, for many of the departing had been with him his entire rise to the High Seat. They were his brothers-in-arms, and his gratitude toward them knew no limits. The silver armbands and coins he distributed were a sorry exchange for the sacrifices they had made on his behalf.

He found Sigurd in the center of the men. "Come here, you lout," Sigurd called. He crushed Hakon in a bear hug. "I hate goodbyes, so consider this a 'so long for now.' And no gifts! You cannot satisfy my greed."

Hakon waved away the thrall who carried with him a box containing a gift for Sigurd. "Too bad. I was going to give you the keys to the kingdom."

"Ha! Now that would have been something. Fare well, Hakon, and please give my regards to Ivar. I am sorry I will miss your betrothal." Sigurd's eyes twinkled playfully.

"I shall tell you all about it when next we see each other. Fare well, Sigurd. The hall will not be the same without your voice to fill it."

"You mean his hot air," said Jarl Tore, who stood nearby.

Hakon turned to him and grabbed his wrist. Before Hakon could speak, Tore pulled Hakon close and spoke into his ear. "We have done well together, Hakon, and for that I give you thanks. Though life is uncertain, I hope it brings us together again. Until then, fare you well and remember our days together with fondness, as I will."

Hakon felt emotion well up inside of him. "I thank you for all you have done, Tore. You will be greatly missed, my friend."

Hakon then found Astrid, who stood beside her mother. Bergliot looked on with a knowing smile and a certain sadness in her eyes, as if she sensed the growing bond between Hakon and her daughter and understood the pain of this parting.

Astrid stepped forward and extended her hands, which Hakon took in his. Her eyes searched the ground at Hakon's feet. Hakon lifted her chin and smiled into her freckled face. She smiled back, sadly. The amusement was gone from her eyes.

"Be safe, Hakon."

"You too, Astrid."

Astrid pulled her hands away and walked to her father's ship.

Bergliot came forward and bowed to Hakon. "Oh, that this were a different time and you were a different man," she said. "Come see us in Lade when you can, my king."

Hakon nodded and smiled, not trusting himself to speak.

She walked away and joined the throng of departing men. The ships left shortly thereafter, and with a final wave, Hakon headed back to his hall, his face a stony mask and his heart heavy. No one dared speak to him, nor would he have responded if they did.

It was time for his own journey to begin.

Part II

His power should every sagacious man use with discretion;
for he will find, when among the bold he comes,
that no one alone is the doughtiest.
Havamal

Chapter 7

"Not much farther," Egil called from his mount at the head of the column.

"And thank the gods for that," Toralv fired back, giving voice to everyone's thoughts.

"Thank your horse, Toralv. Not the gods," chided Egil without looking back. "How she managed to carry your fat arse this far, I'll never know."

Toralv laughed and patted his steed. "She treats me well, this one. I'll grant you that."

It had been a long trip, and the men were tired. They had first sailed back to the beach where they had captured Erik's vessels and where the bones of Erik's men still lay. From there, half the army marched north, while Didrik and Ottar took the remainder of Hakon's men back to Kaupang. All in all, they had been on the move for twelve days.

Hakon glanced at the small army walking behind him. Like Toralv's girth, his army was swelling. Behind him walked roughly fifty warriors. Most had been Sigurd's and Tore's men, veterans of battles with Erik who now followed Hakon and had been hand-picked by Egil for this journey. A few, though, they had recruited along the way. These mostly consisted of brawny local boys, second and third sons who abandoned their plows and shovels and rocky plots of land in search of fame and fortune with Hakon. Though Hakon had been reluctant to take them on, Egil felt certain he could mold them into warriors, and so they had gathered their measly possessions and come along.

Hakon's small army traveled on a tree-lined path that now wound up a small hill. At its crest they stopped to take in the view that stretched before them. Unlike the rugged west coast, where men scratched a measly existence from the few plots of grass they could find, the Uplands was a wondrous place, filled with rich rolling hills and vast forests intersected by rivers and lakes of sparking blue. This rich land was the envy of many kings, including Hakon's father and grandfather, who had fought for it more than once.

"A few more days, a wedding vow, and a romp with Groa, and you will be master of all you see before you. Not a bad bargain, eh boy?"

Hakon grimaced, unamused by Egil's comment.

"Ah come," he said, his grin remaining. "Why so glum?"

Hakon ignored him, for Asger, a blond, pimple-faced teenager who knew these parts from traveling to the regional law assembly, or thing, during summers, had just returned. He was one of the new boys, and Hakon had sent him to scout ahead for signs of trouble. "What news?"

"None, lord. Just locals going about their business."

"Can we reach Ringsaker by nightfall?"

The boy shook his head, and his stringy hair whipped his mottled cheeks. "It's too far from here, lord. But if we follow the Vorma," he pointed to the river that snaked through the land in the near distance, "we'll reach the south end of Lake Mjosa by nightfall. Ringsaker is another two days' hike along the lake's far shore."

"Very well, Asger. Lead on."

They hiked down the hill and out into a flat valley filled with scattered farmsteads, their fields flowing around islands of woods. There were no signs of inhabitants, but this wasn't surprising. Large groups of armed men usually drove people into hiding. The men picked young apples from a farmer's trees, but otherwise left the homes in peace. By afternoon, they reached the banks of the Vorma and followed it until they found a suitable place to ford. Once across, they headed north until they came to the southern end of Lake Mjosa, where they camped.

The next morning broke overcast and cold. The men donned their cloaks and moved off in silence, following a track that clung to the northern shore of the lake. Hakon rode in silence at the head of the column, his thoughts on the people and events that awaited him. Just picturing Ivar and Groa in his mind set his blood to boiling. It would take every ounce of self-possession to see this wedding through. And when it was over, and Groa was his wife, he knew not how he would handle himself, for every time he looked at her he would see Aelfwin in his mind and his heart would ache with the memory. The whole thing was rotten and ate at him like a festering disease, pushing him deeper and deeper into a black mood. His men adopted his glum disposition, trudging along without a word.

The weather soured in the afternoon. Dark clouds rolled in over the lake and a soft rain began to fall, forming muddy pools beneath their feet. The men pressed on until they found a forest thick with oaks in which to camp. Some of the men tried to make fires, but the sky erupted with bolts of lightning and thunder, and the rain fell harder, spoiling their efforts.

"Thor is angry at something," remarked Toralv as he huddled beneath his travel cloak at the base of a tree and cast his eyes to the sky, receiving a drop of rain in the eye for his trouble.

"Not as angry as I will be if this damned storm robs me of sleep," answered Egil.

"I will warn the men to stay clear of you tomorrow," Toralv responded as he wiped his face, "for this rain isn't stopping anytime soon." He seemed nonplussed by the notion.

"So now you can read the weather, can you?" Egil grumbled.

Toralv closed his eyes. "A blind man could read this weather."

Egil cast a muffled curse at his young comrade and let the matter drop.

But in the end, Toralv had the right of it. The rain fell throughout the night and finally ceased early the following morning. Cold and soaked, the men moved out again under a leaden sky that seemed ready to burst at any moment.

At midday, they stopped to eat some food under the canopy of some trees.

"How much farther, Asger?" Hakon asked.

"Not much. Once we clear these trees, we should be there."

Hakon surveyed his army. The men were tired and dirty and grumpy. Their wet clothes clung to their bodies; their hair hung limply on their shoulders.

"We should stop," Egil said. "Mayhap bathe and dry our clothes before we come to Ringsaker."

Hakon had thought the same thing, but he was not confident the weather would hold. "Bathe ourselves only to get pissed on again? No, we keep going," he said. "We can bathe once we get there."

"We'll be a fine-looking lot, arriving in Ringsaker in our current state."

"I care more about getting warm than I do about looking fine for Ivar and his people. We keep moving."

Egil cleared his throat and spat a large wad of phlegm onto the ground. "So be it."

True to Asger's word, the forest soon gave way to a large open meadow in which stood the high-beamed walls of Ringsaker. A number of wooden stakes ringed the walls, each adorned with a decapitated head — some freshly hewn, others old and withered, their empty eye sockets and open mouths gawking at a world they could no longer see. The place was exactly as Hakon remembered. More fort than estate, with an air of evil that hung over it like a stench and set Hakon's nerves on edge.

"Ivar is keeping some strange company," commented Egil, nodding with his chin to a sea of leather tents that stood just to the north of Ringsaker. "Some of those belong to Swedes."

"Are you certain?"

"Aye."

"Why would Swedes be here?"

"Mayhap they've come to wish you well," mused Toralv sardonically.

Egil snorted and turned to the men. "Keep your weapons near."

"You speak as if we're marching into battle," Hakon said under his breath.

"Battle? No. Enemy territory? Aye."

A horn blast alerted everyone of Hakon's approach. To their right, men and women emerged from their tents and studied the approaching group. Up on Ringsaker's walls, spear-warriors gathered. Hakon tensed and scanned them for any signs of malice. Though he saw none, their mere presence did little to alleviate his misgivings.

Just then, Ringsaker's eastern gate creaked open to reveal a large throng of people. Ivar stood at the head of the group, looking as if he'd aged ten years since Hakon had seen him last, though it had only been a few moons. Ivar had never been tall, but his rotund body had always been upright. Now it seemed to droop like a leaf heavy with rain, an effect accentuated by the silver hair hanging limply from his head and the heavy fur cloak draping his shoulders. He lifted his sullen face to gaze upon the arriving guests. It was clear even from a distance that the self-styled king was not well.

Ivar leaned on the arm of his tawny-haired daughter, Groa, who had inherited her father's squat, round frame. She might have been handsome of face, with her keen blue eyes and full lips, were it not for the portliness that rounded her cheeks and thickened her limbs — a portliness that had ballooned alarmingly since their last meeting.

Behind them, Ivar's wife, Holmfrid, and his son, Thorgil, stood tall and proud. They were both handsome, with thick brown hair, high cheeks, and dark, hawk-like eyes. They might have been brother and sister, were it not for the strands of silver at Holmfrid's temples.

"Would that you were marrying Holmfrid," Toralv whispered from the side of his mouth. "I bet she could teach you a thing or two."

"Keep your lips tight," Egil hissed.

Hakon grinned and dismounted.

"You're late," said Ivar weakly. "And you stink. And yet you smile upon us as if this is all a joke." The effort of those few words brought on a deep, rattling cough that bent him at the waist.

Hakon's smile faded and he looked at Groa for explanation. She glowered at him but offered no words. He could see now that pimples had sprouted on her forehead and cheeks. The months since he had seen her last had not been kind to her.

"We were delayed," Hakon finally said by way of explanation.

Ivar wiped spittle from his lips with the back of his sleeve and surveyed Hakon's men. "Where is your Christian priest? Do you not need one for the ceremony?"

"It is good that you remember our bargain, Ivar. Sadly, I had not the time to arrange for a priest to come."

Ivar waved away Hakon's response as if it were a bothersome fly. "It is of no consequence. Come. The guest hall is ready for you and your men." He waved vaguely in the direction of the hall. "I will have my bathhouse heated for those of you who wish to bathe. We shall feast at nightfall and can speak more then. Thorgil, see to their horses." With that, Ivar turned and, with the assistance of his daughter and wife, hobbled away.

"Your father is not well," Hakon said to Thorgil when Ivar was out of earshot.

"Father is fine," responded Thorgil. "It is just a cough."

What Hakon had just witnessed was more than a cough, but he kept his thoughts to himself.

"Bjarni," Thorgil yelled to one of his men, "see to their horses!" He then clasped Hakon's shoulder and led him toward the guest hall. "It is good to have you here. Frankly, my family was wondering if you might show at all."

His words sparked a flame in Hakon's gut. "The thought had occurred to me, but I am no oath-breaker, despite the pain it brings me to keep it."

Thorgil smiled maliciously. "Aye. I remember what my father did to your precious thrall girl. It would be enough to make any man second-guess their union to this family, eh? You are strong inside, Hakon."

The barbed comment struck deep, and Hakon struggled to keep his composure. "You walk on thin ice with that limp of yours, Thorgil." He motioned with his chin to Thorgil's leg, which had been wounded in the battle against Erik. "How is your leg, by the way?"

Thorgil's smile vanished. "Healing," he said curtly.

They arrived at the door to the guest hall and Thorgil gestured for Hakon to enter. "Pardon me if I don't show you around, but I think you're familiar with this hall already. Sadly, you won't find any thrall women here this time around."

It was in this very hall that Hakon had reunited with his childhood friend, Aelfwin. Hakon swallowed the bitter reminder of that memory with a scowl. Thorgil grinned, knowing full well his words had struck home. Just then, Toralv brushed past the two of them and slammed into Thorgil's bad leg with his saddlebag. Thorgil's leg buckled, and he grabbed the doorframe to steady himself.

"I beg your pardon, Prince Thorgil."

Thorgil's dark eyes flashed. "You clumsy —" He bit back his words and turned to Hakon.

"Looks like that leg of yours is still a bit tender," Hakon said.

Thorgil ignored him. "We eat at dusk. Do not be late."

"Horse turd," grumbled Toralv when Thorgil was gone. Hakon smiled and put the retreating Thorgil from his mind.

Inside the guest hall, all was exactly as it had been three moons before. Nothing had changed. Not the positions of the cots or the scant furnishings. Not the spot where the water bowl sat or the spider web in the corner. Nothing. It was as if he had entered a bad dream to which he knew the ending and from which he couldn't escape. Hakon steeled himself against the memories and threw his pack on a nearby bed.

Hakon's men entered behind him and spread out through the hall. Some stretched aching limbs and backs. Others stripped themselves of their wet clothing or set to work coaxing a fire from the small hearth in the middle of the hall. With fifty men, quarters were tight, but at least they'd be warm and dry.

As the men relaxed, Egil called Toralv and Hakon to him. He stood by the door, looking outward into the courtyard where warriors mingled and thralls scurried to do their masters' bidding. "Listen," he began quietly, then glanced over his shoulder to make sure no one was near. "Toralv, find an alternate escape from this hall, but do so discreetly. I don't want to panic the men. Make sure even you can fit through. If there is none, make one, but conceal it."

Toralv frowned. "Think you that Ivar would try something at his own daughter's wedding?"

"It is not Ivar that worries me," he said. "Something else is amiss. I am not sure what it is, but I feel it in here." He tapped his chest.

Hakon knew better than to ignore the intuition of an old warrior. "Toralv," he said. "Wait until darkness comes. Then go about your business as Egil suggests."

"What about the feast?"

The stern stares of Hakon and Egil gave him his answer. The giant youth scratched his bearded chin, looking disappointed. "If you say so. Just bring me back some food and drink."

As the sky's light dimmed, Hakon and his men left the guest hall for the feast. All had now washed the grime from their bodies and brushed the mud and twigs and leaves from their clothing. Before they left, Egil warned them to stay alert and not to drink overmuch. With Egil's warnings fresh in their minds, they deposited their weapons outside the raucous mead hall and entered. The other guests had already arrived and stood shoulder to shoulder, talking and laughing and drinking. Those nearest the door stopped and stared, their conversations halting in mid-word as the newcomers filtered into the hall. The effect rippled across the murky interior until everyone stood silently, staring at Hakon and his men. Hakon ignored their boorishness and led his warriors into the throng.

"Hakon!" called Ivar from across the hall, his voice barely audible. "Come!" He waved Hakon over to the dais before launching into a new coughing fit. "You men," Ivar called to Hakon's men when the coughing had subsided. "Make yourselves welcome in my hall. My food, my ale, and my thrall women are yours for the taking."

Hakon sat beside Ivar as his men drifted into the crowd. No sooner had he sunk into his chair than a thrall girl placed a mug before him. She was pretty enough, despite the ugly cut and fresh bruise that marred her left cheek. Hakon offered her a smile. She averted her eyes and hurried away.

"Still making eyes at the thralls, I see." It was a pointed reference to Aelfwin.

Hakon jabbed back. "Keep beating your thralls, Ivar, and you'll find poison in your cup. It's far more healthy to make eyes at them."

"Hmm. It's rare to find wisdom in the words of a boy. Tell me, how was your journey?"

Hakon shrugged. "Easy enough for a boy like me. I suspect it wouldn't have been quite so easy for you."

"It's impolite to disrespect a man in his own hall."

Hakon smiled. "Which is worse? A host disrespecting his invited guest, or a guest disrespecting his host?"

Ivar grunted and took a deep swig from his cup. "At least my daughter isn't marrying a fool."

A truce, then.

A coughing fit suddenly wracked Ivar's body. It was deep and rattling and bent him at the waist with its force. When it ended, he wiped his lips with his sleeve and took a swig of ale. His face was crimson as he sat back up.

Hakon thought to say something but knew the older man would just wave his comment away. Instead he bit into some hard bread and paused to look about the hall. At one table, Ivar's hirdmen laughed and arm-wrestled and flirted with women. The older boys looked on with wide-eyed envy at the boisterous warriors and the girls who made eyes at them. It was not all that long ago that Hakon had done the same in Athelstan's hall, praying for the chance to prove himself and find his way to the warrior's table. Near the boys stood a group of finely dressed women and men who Hakon recognized as the landholders of Ivar's realm.

Off to his right sat a different group, probably the Swedes, a handsome lot, tall and stately and finely garbed in colorful clothes that exposed their foreignness. Among them sat a handsome man with a shock of white-blond hair, ruddy cheeks, and eyes the color of blue ice. Those eyes studied Hakon now. Thorgil sat by the young Swede's side and whispered into his ear. The sight of those two together put Hakon on edge.

Hakon gestured with his chin. "You have Swedes here. Why?"

Ivar grunted. "Tensions started rising on the border almost immediately after the battle with Erik. To calm the hostility, we invited some of the friendlier clans to the wedding. That man with Thorgil is the son of the jarl who lives on our border, just to the east of here. His name is Gudmund. His father is a weasel, but Gudmund is a decent enough fellow for a Swede. Pretty deadly with a sword, or so I'm told."

The Swedes had long coveted the rich land and forests of the Uplands, but through a combination of politics and war, Ivar and Hakon's father, Harald, had managed to keep them in their own lands. When Erik took the High Seat and brought chaos to the realm, the Swedes had risen again, which is what made their presence at Hakon's wedding so odd.

"Are they hostages?"

"Gudmund is."

"Who did you give in exchange?"

"The son of one of my nobles. Someone of consequence, but dispensable."

"And has the unrest abated?"

"For now."

Just then, Gudmund smiled at something Thorgil said. "Thorgil seems pretty partial to this Gudmund."

Ivar waved the comment aside as if swiping at a fly. "It is called diplomacy."

Hakon grunted. He too was beginning to feel as if something were not quite right. Like Egil, he could feel it in his gut. The feeling turned Hakon's mind to Toralv, who had stayed in the guest hall to craft their escape hatch. He doubted Ivar would try anything so soon, but it didn't hurt to be prepared.

Hakon took a sip of ale, then stared into his cup. *Did it too taste odd?* Hakon lowered his drink and forced his mind back to the present.

"Where's Groa?"

"Resting for her big day." Ivar coughed.

The comment turned Hakon's stomach. "Which would be when?"

"On the morrow, at midday."

"You waste no time."

Ivar managed to look vicious and bemused at the same time. "Oh, it would have been a long, drawn-out feast but for your tardiness. Sadly, I can entertain my guests no longer — it is time for you to take my daughter's hand and for my guests to leave before they devour all my stores. Besides, I have not felt myself lately and need my rest." He sipped his ale and cleared his throat. "Tell me of Erik. I assume he and his wretched family are gone for good?"

"Aye. They are gone."

"Dead?"

"Exiled."

"Exiled." Ivar said the word slowly.

Hakon sighed. "Spare me your comments, Ivar. I have heard it all before."

"I'm sure you have, and you shall hear it again. Without Sigurd and Tore and me, you would still be a castaway in Athelstan's court. A nobody." His cheeks had reddened with the effort of saying those few words without coughing. "We gave you the chance to rid us of Erik and, in so doing, become the king of this realm. But you didn't keep your end of the bargain. Now Erik and his family lurk, lying in wait for their chance to come again." He could hold out no longer and launched into a coughing fit so great, it made nearby guests look on in concern.

Hakon felt none of their pity and leaned closer to him as soon as the coughing stopped, whispering fiercely, "Let us be clear. It was Sigurd who brought me back from Engla-lond, not you. You had not the foresight or the balls to trust a Christian. Only after I was here did you leverage me for your gain, but you took something from me in return. Do you think I care how the potential return of Erik or his sons inconveniences you?"

The truce was over.

Ivar smashed the table with his fist, rattling plates and cups and capturing the attention of everyone in the hall. Conversations stopped. "Damn you, Hakon. The battle with Erik took something from me as well." And that was true, for Ivar's son Brand had died in the fight.

Still whispering fiercely, Hakon said, "The Christians call that an eye for an eye, Ivar, though to me it was not enough. I wish the battle had taken the lot of you. I will see you on the morrow."

Hakon stood, satisfied with just how much he had angered his future father-in-law, the man who had beaten and killed Aelfwin and then reveled in the pain it had inflicted on his daughter's future husband. Off to Hakon's right, the Swede sipped casually from his cup even as his icy eyes studied Hakon. Hakon nodded to the fellow and stepped from the dais. His men fell in with him. The other guests watched in silence as they departed.

Chapter 8

Hakon and Groa wed the following day. It was a Friday, known to the Northmen as Frigga's day in honor of Odin's wife, the goddess of marriage. The guests gathered on the shores of Lake Mjosa under gray clouds. From the cover of nearby trees, Hakon watched them assemble, his spirits as morose as the weather.

"You ready, boy?" This came from Egil, who, as Hakon's senior friend at the wedding, agreed to escort Hakon as far as the altar, where he would hand Hakon to Groa.

"Aye," he muttered.

Hakon had been dreading this day for months, and it couldn't have started worse. That morning, he had been taken from the guest hall and symbolically cleansed of his former self by female attendants. They had come at sunrise and ushered him to a small structure in which stood a bench and a tub of steaming water scented with mint leaves. He would have preferred to be left alone, but the women would have none of it. They turned their backs as he submerged himself, then they set upon him with brushes, soap, and comb.

Once he was bathed and dried, they pulled his golden hair into a tight braid that they interlaced with blue-dyed ribbon. They applied an azure eye powder to his eyelids, giving him a mystical, girlish appearance. Even his adolescent beard did not escape their care. Though still not very long or full, they combed and cut and greased it until it hung stiffly from his jawline. To complete his appearance, the atten-

dants draped a woolen cloak dyed deep blue across his shoulders —
a gift from Ivar.

From somewhere a horn blew, tearing Hakon from the memory of
his morning and beckoning him to his new life.

Egil spat. "Alright then — let us be on with this."

Hakon stepped out from under the trees and walked toward the
gathered guests, who eyed him appreciatively.

"Slowly now," Egil coached from the side of his mouth. "This is a
ceremony."

Hakon sighed and forced himself to step more slowly and take his
time. It pained him, for the urge to rush his way through the proceed-
ings was strong.

The crowd parted, giving way to the groom and his attendant. Here
and there, he recognized a face in the crowd and nodded dutifully,
though his stomach twisted and his soul screamed. Despite the chill
in the air and the gray skies above, his cheeks were hot with embarrassment and sweat trickled down his spine.

As they reached the altar, another horn blasted. Groa emerged from
a different tree line, accompanied by a hunched and decrepit godi. The
priest led her forth, carrying in his gnarled hands a wooden bowl. Groa
followed with stiff, deliberate dignity, her soft chin up and shoulders
back. Her blemished skin glowed from scrubbing. Red paint accentuated her brown eyes and matched the flowing red overdress that clung
to her roundness. A silver bridal crown garlanded with cords of yellow
and green encircled her head. Behind her walked her father, with his
dwarf-like stature and labored shuffle. Taking up the rear were Holmfrid and Thorgil, she with her long, elegant limbs and proud, upright
bearing, he with his handsome face, muscular build, and conspicuous
limp.

The godi passed Hakon and walked to the opposite side of the boulder that served as their altar, bits of bone rattling in the tangles of his
hair. Groa stopped beside her husband-to-be. She glanced quickly at
Hakon and offered a brief smile. He looked back at her, not attempting
to hide the anger in his eyes. Her smile faded and she turned back to

the godi, who had placed his wooden vessel on the rock before them and produced a curved sacrificial knife from the folds of his sleeve. He ran his ancient thumb along the blade to test its sharpness. Drops of blood splattered onto the rock.

Seemingly satisfied, he raised his arms high and called to the sky with a voice that surprised Hakon with its strength, "Blessed Aesir, creators of man and earth, sky and sea, since the dawn of time you have provided for us and watched over us from your heavenly hall. Look down upon these two now and bless the bond that is about to unite them. Frigga, Mother of Gods, Goddess of Weddings, bless this day as a day to live in men's memories for time eternal. Odin, Alfather, oh Great Communicator, look upon these two and provide them with the wisdom to learn from one another and the tongues to speak the words each would hear. Freya, plant your seeds of fertility that will carry the Yngling bloodline through the ages."

A group of young men appeared, pulling, kicking, and prodding a squealing sow — the symbol of Freya — to the altar. The priest scooped up the bowl and knife, turned to the sow, and with a hand practiced in the trade of killing, sliced the animal's neck. So precise was the cut that the sow barely noticed, allowing the priest to fill his bowl undisturbed while the life drained from her body. In three swift movements, the priest placed the bowl back onto the rock, reached into his robe, and produced a bundle of fir twigs. These he dipped into the sow's blood, and while chanting in a tongue Hakon didn't recognize, flicked the blood onto those gathered around the rock. Hakon turned his head and cursed as the flying droplets peppered his clothes. Beside him, Groa raised her face to the gore as a child might turn her face to a cleansing rain, then turned and smiled with glee at Hakon. He stared at her with disdain.

"The rings," prodded the godi.

Egil nudged Hakon. Coming to himself, Hakon unsheathed his sword and handed it, pommel first, to Ivar. Ivar did the same with his own sword. Hakon then placed a golden ring upon the pommel and offered it to Groa, who snatched it in her hands and forced it upon her chubby ring finger. Groa then offered her family's ring to Hakon on the pommel of Ivar's sword.

"Turn to your guests and hold hands."

Hakon grabbed Groa's hand, which was clammy and somewhat limp. The godi then wrapped a single strip of lamb's wool around the couple's grip to signify the new bond and its innocence.

"May all present see that Groa Ivarsdottir is now bound to Hakon Haraldsson in matrimony. Let the wedding procession begin!"

With hands bound, the bride and groom led the guests to a path in the nearby trees that ended at a large clearing. Within the open space stood row upon row of eating boards and benches and, on the far side, a dais upon which sat another long table and bench. Colored ribbons hung from the canopy of branches, dancing in the light breeze over the feasting ground. It was far more beautiful than Hakon had expected from Ivar, but then, he doubted Ivar's hand had graced this place.

Before they could enter the clearing, there was one final step to perform. Hakon unwrapped his hand from Groa's and unsheathed his seax. Holding it before him, he stepped over a branch that lay across his path — the threshold of marriage — to show his new wife and the guests that she would forever be safe in his care. Once "inside" the field, Hakon drove his blade into the top of a nearby stump. The godi inspected the sword closely and proclaimed the blow strong and true, a sign that the marriage would enjoy similar qualities. Hakon rolled his eyes as the guests cheered, for he doubted that the godi had ever proclaimed any wedding less than favorable for a married couple. Hakon yanked his blade from the wood, sheathed it, and led Groa over the threshold and into their new life together.

When the guests had taken their seats, Groa came forth with a silver bowl of mead. This she carefully passed to Hakon, who drank deeply before passing it back to Groa. She too drank from the sweet liquid.

Hakon reclaimed the bowl and held it aloft. "Greetings to all of you. Long ago, I dreamed of becoming the king of my father's realm, and with your support, that dream has come to pass." He mustered what emotion he could, but the words still rang flat and impassive in his ears.

"And so I lift the mead bowl to you, to my new father, to my new family, and to my new bride, in thanks. May God bless this union. Skol!"

"Skol!" the crowd replied in unison.

Ivar stood then and raised his cup slowly to Hakon. "Let us not forget that without this young warrior and king, we would not have united in a common cause, and Erik would yet rule this land. The gods have smiled on us all. Let them continue to smile on Hakon and Groa as they lead us into the future." He lifted his cup higher. "Skol!"

"Skol!" the crowd responded.

Before he could drink, a new fit of coughing wracked Ivar. So strong was it that Thorgil, Groa, and Holmfrid rushed to his side. The nearby guests looked on helplessly as Ivar waved his family away.

"Please, eat," Holmfrid urged when the fit had ended. "Ivar will be fine," she added, though he did not look fine, slouching in his seat with his red face and watering eyes. Holmfrid turned her attention to Thorgil, who sat beside her, and whispered something in his ear. He smiled briefly, which Hakon thought strange. Hakon's gaze found Gudmund, who sat at the table closest to the dais. The Swede's icy eyes stole glances at Holmfrid and her son. Near the Swede sat Hakon's men, who kept one eye on their cups and the other on the guests. There would be no revelry this night for them.

Groa, of course, was oblivious to it all. Her attention was on her husband's plate, where a cooked trout lay. "Why do you eat fish while your guests eat pork? Do you not like pork?"

"It is Friday. I eat only fish on Fridays." He could have gone on to explain that abstaining from meat was a small sacrifice to Christ to honor Him for the sacrifice He made on behalf of all men, but he knew Groa would not understand. Instead, he said only, "It is the way of Christians, which you will learn soon enough."

Her face pinched. "It is a stupid religion that keeps you from eating as you like on your wedding day."

Hakon shoved some fish into his mouth to keep from speaking the words he truly wanted to say. Thankfully, a man stood just then and made his way to the center of the field. The man bowed to the dais, then launched into the poem of Frey, the god of virility and prosperity. In the well-known story, Frey ascends to the seat of Odin and looks out over his kingdom. As Frey looks to the north, he beholds a young maiden named Gerda, entering the house of the frost giant Gymir:

> *"In Gymir's court I saw her move,*
> *The maid who fires my breast with love;*
> *Her snow-white arms and bosom fair*
> *Shone lovely, kindling sea and air.*
>
> *"Dear is she to my wishes,*
> *More than e'er was maid to youth before;*
> *But gods and elves I wot it well,*
> *Forbid that we together dwell."*

"Ugh," Groa groaned. "This again? Father?" she called to Ivar, who was slumped over his plate, barely able to lift his head. "Have we not heard this tale last night and the night before? Does he not know anything else?"

The skald, who had overhead Groa, stopped and looked at Ivar, not quite sure whether to continue or sit. Ivar glanced tiredly at his daughter but had not the energy to protest, so he waved the poor man away. The skald bowed and returned to his seat, accompanied by the laughter of the wedding guests.

Groa snorted. "I always hated that story." She then turned back to her food, oblivious to Hakon's incredulous look.

Hakon drank deeply from his mead cup. Nearby, Ivar coughed again.

The following morning, Hakon's eyes opened slowly. He blinked, hoping to relieve the throbbing at his temples but managed only to intensify the pain with the sudden movement of his lids. For a long moment he lay in the darkness, trying to remember where he was and why his mouth felt as if he had swallowed mud.

Slowly at first, and then with increasing rapidity, images flooded his aching head. Images of Groa's sour face amid singing, boasting, drunken revelers; of plates of food and cup after cup of mead; of Ivar, wracked by coughs, being escorted by Holmfrid from the field; of Gudmund and Thorgil huddling together; of the guests seeking refuge under the trees as the heavens opened up and wind and rain doused the cooking fire.

His mind navigated the visions, placing each in its proper order until it came to rest on a hazy memory of Groa lying in bed with her bridal crown still affixed to her head and her silent attendants standing nearby, each with a candle in her hand. Like Odin's ravens who reported to Him on the news of the world, the attendants were there to witness the wedding's consummation and to report that to Ivar. For only then would the wedding be recognized as valid. Hakon remembered fumbling with Groa's bridal dress and how awkward he felt when the dress opened to reveal her milky skin and round breasts, the plumpness of her girlish belly, the tuft of course hair between her legs. He too was naked, his manhood stiff between his legs. How foreign this experience was to him and how clumsy his groping, made clumsier by the vigilant audience of attendants.

It was then that Aelfwin entered his mind. And as quickly as he stiffened, he softened in Groa's hands. She looked at him aghast. The attendants stood by, silent observers to his incompetence. He closed his eyes, trying to concentrate. His head swam from too much drink. He recalled nothing more...

Now, he studied Groa's sleeping form in the soft glow of a sputtering candle. She slept facing away from him, buried beneath the fur covers with her greasy hair splayed on her pillow like the legs of a spider. The attendants had vanished.

His stomach gurgled and a sudden warmth filled his mouth. He breathed deeply to quell the rising bile, but it was no use. Sitting up, he peered at the dark outlines of the room, desperately searching for a place to empty his stomach, but found none. He could run for the door, but even if his pounding head allowed such movement, his nakedness would prevent his leaving. The bile rose and his stomach lurched. Whirling, he dropped his feet to the floorboards and spewed his gluttony forth.

Hakon did not need to look at his bride to see the horror in her round face. He could hear it in her gasp and see it in the white of her stubby knuckles as they clutched the bearskin blanket beside him. He was not sure what was worse: the sickening sight before his eyes or the embarrassment of his unwanted effusion. And yet, there was a part of him that smiled upon the destruction, a feeling that he had, in some way, struck back against all that was unholy and unwanted in this union.

"Tsst," she hissed. "I did not marry a king. I married a boy who cannot hold an erection or his mead!"

If Hakon could have jumped to his feet and spat forth his indignation at her comments, he would have. There was so much he could say to make her hurt, to make her suffer for what she and her family had done to him. He could tell her that she disgusted him, that she made his skin crawl, that the smell of the oil in her hair gagged him. He could tell her that the reason for his gluttony in drink was to numb himself against the thought of having to bed her. He could tell her that she was too fat, that her table manners were no better than a swine's, that his true love had died as a result of her father and that he would never forgive him that wrong. But try as he might, he could muster no more than a groan.

The bile rose again. He took a deep breath but failed to stem the surge. He bent and vomited a second time. Resting his aching head in his hands, he spat the foulness from his mouth.

It was then that they heard the shouts. And in that instant, everything changed.

Chapter 9

By the time Hakon reached Ivar's hall, his thralls and warriors had already gathered. A teary Groa, who had run to the hall as soon as she heard the commotion, sat weeping on a bench with Holmfrid by her side. She glanced at Hakon as he entered, then buried her head under her mother's arm. From the hushed chatter, Hakon understood that something had happened to Ivar; but just how serious it was he could not tell.

The godi emerged then from the sleeping chamber and whispered in Thorgil's ear. He nodded gravely.

"It is confirmed — Ivar is dead," Thorgil proclaimed to the somber audience. "Prepare a ship. We shall honor my father with a funeral to be remembered. You." Thorgil pointed to the pretty girl with the bruised face who had served Hakon at his arrival feast. "You shall accompany my father to his next life."

"No," gasped an older thrall woman who stood by the girl's side. "Please."

Thorgil's hard eyes fell on her. "And you will prepare her for the ceremony." Thorgil turned to the others. "Gather my father's horse, bridle, and saddle and bring them to the ship. I will gather his sword and armor."

Groa's tears grew to uncontrollable sobs. As much as he despised her and as much as his head hurt, it was hard for Hakon to look upon her sadness and not feel some pity for the loss that now disrupted her wedding and her life.

"Allow me to serve him in death as I've served him in life," said an old warrior with hair the color of steel. "It would be an honor."

Thorgil nodded curtly. "I thank you, Einar, as I'm sure my father will thank you when you meet him again."

Hakon had heard enough. His head pounded and his stomach churned. This news only made him feel worse. He slipped from the hall and into the crowd of guests now gathered in the courtyard. Gudmund stood near the front of the crowd, studying the scene and Hakon intently. Hakon met the Swede's gaze until Gudmund looked away. Hakon brushed past him and found his men.

"Is it true?" asked Toralv, his powerful arms folded across this chest. "Is Ivar dead?" His young face was almost amused. Clearly, he cared little that the chieftain had died.

"Aye," Hakon confirmed, his own emotions mirroring the look on his friend's face.

"Some cough," he grinned.

Hakon fought to keep his own amusement concealed. The last thing he needed was for his grin to anger some hotheaded hirdman of Ivar's.

Egil spat to show his displeasure. "Keep your lips tight, both of you," he snarled. "Like him or not, it is not the death for a warrior like Ivar."

Glorious death in battle was the death that all warriors and kings sought. Hakon, of course, shared no such sentiment for Ivar. Instead, he snorted at Egil's comment. "Ivar got what he deserved."

Egil frowned.

Behind them, Holmfrid and Thorgil appeared at the doorway to the hall. The gathered crowd went silent, and Hakon and his men turned to watch.

"Ivar, son of Eystein, King of the Uplands, is dead," said Thorgil. A fresh wave of groans and weeping swept through the crowd. "I am sorry to bring such sad tidings to what should be a merry occasion — my sister's wedding. We are preparing the funeral now and will feast tonight in celebration of my father and his exploits. If you have gifts you wish to provide for him on his journey to the otherworld, please leave them here at this door. We will be sure to add them to his funeral ship."

"You should go to him," Egil whispered to Hakon. "Proclaim Thorgil as the new jarl and make him swear an oath to you."

Hakon held up his hand. "Patience. I will wait until Thorgil has said his farewells. Then I shall go to him."

Egil moved closer to Hakon. "Just do so before the damned Swede gets to him."

In his mind's eye, Hakon saw again Gudmund and Thorgil huddled together at his wedding feast. "It may be too late for that."

At dusk, a single drum began to beat, calling forth six members of Ivar's hird. They carried from the hall a wooden stretcher on which lay the squat body of their fallen king. Proud Holmfrid followed behind in a white lace dress covered at the shoulder by a wolf mantle. Behind her limped Thorgil with his jaw set tightly and Groa with her eyes swollen from crying. Einar followed them, his chin high and his eyes forward, a slight grin on his face, as if he was privy to a joke the others had not yet heard.

The somber procession walked between two torch-bearing lines of warriors from Ringsaker's gate to a small pier on the shore of Lake Mjosa, not far from where the wedding had recently taken place. The torches sputtered in the gathering wind, casting an eerie, dancing glow on the group as it headed out to the end of the pier, where a small ship and the old godi waited. The warriors passed the jarl's body carefully onto the boat and laid the stretcher on a bed of clean, dry hay that had been piled beneath the mast. They then placed his sword, helmet, shield, armor, and a number of his personal effects within arm's reach of his body. He would need them in Valhall, the hall of the slain, though it seemed more likely to Hakon that he was headed for the fiery underworld called Hell. Bystanders lined the dock and the shore, still and silent. Some of the women wiped the tears from their cheeks. An infant cried.

The chosen warrior, Einar, climbed aboard and faced the godi. Two warriors joined him, each holding an arm. Though Hakon could hear no words, his stomach tightened, for he knew what was to come. And so it did, with a spoken blessing and a deft swipe of the godi's blade. The warrior's body twitched for a moment or two, then fell limp. The attendants laid him gently beside his master, his tunic stained crimson. On the dock, Thorgil wrapped an arm around his mother, who buried her face in his chest.

Next came the thrall girl, though she did not go complacently. Two warriors had to drag her writhing, screaming body from the hall and out onto the dock. She fought like a shield-maiden as the warriors physically held her down and the godi slashed her throat. Even then, she writhed and fought like a dying fish, forcing her guards to hold her so she wouldn't fall into the lake. When the lifeblood finally drained from her wound, the blood-soaked warriors dragged her body into the boat and tossed her corpse at the feet of their dead lord. Hakon said a silent prayer for her soul in the hope that God might see her plight. He knew not if God paid attention to such pleas, but it was worth the effort.

The funeral pressed on. The old godi raised his arms above the corpses and spoke words too far away for Hakon to hear. He then climbed from the vessel as Thorgil tossed a torch onto the dry hay that lay beneath his father. Warriors grabbed the lines and oars and pushed the ship from the dock until it bobbed a safe distance away. More warriors tossed torches into the ship until the flames danced high into the air and their reflection stretched far across the surface of Lake Mjosa.

Ivar's family watched for a time, then Holmfrid took the weeping Groa back to the hall. Little by little, the other onlookers peeled away until only Thorgil stood on the pier, silent and watchful. Hakon, who had been sitting on the shore, approached.

"I am sorry for your loss, Thorgil."

Thorgil's eyes remained fixed on the flames. Though the inferno had abated somewhat, Hakon could still feel its heat upon his skin.

"Cease with the platitudes, Hakon. You hated my father."

"A new jarl of the Uplands should be appointed," offered Hakon, ignoring Thorgil's surly comment, true though it was. "Before other challengers arise. It is right that the Uplands should go to you. Oath-swear to me and I will proclaim my support for you tonight, to your gathered guests."

Thorgil remained silent for a long, uncomfortable moment. When he spoke there was no mistaking the edge in his voice. "Could this not wait until my father's ship is done burning and his memory has been celebrated?"

"I thought to ask you earlier," Hakon admitted, "but felt it best to wait. It can wait no longer. Word of Ivar's death will travel as quickly as the fire that engulfs him. I must look to the welfare of this realm." He thought to mention the Swedes, but something told him to hold his tongue on the matter.

"So that's it? I simply bow my head to your knee and my father's realm is mine?" he finally asked.

Hakon steeled himself for his next words. "Aye. Though there is one more thing I require."

"And what might that be?"

"I want the marriage to Groa annulled."

Thorgil turned. His brows angled menacingly toward his nose. "Annulled?" The fire behind him made it look as if his dark hair was ablaze.

The effect unsettled Hakon, though he stood his ground. "The wedding to Groa was never consummated, so a divorce is not necessary."

"Never consummated? You lie!"

Hakon scowled back at him. "I will ignore that accusation. You need only ask Groa or the attendants to know I speak the truth."

"And if I don't agree to your condition?"

"Then you are on your own. I will not recognize you as jarl. The Swedes will come, as will other challengers from neighboring fylker, and I will not support you."

"You would break the oath you made to my father and risk the loss of the Uplands to the Swedes, not to mention the fury of the Tronds, just to rid yourself of my sister?"

Hakon pointed to the burning ship. "My oath died with your father. I have no oath with you."

"And what of Groa?"

"She may keep the bride-price that I promised and the morning gift. It is enough for her to live comfortably for the rest of her days, or until you find a suitable husband for her."

Thorgil spoke not a word. Behind him, the flames on his father's ship popped, throwing red ash into the air.

Hakon forged ahead. "Say yes to me and we will publicly declare you as jarl tonight. I will continue to support you, and you will be free to offer Groa to another. Say no to me, and you will have to fight for the jarldom, unsupported. Groa will languish here in the Uplands, wife to me in name alone."

Thorgil's expression had transformed from fury to disgust. "A third I see," he said, "and it is this: I will take my father's jarldom, and you will take my sister and leave on the morrow with your head on your shoulders. Take her not, and you will die a slow and awful death here at Ringsaker, but not before you witness the death of your men."

The lots were now cast. The line had been drawn. Still, Hakon tried one last time. "Your anger speaks for you, Thorgil. Swear an oath to me and you will have my support. Kill me, and you will bring Sigurd, Tore, and my nephews down upon you. It would not be long before your own head rots on the stakes outside of Ringsaker."

Thorgil spat on the dock at Hakon's feet. "At least I will die knowing I killed you. Now go from this place before I change my mind. I want you and your new wife gone at first light."

Chapter 10

They left the following morning, when it was yet dark and the morning's chill clouded their breaths. The parting was as chilly as the air, with Thorgil and his spear-warriors watching in silence as Hakon and his men gathered in the courtyard, bleary-eyed from a night of uncertainty. His men had not attended the feast, nor had they slept. Rather, they rested in the guest hall, armed and ready for an attack they all felt was imminent. But for whatever reason, Thorgil never came. Mayhap the ale from his father's burial feast had gotten the better of him, or mayhap he relished just knowing he had Hakon and his men within his grasp, like some cruel cat toying with a mouse.

Hakon shifted his gaze to Groa, who sat on the seat of an ornate oxcart with a heavyset female attendant beside her, holding the reins. The cart held in its bed three large chests — Groa's worldly belongings. She looked miserable.

"You will regret the day you tried to dishonor me and my family, Hakon."

Hakon turned in his saddle. "I welcome our next meeting, Thorgil, and pray to God that the Swedes don't kill you first."

Thorgil laughed. "They won't." He turned to his men. "Open the gates!"

The gates opened inward to reveal six female bodies dangling by their necks over the entrance — the wedding attendants. With them, all knowledge of Hakon's incompetence had perished save for what resided in Groa's mind, and she knew better than to speak. Hakon eyed them coldly, then kicked his mount into motion, chased as he rode into the morning's chill by the sadistic laughter of Thorgil and his men.

They rode south for an hour until they reached a small, nameless settlement on the lake's edge. Open pastures and hills green with forests surrounded the settlement, which smelled of pine smoke. The company rode past it in silence, following the contours of the lake until it began to bend more to the south. After a time, Hakon called for a stop and ordered his men to water their horses and fill their water sacks. He then dismounted and walked over to the oxcart, studying its masterful workmanship before turning to the women sitting stiffly on its wooden seat. They kept their eyes averted from his sharp gaze.

"This is as far as you come."

Groa turned to Hakon. "Pardon?"

"This is as far as you come," he repeated calmly. "You will now turn this cart around and ride as quickly as you can back to Ringsaker."

The surprise in Groa's face quickly turned to indignation. "We will do no such thing."

Hakon looked Groa full in her pudgy, pimple-strewn face, keeping the tone of his voice as level as he could. "If you do not turn this cart in the next few seconds, I will kill the oxen where they stand." He pulled Quern-biter from its sheath and made a show of testing its blade with his thumb.

The female driver was no fool and understood instantly that for two women with a full cart of goods to be stranded in the wilderness was a dangerous thing. She immediately started coaxing her beasts into a wide turn, ignoring Groa's protests. Hakon walked beside them, guiding an ox by the yoke.

"I will not forget this, Hakon," called Groa from her seat as the cart lumbered along. "Nor will my brother."

"Trust me. You will be better off in Thorgil's care."

"May the gods curse you!" she spat over her shoulder.

Hakon stopped and let the cart move onward. He thought to say something to his wife in parting, but he could think of nothing to say that would sufficiently and cleverly capture his true feelings. So instead, he crossed himself to ward off Groa's curse and let the cart roll back the way it had come.

Toralv stepped up beside his lord. "You are mad, Hakon."

Hakon didn't respond.

"Should we follow them to ensure they make it back to Ringsaker?"

"And risk being seen by Thorgil? Now who is mad? No — we let them ride alone. It is yet early and Ringsaker is not far from here."

Toralv grinned. "How noble of you."

Hakon turned to his men, who all stood watching the oxcart. "Stop gawking and fill your water sacks. We leave soon."

Hakon walked to the lake's edge and dipped his hands in the chilly water. It rippled softly, distorting his reflection as Toralv's words echoed in his ear. Was he mad? Since the spring, he had lived with the oppressive weight of this marriage on this mind and of the spirit-crushing presence of Groa in his life. And now he was free — a thought that brought a wide smile to his face and a loftiness to his spirits that he hadn't felt in quite some time. Perchance he was slightly mad, but if madness felt this liberating, he could accept that.

Egil knelt beside Hakon then. "What are you doing, boy?" he whispered harshly, and as quickly as Hakon's spirits had risen, they fell.

Hakon looked at the old warrior. "Sending Groa back."

Egil's eyes narrowed. "I can see that. You understand that the decisions you make affect us all. That decision," Egil pointed in the direction of the oxcart that had now disappeared into the woods, "will bring with it a storm. Only in this storm, the rain will be steel and the thunder will be the sound of armies on the march." His voice started to rise, which in turn pulled men's eyes in their direction. "That is, so long as we make it to Kaupang. As soon as Thorgil sees Groa, he and his men will come looking for us, for there will be nothing more to hold them back. You just cut the thread that was keeping us alive."

"And a thread it was, Egil. You saw yourself the Swedes in his midst, and the death of his father. Strange how it all happened so quickly after my ascension to the throne."

"Yet it was the only thread we had. Now we're out here alone. In his lands. With his sister rejected and his honor smeared." Egil looked up at the trees. "If I were him, I'd send a ship. The wind blows in our direction. Groa will most certainly tell him which way we're headed and a ship will be faster. If we follow the lake, he will catch us. But I suppose you thought of that?"

If his newest shield-warriors did not understand the fragility of Hakon's relationship with the Uplands, they did so now. And so too did they understand the peril in which Hakon had just placed them. Hakon ignored their eyes as he climbed onto his mount.

"Are you finished, Egil?" he asked loud enough for all his men to hear.

Egil stared at his lord.

"Good. There are settlements nearby. Fishing settlements with boats. We ride for them."

Toralv, who had been watching the exchange, turned to the men. "You heard your lord. Get ready to leave."

Hakon's men needed no coaxing. They grabbed their gear and followed.

The group moved south along the shore of Lake Mjosa until they found a settlement with several rowboats. Fishermen toiled near the boats, piling netting and baskets into the open spaces beneath the benches. The men stopped their work at the sight of Hakon and his men.

Hakon rode forward, his hands visible to show he meant no harm. "I am Hakon Haraldsson, son to Harald Fairhair and the man who expelled Erik Bloodaxe from the realm. We have need of your boats."

The elder among them glanced at his comrades, then stepped forward. He was a poor fellow with graying hair, weather-creased skin, and tattered clothes. Even from a distance he smelled like fish. "I have heard of you. And I can see that you are a powerful lord who can take what he desires. But I beg you, please don't take our boats — they are our livelihood."

Hakon lifted the bag attached to his belt. "We also have need of your services. I am no robber. I do not steal. Rather, I will pay for the crossing. A gold coin for each of you."

The man's eyes widened. It was more than they could make in a year's worth of work. "What of the beasts? We can't take them in the boats."

"They stay."

"And once we reach the far shore? What will befall us then?"

"Old man," called Egil, "if we meant you harm, you would now be dead." He grabbed the hilt of his sword. "What say you?"

"Climb in," said the man wisely. "We can take eight to a boat. No more."

That wasn't enough, of course, but Hakon had a plan.

"Have you extra oars?"

"Aye."

"Fetch them quickly."

The old man scurried away as Hakon dismounted. He instructed Egil to do the same. "Toralv," he called to his friend, handing him the reins of his mount. "Choose eighteen men, including some of the new boys, and lead the beasts due north, into the mountains. Quickly. Circle back when you think it safe and make for Kaupang. The boys will be your guides. Go now." Hakon patted Toralv's knee in parting — there was no time for extended goodbyes.

He then walked to the closest ship and untied the ropes attached to its prow. Others joined him. "We must go now," he called to the fishermen as Toralv formed his retinue and rode away.

After an hour of hard rowing, the fishing boats reached the far shore of Lake Mjosa. It had taken them longer than expected due to the weight of the men and their belongings, as well as a wind that drove in from the north and splashed water over the low gunwales. Soaked but heartened that they had reached the far shore undetected, Hakon paid the fishermen their due.

"Thorgil, lord of Ringsaker, may ask if you've seen me. It is important that you tell him I have ridden north. Show him the tracks if you must. If he learns you have helped me cross the water, he will kill you. All of you. Do you understand?"

The men nodded.

"Leave now, and forget you ever saw us."

Without a word, the men climbed into their boats and rowed away. Hakon watched them until they were out of earshot, then turned to his own men. "We head to Kaupang. Egil, choose two scouts to guide us, and make sure we avoid contact."

The group set off at a jog along a narrow trail that led away from the lake and toward a rocky range of hills. About them, the long grass waved in the growing wind — a wind that carried with it the smells of cooking fires from unseen dwellings nearby. Hakon wondered briefly if the fishermen would reveal their location to Thorgil, then he pushed the thought from his mind — he could not worry about that now. His focus was on putting distance between his men and Thorgil before that bastard learned of their whereabouts. Nothing else mattered.

When they reached the base of the first hill, one of the men whistled softly. Hakon turned. Across the water, Thorgil's ship appeared. Egil had been right. Hakon and his men knelt slowly and watched as the ship glided south, hugging the far shore. Hakon crossed himself and whispered a prayer of thanks, then turned his back and followed his men southward toward Kaupang.

Chapter 11

Hakon and his small band reached the remains of Skiringssal by way of a cart track they had been following all morning. They were tired, hungry, and wet. A thin mist was all that remained of the heavy downpour that had started early on the second day of their flight and lasted for five days without a break. The cold rain had drenched their clothing and their boots, robbing them of sleep and warmth and animals to hunt. The men subsisted on nuts, berries, and the occasional fish, their spirits falling like the hard rain. But there was some good to it too, for the rain formed pools and swelled streams and covered the tracks left by Hakon and his men, making it next to impossible to track them.

And now, with Skiringssal in sight, their moods lifted.

Hakon called a halt and scanned the scene before him for signs of trouble. In the short time he had been away, things had clearly changed. The "Shining Hall" had been transformed into a protective fortress of sorts, its blackened beams now pointing outward to form an ugly but effective defensive ring at the base of the rise where the hall had once stood. Inside this ring was a sloping mound of earth where guards now stood. Hakon studied the group from the protection of the trees. In the mist, it was hard to tell whether they were friend or foe.

Just then, a man turned and gazed in their direction, and Hakon smiled. "Come," he called to his men.

The group stepped from the canopy of trees and slogged forward over the wet ground. In the fortress before them, the warriors gazed at the newcomers, weapons at the ready.

"State your business," called the man Hakon had seen.

Hakon removed his soaking hood and grinned at this nephew. Gudrod's mouth dropped open. "Hakon?"

"Aye."

Gudrod walked forward to greet his uncle. "Did Groa kick you out so soon?" he asked, smiling. "Why are you here?"

"Are those the only words of welcome you have for your uncle, Gudrod?" called Hakon.

"Forgive me, but I did not expect you, and especially not in this manner. Where are your horses? Where's Groa? Where are your men?" He scratched his soaking head. "Were you not just at your wedding?"

"I will tell you everything once my men and I have had a chance to rest, eat, and warm ourselves."

Gudrod grabbed his uncle's wrist in greeting. "Come, then."

Hakon waved to his warriors, who followed Gudrod and Hakon down a muddy path in the direction of Kaupang.

They had not gone far before Hakon stopped. "Is that hammering I hear?"

"Aye. Your ears are keen."

"You and Trygvi have been busy."

"Busy is not the half of it. Since you left, we've been either building the town or burying the dead the Danes leave behind." He waved vaguely at a cemetery off to his left.

The sight startled Hakon. "More dead in Kaupang?"

"No, thank the gods. Elsewhere. North. South. East. Pretty much everywhere but here."

"Ragnvald?"

"Aye," Gudrod said with an edge in his voice. "Never stays long enough to meet us in a fight. The bastard just preys on the settlements all up and down and across the Vik, taking booty and the able-bodied as thralls and leaving nothing but destruction behind. The wounded we bring back here and try to help. Most die."

"Where is he now?"

Gudrod shrugged. "Our scouts tell us he is north of here, though exactly where is not clear. He seems to be everywhere and nowhere at once."

They crested a small rise thick with pine trees and gazed out at a new Kaupang. Hakon could barely believe his eyes. The last time he had been here, the structures still smoldered and the smell of death hung thickly in the air. But Gudrod and his cousin had done much to eradicate that sad memory. Damaged dwellings had been repaired or removed, and new ones were even now being erected. A new wharf had also been built and from it stretched a freshly planked walkway that led up into the town. Though no trading ships moored in the inlet, they would soon enough if Gudrod and his cousin could keep Kaupang safe.

"I am impressed," said Hakon.

Gudrod smiled. "We owe most of this to the locals. They have worked hard to rebuild what was lost. Now the place lives again." He smacked Hakon's shoulder. "Even the whores have returned!"

Hakon laughed and followed his nephew into Kaupang. He wove through the toiling people, looking for the telltale signs of the town's former struggles. He saw few. Every blackened plank, every broken reed, every bit of burnt thatch had been removed, scrubbed,

or repaired. Along the wood-planked walkways, traders hawked their wares and weighed the hack silver buyers brought to them. Hakon saw walrus tusk from the far north, amber and furs from the forests, beads and other jewelry, combs made of ivory, weapons and thralls, and myriad other items besides.

"You make Kaupang a worthy prize for Ragnvald."

"Aye. We do. But we're accounting for that."

"How?" Hakon asked as they passed a blacksmith banging mightily on a crimson rod in his smithy.

"We are building our defenses, as well as a beacon system that stretches up and down Viksfjord, and even beyond. See there?"

Hakon looked in the direction that Gudrod pointed, across Kaupangskilen to the opposite bank. There he saw for the first time a hill fortress not so unlike the defensive mound that used to be Skiringssal. It sat on the highest point of land, surrounded by trees, but with a commanding view of the Viksfjord and its myriad islands.

"There is another such fortress to the south, on the headland overlooking the mouth of the Viksfjord, and yet another across Larviksfjord at Stavern. The four fortresses — Skiringssal and these three — form a defensive perimeter around the town and the hall, and we're building another inland."

Gudrod then turned and motioned with his bearded chin to the hill behind the town. "We've also built defenses around the main hall."

Hakon could see now the new main hall — a huge structure squatting like an upside-down ship on the hill. Behind it, at various elevations, stood other, smaller structures. Below the hall, a network of log walls stretched at various levels around the hill. They had been meticulously woven into the landscape, hiding behind trees and ferns, beside rocks and other contours of the hillside. The only way up to the hall was to pass through that network. Put trained warriors behind those walls and Trygvi and Gudrod could deny access to most armies.

"The walls stretch all the way around the hill?"

"Aye. Ragnvald — or anyone else for that matter — would be a fool to come. But we hope he does. It would be nice to be rid of him once and for all."

"Where is your cousin?"

"Trygvi? Out on the water. You know him — he's a fighter, not a builder." Gudrod smiled. "Come."

Hakon dismissed his men and followed Gudrod up the winding path and into the main hall, where thralls took his gear. Gudrod ushered Hakon to a table by the crackling hearth. Egil joined them.

As the heat warmed their skin and steam rose from their damp garments, a young thrall girl brought forth warm bread, butter, and ale.

She lingered longer than customary by Gudrod's shoulder. He patted her rump. "Go along, Siv. Our words are not for your ears."

Hakon couldn't contain his smile. "She's my age, Gudrod. What use have you for her?"

"Many," he said with a laugh before taking a long draught of ale. "So then," he said, leaning forward and growing suddenly serious. "What news? Where is Groa?"

Hakon glanced at Egil, then launched into the story of Ivar's death and how he sent Groa on her way. He omitted the details of his conversation with Thorgil — there was no need to make matters worse, for he could see during the telling of his tale that Gudrod's mood was darkening. When he finished, Gudrod glanced at Egil again, then back at his younger uncle. "I could tell you all of the reasons why your actions are thick-headed, but I can see from his expression that Egil has already done that." He spun his cup mindlessly in his hand. "You have done what you have done and now we must act. Right..." Gudrod rose suddenly from his bench, tapping on his cup with a ringed finger as he began to pace. "Thorgil will not take your actions lightly. You and he have never gotten along, and this will only anger him more. If I were him, I'd build my strength quickly and finish you."

Hakon's mind turned to the Swede in Thorgil's hall. That would be a likely choice, but given the bad blood between the Uplanders and their eastern neighbors, he doubted they would trust each other enough to fight for control of the realm together. Besides, what would happen if they succeeded in defeating Hakon? Surely they must then fight each other as they always had? Would Thorgil really take that risk? But if not the Swedes, who then? The Danes? Ragnvald? Hakon had been chewing on these thoughts since leaving Ringsaker and time and again had come to the same conclusion: the possibilities were numerous, and none of them were good.

"Which means," Gudrod continued, bringing Hakon back to the present, "that we must ally ourselves likewise."

"Sigurd will support us," said Hakon a bit too readily.

Gudrod stopped and frowned at his young king. "Will he? He brings you back from Engla-lond. He supports your entire campaign. He finds a way for you to control the entire realm. And you do what?" Gudrod's cheeks reddened. "I would not think of him as a ready ally any longer. Besides, he is back in Lade and far from here." Gudrod stopped himself and took another guzzle of ale, wiping the froth from his blond mustache with his sleeve. "If I were Thorgil, I'd find an ally soon and attack before the harvest is in. Or mayhap just after. Which means we must prepare ourselves quickly." Gudrod shook his head. "You have picked a fight, Hakon. Now we must prepare ourselves. I will send out a summons on the morrow to the neighboring areas. It is time to introduce them to their new king."

"I do not believe Thorgil can act so quickly," said Hakon.

"Then you are twice the fool," Gudrod countered flatly. "Ivar was cunning, but his son is rash. Acting without thought is exactly what Thorgil is good at. Remember, Trygvi and I lived with them for a time. Do not underestimate him."

Gudrod paced some more. "And now we have another problem on our hands."

Egil and Hakon looked at each other. "Which is?" Egil asked.

"Come. I think it best to show you."

They exited the hall and walked in silence to a structure that stood behind it, a little ways up the hill. It was a low-lying, windowless hut built of thick oaken planks. Even its roof was made of beams rather than the customary thatch. Hakon would have thought it a storage shed or larder, were it not for the two warriors who guarded its door.

"What is this place?" Hakon asked as they stopped before the door and Gudrod nodded to the guards.

"You'll see," he answered.

One of the guards opened the door and the other leveled his spear at the darkness within. Hakon peered into the gloom. He could see shapes moving — people — but could not discern anything about them other than their stench, which was awful.

"Come out," Gudrod commanded.

The people shuffled about inside and spoke a few muffled words to each other. Eventually, someone came toward the door and poked his head out of the shadows.

Hakon froze. The tall, squinting man looked like a half-starved mole risen from his subterranean den. Dirt smeared the man's gaunt face and matted his graying hair, but there was no mistaking his identity.

"Father Otker?"

"You know this man?" Gudrod asked.

Hakon nodded, unable to conceal the shock and joy that fought for purchase of his emotions. "Aye," he said as his wide smile spread across his face. "I do."

Chapter 12

The wisps of gray that were Father Otker's eyebrows rose in surprise. "Hakon? Is that you?"

Hakon grabbed the older man by his thin shoulders and laughed. "It is I!"

A grin stretched across Father Otker's grimy face as a tear slipped from his eye and rolled down his sunken cheek. "Then we are saved. God be praised."

Hakon turned to his nephew. "How long have these men been in here?"

Gudrod shrugged, as if it were of no consequence. "Several days." As he spoke, more monks emerged from the darkness on wobbly legs, squinting into the soft light. Hakon counted the frail, dirty men. Twelve in all, including another face Hakon thought never to see again: the young novice Egbert. Winters ago, the freckle-faced red-head had healed Hakon after a fight with King Athelstan's younger brother, Edmund. And now he was here in the North with his orange curls shooting in all directions and his freckles carpeted with dirt.

"Twelve in all," he remarked in Latin.

"Aye," responded Father Otker. "Like Christ's apostles. Only you are not Christ and this isn't Galilee. But these men are as wicked as the Romans. What is the meaning of holding us prisoner? I am King Athelstan's emissary," he said to Gudrod, not attempting to conceal his ire.

Father Otker had always been a spirited man. It was good to see he had not mellowed with age.

Gudrod looked at Hakon for an explanation, for he did not speak the Latin tongue.

When Hakon had translated Father Otker's words, Gudrod shrugged again. "This one," he pointed to a round fellow, "told us that they had been sent by King Athelstan. We had a hard time believing so motley a crew could be vassals to a king, especially one as renowned as King Athelstan. They explained that they knew you and would prove it, so we told them they would have to wait."

"Didn't the ship's captain vouch for them?"

"There was no one with them. We found these men alone on the beach."

Hakon turned to Father Otker and in the Latin tongue said, "My nephew says that he found you on the beach. Where was Halldor, the ship's captain?"

"He dropped us off before the town. He said he had gone far enough. He told me to tell you to keep your silver."

"You are lucky, Father Otker. The North is not kind to strangers, and especially foreign priests. It is lucky that I came when I did, for my cousin might have kept you here many more days. Nevertheless, I apologize for your treatment, but I praise God for your welfare. You are welcome under my roof, and you shall feast with me tonight." He turned to Gudrod. "Prepare some food and some soap so these men might bathe. And move them to more comfortable accommodations. They are not prisoners — they are my guests."

Gudrod stood his ground. "They are Christian priests, Hakon."

"Yes, they are. I summoned them," said Hakon, deliberately putting more edge in his voice. "Now do as I ask."

Gudrod's hard eyes studied Hakon's face for a long time. Hakon readied himself for the vitriol that never came. "Geir," Gudrod finally said, speaking from the side of his mouth, "see that these priests are bathed and moved to my guest hall. Then bring them to my hall for food."

Eric Schumacher

With a final sour glance at Hakon, he stomped away. Hakon watched him go, not sure whether to feel elation or foreboding. Beside him, Egil spat into the underbrush.

Toward evening, the priests came to Gudrod's hall. They had bathed, washed their habits, and re-tonsured their hair. In the hall's smoky gloom, Hakon watched the unwelcoming eyes of the warriors as they studied the robed men. Some stared curiously from their eating benches, others coldly. Still others spat loudly into the hearth fire, which hissed in response, as if sharing in their disgust.

If the attention bothered Father Otker, he showed no sign of it, for he strode into the clouded hall like the king's champion come to claim his prize. The others peered around sheepishly as they followed their leader into the cavernous space. Gudrod made no move to welcome them, so Hakon rose instead.

"My friends! Welcome. Come and dine and relax." Hakon motioned the monks to the eating board below the dais where he, his nephew, and a few honored guests sat. "Make room," he called to some of the warriors and women seated at the table.

"I trust you are feeling better?" Hakon asked them in Latin as they took their seats.

"Much," answered Father Otker.

"My apologies again for your maltreatment. Your appearance here took my nephew by surprise. Are your new accommodations more suitable?"

"The sleeping quarters are more than sufficient. Thank you." He motioned with his sharp chin toward Gudrod. "I heard you call him your nephew before. Who is he?"

"This is Gudrod Bjornsson." Hakon motioned to his nephew, who heard his name mentioned and looked questioningly at Hakon. "They asked your name," Hakon explained before returning to Latin. "He is the son of Bjorn the Chapman, one of my half-brothers who was slain by Erik Bloodaxe a few winters ago. You may remember the story? It happened around the time of my baptism."

"I remember." Father Otker bowed to his host.

Serving maids brought forth bowls of venison stew, utensils, and a cup of ale for each of the monks. Unable to contain his excitement, Egbert tore a chunk of bread from the flat loaf and dunked it into the steaming bowl before the last of the monks had been served.

"Brother Egbert! You forget yourself."

The warriors seated nearby didn't understand Father Otker's words, but they could hear the rebuke in its tone, and their eyes turned on the old monk.

"I'm sorry, Father." Blushing, Egbert dropped his bread into his stew and joined his brothers in a quick prayer of thanks for their safe arrival in the North, for the food before them, and for their fortune in finding Hakon.

"What are they doing?" Gudrod growled. He was normally a level-headed man, but the monks were eating at his composure.

"They are giving thanks to God," Hakon explained.

"They should give thanks somewhere else. I do not want their Christian prayers in my hall." Hakon could see Gudrod's displeasure mirrored in the malicious gazes and murmurs of the hall's guests. One man rose from his table and strode from the hall.

"The people have never seen monks pray," Hakon said to the confused monks. "They don't like it."

"They will need to learn to accept it," Father Otker responded simply.

Hakon held up his hands to stop his former tutor. "Father Otker — it is wiser to tread lightly. Your appearance here, as you have already experienced with your mistreatment, is not exactly welcome. In time, the people will learn."

The old monk held his tongue and went back to his meal. Beside him, Egbert and the others ate haltingly, picking at their food while stealing glances at the Northmen.

Gudrod leaned in to Hakon then. "You'll be lucky if they survive a week."

Hakon snorted derisively. "By the looks of that cell you had them in and the welcoming manner of your warriors, I'm surprised they've survived this long, Gudrod."

Gudrod pushed his bowl away and stood, spilling his chair as he did so. It landed with a clatter. "First Groa. Now this. You play a dangerous game, Hakon."

With his departure, Hakon sat alone at the head table, looking out at a hall full of tense, unhappy guests. He was acutely aware of the whispers and glances being cast in his direction, and he knew that to sit alone and appear defeated would only make matters worse for him and the monks. So instead, he rose and called for the skald, a man named Hrolf, to recount the bawdiest stories he knew. Most of the guests seemed to welcome the distraction and turned their attention to the renowned word-weaver. Hakon used that moment to move to the monks' table.

"Tell me, Father," Hakon said as he slid onto the bench across from Father Otker. "What word of King Athelstan?"

Father Otker finished chewing a piece of venison and wiped his mouth with the back of his sleeve. Around him, the guests guffawed at one of the skald's stories. "By the grace of God, Athelstan still rules, and with each day his kingdom flourishes. After you left, he put the Scots to sword by land and sea and won great victories against those scoundrels. He continues to build on his successes and praise the Almighty with the construction of new churches and monasteries. God truly smiles on him, Hakon, and on us."

"That pleases me to hear. And Louis? How is he?"

Louis was the son of Athelstan's sister, Eadgifu, and the king of the West Franks, Charles III, whom many called "the Simple." When Charles had lost control of his kingdom, Eadgifu brought Louis to the court of her brother to be raised. Hakon arrived the same year, and the two became fast friends, despite their dissimilar heritage.

"He too flourishes, though I fear he grows anxious in the court of Athelstan. Like you, Louis has matured and now yearns to fight for his kingdom as you have done here. With God's grace, I pray it comes to pass."

Hakon's mind turned to a time long ago, when he and Louis pretended to stand guard on Winchester's ancient walls with the local fyrd. The memory brought a smile to Hakon's face. "I too will pray for that," he said. "He will make a wise king one day." Hakon sipped from his ale cup. "So tell me — how is it that you and your men are here? And so soon? I did not expect to see priests here until next summer, if they came at all. I believe there is a tale there."

Father Otker wiped his mouth and placed his elbows on the table before him, folding his fingers together. "I wish I had a grand story to tell, but it all came about simply and quickly. King Athelstan summoned me one day to his chambers and told me of the missive you sent to him. He asked if I might want to undertake this journey, given my knowledge of you. After praying on it, I accepted the offer and asked to bring eleven others with me. Brothers of my choice."

"And how did you choose?"

"Oh, that part was easy. I chose my comrades by skill. All are capable of running various parts of a monastery. Teachers like me. A gardener." He motioned to Wulfstan. "An infirmarian." He motioned to Egbert. "A carpenter." Next to Egbert, a dark-haired man nodded. "And so on." Father Otker motioned vaguely to the rest. Some listened carefully to their leader's words. Those out of earshot slurped at their stew. "Within a few days, I had my eleven. Since the ship was there and summer was waning, I thought it best to leave as soon as we could. And so we are here."

"I see. So the plan then is to start a monastery?"

Father Otker smiled and held up his thin hands. "Patience. Such things take time. I thought to start with a humble church, provided that sits well with you."

Hakon looked out at the warriors in the hall, then back at his former tutor. "My original thought was to have you and your men spread the word of Christ as missionaries. But I've revised that thinking. I believe, for the time being, you will be safer here. At least until the people grow accustomed to your presence."

"So be it." Father Otker smiled. "We will establish ourselves here, God willing."

"Where should we build this church?" asked the portly gardener named Wulfstan. He was a man in his mid to late twenties, with fair complexion, hair the color of young wheat, and a youthful enthusiasm that gleamed in his blue eyes.

"Close to the town would be best." Hakon smiled at Wulfstan. "Kaupang has been a trading post for generations. My brother Bjorn, father to Gudrod whom you just met, built it into a prosperous town. And as you probably saw upon your arrival, we are expanding it daily. It is here that many people come to trade, to meet, and then return to their homes."

"Will you remain here?" asked Egbert as he scratched at his newly tonsured scalp. "With us?"

"For a time, Egbert. Though I have much to do in other parts of the realm. You will be safe here after I leave. Gudrod possesses his father's same skill for commerce, and his cousin Trygvi is a formidable warrior. God willing, the two will transform this place into a center of commerce and strength."

To a man, the monks looked dubious at Hakon's mention of safety.

"Your missive mentioned a wedding?" This question came from Wulfstan.

Hakon nodded. "It did, though the wedding is no longer."

"I am sorry, my lord," replied Wulfstan.

"You need not be, Wulfstan. I broke off the marriage myself. It is a long story," Hakon hastened to explain to the confused monks, "that I will recount one day, but not today." He sipped his ale. "For now, we must get you started on your mission. And the first step," he raised a finger, "is to teach you the language of the Northmen. You cannot convert people whose language you do not speak."

"We are a step ahead of you," Wulfstan said proudly in a dialect of the Northmen's tongue. "I was raised in Nottingham and have been teaching my brothers." Nottingham was in the Danish-controlled area of Engla-lond known as the Danelaw. Though Athelstan had wrested the area from its Danish overlords years before, many there still spoke the Danish tongue, which was not so dissimilar from the Norse tongue.

"We are learning," Father Otker agreed in Norse, then switched quickly to Latin. "Did you think I would overlook such a basic need?" He smiled.

Wulfstan winked. "They have a long ways to go, but I'm determined."

Hakon laughed.

Chapter 13

The summons went out to the local areas and several days later the bonders arrived. It was raining outside again, so Hakon held the meeting in Gudrod's hall. Though the hall was large, the men stood shoulder to shoulder from the dais to the door. The stench of stale ale, venison, leeks, and body odor hung thickly on them. It was early and the mood of the men was as sour as the air.

"By now," Hakon began, getting straight to the point, "most of you have heard of or seen the priests from Engla-lond who have come to our shores." At his words, the assembly cast malignant glances at the priests, who stood off to Hakon's right just below the dais. "If you have not seen them yet, then you see them now before you. They are men like you and me, only they wear funny robes and strange hair and bow their heads to a different god."

Hakon's joke met with sullen silence. He cleared his throat and continued. "These priests are guests under my care. They will build a church here in Kaupang and live among you. And they, like you, will be protected by the law."

"And what of us? How are we to be protected from their sorcery?" This question came from one of Trygvi's hirdmen, a tall, lithe man named Vidar whom many called One-Eye because of the serpentine tattoo that snaked up his neck and encircled his left eye. The tattoo was rumored to honor his patron god Odin, who sacrificed his own eye at the Well of Urd to gain its cosmic knowledge.

"If you fear their so-called sorcery, Vidar, then pray well to your patron god for protection. For surely He will protect you, will He not?"

The mockery brought a scowl to Vidar's face and muffled curses to the mouths of those around him.

Hakon pressed on. "The priests shall live among us, and observe their customs, and be treated as guests in our realm. On the day they call Dominica, or the Day of God, they will hold a religious service, which is called 'Mass.' All are invited. Men and women. Young and old. If you are curious, go. If you are not, don't. No one will force you to attend."

"What do they say in this Mass? How do we know they are not cursing us or calling on their God to smite us?" This came from another man whom Hakon did not recognize.

At this, Wulfstan stepped forward. "My name is Wulfstan," he began in the Danish tongue. "I was born in a Danish household in Engla-lond and, as a child, learned the stories of your gods. When my parents died, the monks who lived nearby took me in, though I followed a different faith. From that experience, and from my experience with the Word of the White Christ, which is written in the holy books we keep, I can assure you that cursing people has never been the Christian way. If it pleases you, we will hold our Mass in your tongue so that you can hear for yourself our words. Or better yet, have some of your men stay with us for a time and hear our prayers. They will hear no curses."

"So that everyone here is clear on this matter," added Hakon, "this is not a debate. It requires no vote. I am not asking whether these priests can stay or go. They will stay. I am asking that you accept their presence and see that no harm comes to them."

The assembly's response came as a low grumble, like distant thunder.

"That is all I wished to say this morning. You may go."

"What of your marriage, lord?"

Hakon stopped and turned to his cousin Trygvi, who had asked the question. Trygvi had returned from his patrol late the previous night and looked as if he'd slept little since then.

"What of it?"

"Will you not tell the men, most of whom fought with you to defeat Erik, what has become of the alliance with the Uplands? We just learned the marriage did not come to pass, but you have offered no explanation to anyone. To us, it appears that you have walked away from your oath to Ivar and, in doing so, have untied the bonds we struggled so hard to achieve — the bonds we needed to defend ourselves against the Danes who now harry us day and night. Before we accept your new guests in our midst, can we not hear from you why you have done these things? Considering that many brave warriors died for your sake, I think you owe us this much."

Hakon had not expected a public challenge about Groa at this assembly, especially from Trygvi. As a result, it took him a while to respond. "Your question is a good one, Trygvi, but it is born from ignorance," he began. "I walked away from my wedding — that much is true. But I did not walk away from my oath, which was to Ivar." Hakon skewered Trygvi with his gaze. "Ivar died before the marriage was consummated. The oath broke the moment his heart stopped. I offered his son the jarldom, but he refused to accept my terms and would not swear an oath to me for it."

"But you owe us!" Trygvi retorted angrily. "You owe every man who gave his life to see Erik defeated and the people of this realm united." A few men — mostly Trygvi's — backed their leader with cries of support. "Now we have the Danes attacking from the south and an angry snake named Thorgil to the north."

Hakon waited for the warriors to settle themselves. "Thorgil *is* an angry snake, Trygvi, and he is *also* ambitious. You have the right of it. So even if I hadn't walked away, he might still have come. In fact, I know he would have come. Mayhap not tomorrow or even in a winter. But mark my words, he would have come."

The crowd hesitated.

"This surprises you, but it shouldn't. For those of you not from here, I suggest you prepare yourselves as best you can. As for the priests, they will preach their holy words to anyone who cares to listen. Any attack on them is an attack on me and will be treated thusly. Are my words clear?"

Trygvi and his men stared hard-faced at Hakon but held their tongues. Hakon's eyes moved to Gudrod, then to Egil. No one spoke.

"Good. Then we are agreed. You may go about your business." Hakon watched the men go, knowing from their silence and stolen glances that they were not pleased. He had been wrong to break off his wedding, but what was done was done — he could not go back on that decision now.

Hakon's gaze shifted to Egil, who had remained behind. The older man stroked his white beard mindlessly. "You have more words for me, I suppose?"

The old warrior waited until the gathering, including the monks, had moved away, then he spoke. "I decided to bend my head to your knee knowing you worshipped a different god. We talked much of gods then, do you remember? I still do not know what I will find when my death comes, but I do know that times are uncertain and your reign is yet young. I see how the Christian religion taints your decisions and puts your young reign at peril. Having these priests here will not strengthen your standing — they will jeopardize it. They already have."

Hakon stared at Egil for a long moment as he considered his response. "Egil Woolsark. Your words mean much to me, for they have guided me since I returned to the North and even before. I have seen the trouble my recent decisions have caused you and others, and it has not been easy to watch. But I have also come to realize one thing — this land will never be without strife. Whether I introduce priests or not, some disgruntled princeling, or Dane, or Swede, will come with his sword and retinue of warriors to claim what he believes to be his. I can therefore only do what I believe to be right."

Egil nodded softly as if agreeing to something Hakon had said. "I have seen much strife in my many winters, boy, and in all that time, one truth has always held true — strife happens where weakness resides. These priests weaken your power, for they will introduce a new religion — an untrusted religion — that will stoke fear and force men to take sides at a time when you need them united behind your standard. I will say it one last time — send these priests away before it is too late."

Hakon sighed and cast his gaze over Egil's bald head to the retreating monks. "I cannot."

Egil shook his head and walked away.

Later that day, Hakon collected his men and rode to Halldor's home, for he had a score to settle with the trader. The home lay near the mouth of the bay that led to Kaupang, shadowed by the surrounding coastal pines and shielded from the sea winds by a rocky headland to the south. A wattle fence surrounded the small hall and its various sheds and pens. The morning's rain had ceased and a few sheep grazed on the wet grass that grew in the shade of the trees. Smoke snaked from the chimney hole in the hatched roof of his modest dwelling, carrying with it the aroma of leeks and mushrooms.

Off to their left, near the water, lay the cargo ship that had transported the priests from Athelstan's realm. It was there that the ship captain worked, caulking the knarr's strakes alongside a handful of his shipmates. Halldor saw the warriors approaching and wiped his pitch-soaked hands on a woolen towel. He did not try to run. Behind him, his crew looked on sternly.

Hakon stopped his horse and looked down at the weathered sea captain. Red-rimmed eyes stared back at Hakon. He looked as if he had not slept in weeks. "You are headed back to sea so late in the year?"

"Aye. We have a few more runs to make. The seas won't grow too rough for another moon."

"You like to take risks then. I've heard that only Danes are plying these waters now."

"Risk is not the friend of traders. But a man must eat."

"You head to Hedeby?"

"Are you here to talk about my business, or do you want to know why I abandoned your monks?"

Beside Hakon, Egil chuckled. "He's got balls, this one does."

Before Hakon could speak, Halldor said, "I will tell you, lord, but you alone."

Hakon glanced at Halldor's crew, many of whom had sharp tools in their hands. "Egil." Hakon motioned with his chin toward the boat. "Take the men and watch them."

Egil shrugged. "It's your neck, lord."

When the men had gone, Hakon considered Halldor quietly, then slowly withdrew his sword Quern-biter from her sheath and leveled its point at Halldor's chest. "Well?"

Halldor glanced about him, as if to see if anyone was listening. Satisfied, he turned back to Hakon. "I see things, lord."

"You see things," Hakon repeated slowly, not quite believing his ears. "What things?"

"Strange things," Halldor continued. "I see battles. Storms of blood. Christian crosses and bodies lying in piles upon the ground. A feast for ravens, lord." The words came quickly, as if he had been holding them inside and could do so no longer. They re-conjured Hakon's own visions, those that had plagued him after the battle with Erik. A shiver inched down Hakon's spine. "The visions first came to me when I sailed with your monks. Even now the visions haunt my thoughts. They will not leave me." He grabbed all of the pendants that hung from his neck and squeezed them in his fist. There was a sudden, desperate look in his eyes that stood up the hairs on Hakon's skin. "I've brought something to these shores that angers the gods, and they are punishing me for it."

Hakon tried to remain unmoved, but frankly, the tale unnerved him. "So you stranded the priests upon this shore, hoping someone would rid you of them." Hakon pushed his sword point against Halldor's chest. "Why did you not just kill the monks yourself, if you thought these things?"

Halldor shrugged. "I did not feel it was up to me to decide their fate, so I left them. Besides, they are holy men, and killing them might bring the Christ-God against me."

"You are lucky they yet live, Halldor. Had they died for your treachery, I would have come for you and your luck would surely have run out then."

Halldor bowed his head. For a moment Hakon contemplated punishment, then just as quickly pushed the notion aside. Halldor's mind was punishing him enough; there was no sense in harming him further. "Remember this day as the day I spared you, Halldor. And remember too that you now owe me. One day, I may come for that payment."

The sea captain nodded, but wisely kept his lips tight.

Hakon called his men back to him, then turned and rode away with Halldor's words echoing in his head. *Storms of blood. A feast for ravens.* Hakon shuddered. The gods were arming themselves for battle.

Chapter 14

True to his word, Hakon gave the monks free rein to practice their faith, and over the following days, Father Otker transformed life for his brethren into something with which they were far more familiar. He divided the days into the liturgical hours as they had done for years in the monastery. Hakon joined them when he could in their services, reveling in the soft, monotone voices that bolstered his faith and reminded him so much of his time in Winchester. On Sundays, the brothers marched to the top of the small rise north of the town and held their Mass. Father Otker stood with the pine trees at his back and recited the service in Latin to his kneeling monks. As he spoke, Wulfstan translated the words to the few townspeople brave enough or curious enough to listen.

Between their prayers, the monks busied themselves with their church. It was slow going with the unseasonal rain, but by the beginning of the harvest month, they had a foundation frame laid down and most of the tall staves driven into the frame. God willing, by spring they would have the withies interlaced into the staves and by the following autumn, the daub walls would be hard and the thatch roof would be in place. When it was complete, it would be the most permanent structure in the town of Kaupang save for Gudrod's mead hall.

As summer slipped into autumn, the monk's routine became less of a distraction and more a part of the daily backdrop of Kaupang. So long as the monks kept to themselves, there was peace in the burgeoning town. Hakon was acutely aware of it, though he was not so naïve to think it could continue. One day a monk would venture too far afield, or a warrior would drink overmuch and step beyond his boundaries. And when that day came, the peace would dissolve.

Hakon had little time to dwell on such things though, for beyond the town, matters were more chaotic. Ragnvald continued to evade his pursuers and feast on the fat of the land. Hakon often joined his nephews in their efforts to catch the Dane, but each time he would vanish before their arrival, leaving nothing but carnage in his wake. Meanwhile, in the Uplands, Thorgil plotted. Upland traders brought word of Thorgil's embassies to the Swedes, and rumors spread that Holmfrid or Groa would be offered up in exchange for their support. In time, Thorgil would have his army, and they would come for Hakon and the High Seat. Part of Hakon wanted to preempt that attack and invade Thorgil's lands, but to pull men from the impending harvest and form an army capable enough to overthrow Thorgil, all with Ragnvald breathing down their necks, was proving impossible. Better to wait until raiding season began the following summer.

As the days slipped ever closer to the harvest, two things happened to lift Hakon's flagging spirits. The first was the arrival of Toralv and his men. Though soiled from their long travels through the mountains and forests of the Uplands, they were hale and in good spirits. Hakon rejoiced in their appearance and celebrated the boys who had guided Toralv and the others safely to Kaupang.

The second event was a baptism, which came about quite suddenly on a Sunday afternoon. Father Otker came to Hakon after the Mass and told him of his plan to baptize those few who had been attending the Mass regularly. Hakon excitedly sanctioned the ceremony, and the following Sunday, the few converts — eight in all — donned simple robes provided by the monks and stepped into the waters at the end of the bay, a few hundred paces upstream from the bustle and filth of Kaupang. Word of the baptism spread, and a crowd quickly gathered to witness the affair.

Excited that the seeds of his faith were beginning to blossom, Hakon was one of the first to arrive. As he watched the monks gather on the shore, he could not help but recall the words of Athelstan: *Like the missionaries of old, you have the opportunity to bring the light of our faith to the North. And I believe with my heart that you will.* His heart swelled with pride at the prospect of finally making those words a reality, then just as quickly plummeted when the converts came forth.

Beside him, Toralv laughed, as did many others who had gathered, for the converts were the dregs of the town: beggars and drunks, cripples and hags. Hardly the people Hakon envisioned as the first converts to the faith. For the Northerners, who worshipped strength and cunning above all else, society's destitute were a poor example for Christianity's power. Still, he kept his lips tight and his thoughts to himself.

Father Otker and Wulfstan performed their tasks dutifully, the father speaking in Latin as his brother called out the words in the Norse tongue to the onlookers. For all their earlier scorn, those same onlookers were not immune to the power of the ceremony. Hakon noticed that more than a few grabbed the talismans at their necks or cast their gazes to the skies, as if expecting the Northern gods to somehow appear. But if the Aesir looked on, they did so in silence. Or perchance it was they who stoked the embers of hostility in the hearts of Kaupang's townspeople, for no sooner had the converts emerged from the water than someone punched one of the new Christians in the jaw. The hapless fellow never saw it coming and dropped to the sand like a bag of stones. Gudrod's warriors rushed to break up the fight before anything more serious could occur, but the message had been sent: the monks may be guests and beyond approach, but the converts would be targeted.

"Still convinced that your faith can take hold here?" Gudrod said as his warriors dragged the bloodied convert out of the fray.

Hakon had no response. Nearby, Egil spat poignantly.

Later that day, after the monks had eaten their midday meal, Hakon approached Father Otker to share his feelings. They sat in a small clearing on the hill near Gudrod's hall, looking down upon the town as Hakon expressed his dismay about the baptism.

Father Otker sat silently for a moment, contemplating a red-breasted robin that hopped along a nearby log. "What troubles you about what you saw?"

Hakon tried to put his thoughts to words, but knew not how to express them without treading on Father Otker's spirits, which were still running high after the baptism. "It was not what I expected," he ventured delicately.

"What was not? The fighting that occurred or the converts themselves? Or mayhap both?" His brows formed crescents over his inquisitive eyes.

Hakon grinned at his former tutor's keenness. "Both, I suppose."

The old man squinted as he smiled. "It is not for us to judge the ways of God, Hakon, nor to pass judgment on those who seek Him. As for the poor fellow who got punched...he was undeserving of such treatment, to be sure, but it could have been worse."

"That is true," Hakon admitted. "Still, it makes me fear for you and your mission here."

"I see." The robin took flight and Father Otker craned his neck as it disappeared into the trees behind him. When it was gone, he turned back to the conversation. "Let me tell you a little story. When we first arrived, we were thrown into that cell without any idea of how long we'd be there or whether we would live or die. For the first time in a long time, I was truly afraid. It was the first time in a long time that my faith had been tested."

"I'm sorry," said Hakon.

"No, no! Don't be! It was the best thing to have happened to me. You see, it was in that dark cell, with my spirits at their lowest, that God spoke to me. Not in the way you might think," he quickly added. "There were no booming voices and grand visions. There was only a passage from Scripture that kept popping into my thoughts. I couldn't get rid of it. It took me a while to understand that God was trying to say something, and even longer for me to listen."

Hakon had heard of God speaking to people but had never known anyone to whom that had actually happened. "What was the passage?" he asked excitedly.

Father Otker smiled. "Luke, Chapter 10."

Hakon stared blankly at his old tutor.

"The story of the Good Samaritan from Scripture," Father Otker reminded him. "Oh, come," he said again when it was clear Hakon didn't remember. "Did I do such a poor job tutoring you? Luke, Chapter 10: 'And Jesus answering said, a certain man went down from Jerusalem to Jericho, and fell among thieves, which stripped him of his raiment, and wounded him, and departed, leaving him half dead. And by chance there came down a certain priest that way: and when he saw him, he passed by on the other side. And likewise a Levite, when he was at the place, came and looked on him, and passed by on the other side. But a certain Samaritan, as he journeyed, came where he was: and when he saw him, he had compassion on him, and went to him, and bound up his wounds, pouring in oil and wine, and set him on his own beast, and brought him to an inn, and took care of him.'"

Hakon felt like a small boy once more, doing his best to unravel Father Otker's words. "I don't understand. How does that pertain to converting the realm and the risks that come with it?"

"Much. Though I admit, it took me a while to see it too. You see, twelve priests cannot march into a kingdom and expect the people to instantly flock to them for conversion. Oh, I wish we could, but we are too few and too foreign. We can only work among the people, show them kindness and the ways of Christ, even if we don't believe as they do."

"As the Good Samaritan did to the traveler."

"Precisely." He raised his bony index finger to emphasize his point.

"Do you have a plan for how you might do this?"

"Aye," he responded. "We start here, and we start soon. With the harvest. There will be plenty of work to do, and every one of the brothers has something to offer, even if it's just helping gather the animals for slaughter. We need only the courage to go out and do it, and the faith that our work will change people's hearts."

Hakon gazed out at the town, wondering whether his people were ready for the priests to work among them. "What about the church?"

"We will keep working on it when we can. But the rain is hampering our progress, and it will only get worse. Part of me wonders whether the Lord wants us to turn our attention to something else. Everything happens for a reason, you know."

Hakon smiled at the words King Athelstan had spoken so often. And then his thoughts turned to the scene on the beach that morning and his smile faded. "It is a risk. You saw what happened this morning."

"I did, but sooner or later, we will need to start getting closer to the people and taking some risks. I'd prefer it be sooner."

Hakon sighed. "Very well. I will make sure my men keep an eye on you, for my own peace of mind."

Father Otker patted Hakon's knee with his bony hand. "God will protect us, Hakon."

Hakon grunted. He was not so sure.

Chapter 15

"My lord!" Egbert called, interrupting Hakon's sparring session with Toralv.

Hakon checked his swing and looked over at the young monk. The dismay on Egbert's freckled face froze Hakon's heart. "What is it, Egbert?"

"It's Wulfstan, lord." Egbert turned on his heel and ran in the opposite direction, not waiting for the warriors to respond.

Hakon looked at his men, then ran after the monk. His men followed. They sprinted along the beach past Kaupang and up the hill to the north of town where the priests held Mass and where a small crowd had now gathered. It was there, in those trees, that they found Wulfstan and the eight townspeople who had so recently accepted baptism. They hung from a stout limb by bound feet, upside-down, their arms hanging stiffly above the ground, their eyes open but seeing nothing. Dried blood stained their faces where it had poured from their sliced necks. Flies buzzed thickly about them. Father Otker stood before Wulfstan's sacrificed body, tears streaming down his cheeks. Nearby, a number of the monks knelt in prayer, their muttered supplications mixing eerily with the call of carrion and the creak of the hanging ropes as they skidded across the branch.

Hakon turned from the scene and gazed out at the inlet, struggling to keep his emotions in check and the bile from rising in his throat. Beside him, Toralv muttered a curse as he grabbed the amulet that hung from his thick neck to ward off the evil that might still lurk in this place.

"Cut them down," Egil growled.

"What happened?" Hakon asked Egbert, who was standing by his side, looking on wordlessly as Hakon's men cut the ropes and lowered Wulfstan and the other sacrifices to the earth.

"I don't know," Egbert responded, his voice quivering with emotion. "Wulfstan went to help some local farmers tend to their flock and never returned. That was yesterday."

"Did no one keep an eye on him?"

"Wulfstan told them he didn't need them. That God would protect him."

Initially, Hakon had sent guards with the monks who went out to help with the harvest, but the monks had grown more secure in their environment, and more careless as a result. Still, carelessness had not wielded the blade that slit Wulfstan's throat or hung him like an animal from a tree. All of this Hakon understood; but at that moment, there was nowhere else to direct his growing anger, and so he let his displeasure be known to Egbert.

"Did you not think to look for him when it grew dark?"

"We did, lord, but it was only this morning — now — that we found him."

The despair in Egbert's voice was like a knife raking across Hakon's heart. It, like the pain of Wulfstan's death, hurt deep inside, yet Hakon could not just run from the pain. He had to press forward, to get to the bottom of this foul act. "Where are the farmers he helped?"

"I don't know." Egbert shook his head, sounding desperate, "I don't know."

"Egil, find them and bring them to me." To Egbert he said more gently now, "Wulfstan and these others need a proper burial. We will bury them here."

Egbert nodded. "Yes, lord." There were tears in his eyes.

Hakon walked down the hill, his mind numb. After a few paces, he sat heavily and gazed out over Kaupang and the waters beyond.

His thoughts harkened back to something Athelstan used to tell him. Athelstan was convinced that God had a plan and that everything had a reason; that misery, grief, and sorrow were but trials of faith and that their purpose was to make leaders stronger. But gazing at Wulfstan's sacrificed corpse did not make Hakon feel stronger — all he felt was a heavy sorrow and a vast emptiness. What purpose could they possibly serve?

"May I sit?"

Hakon looked up at the towering bulk of his friend Toralv and nodded.

Toralv grunted as he sat heavily on the ground beside his king. "Much has happened since we parted company at Lake Mjosa, Hakon. And not much of it good, eh?"

Hakon snorted. "Aye, much has happened," he admitted. It was a cold morning and Hakon's breath clouded before him as he spoke. Fall's crispness was in the air.

Toralv leaned back on his elbow. He was looking at Hakon, but Hakon refused to look back. "When you sent for the monks, you knew this might happen. By all the gods, *I* knew this might happen. They are not welcome among our people. Elsewhere, sure. But here?"

Hakon glanced at his friend. "I could have prevented this."

Toralv sighed. "Aye. You could have left well enough alone and never sent for them. And you could have sent them away once you understood how your people felt about their presence here. That would have prevented this. But you need not worry about those things any longer. What's done is done. Your thoughts should be on those that yet live and the people you rule." Toralv picked up a stick and tossed it down the hill. "And the men who have gone directly against your word."

Toralv watched his friend and waited, as if expecting a response, but there was nothing Hakon could say. He had no profound words or ideas to combat Toralv's frank and accurate observations. Besides, he was struggling to quell his own fury and sadness at the loss of Wulfstan, not to mention the overwhelming burden of how to keep the other priests safe. So instead he silently stewed, keeping his lips tight and his eyes focused on the land and waters to the south. Eventually Toralv tired of waiting and lumbered away.

That afternoon, Egil brought a farmer to Hakon, pulling him forcibly by a strip of leather that bound the man's arms at the wrists. The farmer's tattered clothes and disheveled appearance spoke of a meager life scratched from what the earth would give him. His spirit, unlike his body, showed no signs of relenting, for there was mettle in the eyes that gazed back at Hakon.

"Cut him loose, Egil."

Egil pulled a knife from his belt and did as he was told.

"What's your name?" Hakon asked the farmer.

"Ulf," the farmer responded as he rubbed at his wrists.

"You are a farmer, Ulf?"

"Aye."

Hakon pointed to the bloated corpse of Wulfstan, who lay on the ground beside an open grave. "Do you recognize that man, Ulf?"

Ulf gazed at the corpse, then turned back to Hakon, his face softer now than it had been when he arrived. "Aye. He offered to help us yesterday morn. I told him he was welcome if he could help salt and smoke our slaughter."

"Did you know he was a guest in my hall?"

"Aye, lord. Everyone knows of the Christ followers."

Hakon considered that response for a moment. "Did it not worry you to employ a monk in your slaughter?"

"Some of my family worried, lord. But we needed the help."

"I see. Do you remember when he left your fields?"

"After the day's work was done. It was getting dark. We had a cup of ale together, then he insisted on getting back. We walked him partway to town."

"Why only partway?"

"A group of warriors appeared, lord. They looked like they were headed to garrison the fortress at Skiringssal, but they stopped when they saw us. They took an interest in your monk and offered to escort him back to Kaupang. They told us that they would see to his well-being, seeing how important he was to you."

The irony in that statement boiled the blood in Hakon's veins. "Did you recognize the men?"

The man set his jaw. It was clear he was struggling with whether or not to answer, so Hakon gave him time. The man's eyes moved to Wulfstan's corpse, then back to Hakon. He looked about him, then finally stepped closer to Hakon and said quietly, "Aye. It was the warrior they call One-Eye, Lord Trygvi's man."

"Can others corroborate your story?" asked Hakon just as quietly.

Ulf's eyes went wide. "Aye, but do not make us testify in public. It'll be our death. Please, lord."

"Did you see Vidar kill Wulfstan, Ulf?" This question came from Egil, who had overhead Ulf's testimony.

"No."

Hakon cursed. He could accuse Vidar of murder all he wanted, but with no witnesses, there was no proof that he was the killer. The accusations would remain just that.

Hakon handed Ulf a piece of hack silver. "I thank you for the information."

The farmer looked down at the rough silver nugget in his palm. It was probably worth as much as he might make in a month or more. He then looked over at the monks, who were now praying over their fallen brother. "I thank you for this gift, lord, but I did nothing to earn this. I have lost nothing and in fact have gained by the hand of that Christian." He handed the silver back to Hakon. "Give it to the monks, lord." Ulf bowed, then retreated.

Hakon's fist closed around the silver as the farmer moved away. "I want Vidar brought to me," he said quietly to Egil, "along with Trygvi and Gudrod."

"Do not pursue this, boy," Egil warned. "It will only add fuel to the fire you have built by your own hands."

Hakon peered at Egil. "A man — my guest — lies dead. Others, innocent townspeople, lie dead. And you are suggesting I am creating the fire?"

Egil met Hakon's gaze, but said nothing.

"Fetch me Vidar and my nephews, Egil."

Egil moved off without another word.

Trygvi and Gudrod came to Hakon that afternoon, just as the monks laid the last piles of earth on Wulfstan's grave. Egil began to announce their arrival, but Hakon held up a hand for silence — Father Otker was finishing a prayer and Hakon didn't want him interrupted. When the prayer ended, Hakon turned to receive his nephews. Their disgust at the scene and at having to wait out a Christian prayer was more than evident on their faces.

"You called for us?" asked Gudrod flatly.

"Aye. As I called for Vidar. Where is he?"

"He is gone," Trygvi reported. "Along with some of his sword-brothers."

"He killed one of the priests, Trygvi. One of my guests, whom I purposefully told everyone, including him, not to harm." Hakon could feel the rage build within his body and did not try to quell it. "Vidar went against my words, and he went against the laws of this land. He does not exist outside the law!"

Trygvi's face darkened. "You don't know any of that. You guess that Vidar killed the priest."

"And yet, he is gone. Did you not think to wonder why he might have left and where he might have gone?"

Trygvi took a step toward his uncle, his face now crimson with anger. When he spoke, he did so through gritted teeth. "Vidar was one of my best warriors, Hakon. Oath-sworn to me. He has saved my life more than once. I do wonder where he has gone and why he has gone, but I hold onto hope that he will return in due time."

Hakon did not back away, but kept his eyes leveled on his nephew's face. "Find him."

He turned to Gudrod, who held his tongue behind a stony mask. "Gudrod, call an assembly for tomorrow, midday. We will meet here. I want everyone — your warriors, Trygvi's, and every free man, woman, and child in this area — to gather on this spot when the sun is at its peak."

Gudrod was not so easily commanded. "And what do you plan to say to the assembly, Hakon?"

"Are you refusing, Gudrod?"

"No, my lord. But I would know what you plan to tell the people before we ask them to abandon their work in the midst of harvest."

Hakon scoffed. "It is not so great a burden. Now be about your task, Gudrod."

The cousins exchanged a momentary glance. Though fleeting, it was filled with malice. "As you wish," Gudrod finally answered.

Without another word, they turned on their heels and walked away, leaving Hakon alone with his misgivings.

A heavy fog rolled into Kaupang during the night. Despite the approach of midday, it continued to cling jealously to the earth, shrouding the town and its environs in a thick, swirling gray that weighed on Hakon's spirits. Drops of moisture collected on his cloak and slickened his hair as he and his warriors made their way to the hill north of town, where Father Otker and his remaining monks waited. Torches illuminated the hilltop, casting a shifting orange glow on the holy men and the nearby graves. The effect put Hakon's nerves on edge.

Wordlessly he watched as the townsfolk came, gathering on the muddied slope that climbed from the town. When the slope was sufficiently crowded, Hakon stood upon a dew-slick bench and spoke to the people. "Two nights ago," he called above the chatter, "someone attacked and killed a guest under my care. One of the monks who went by the name of Wulfstan." Hakon paused to let his words take effect. A hush settled on the crowd. "He had been on his way back from helping someone prepare for the winter. With him, other members of this community died. They were sacrificed like animals and hung from these trees." Hakon waved at the trees behind him. "The attack on free people is a crime. I warned you all that the monks were not to be mistreated. That they were guests under my roof. And yet, some of you disobeyed!"

By now the crowd had grown deathly still, sensing that something greater was playing out before them. Hakon turned to his nephew, Trygvi, but spoke so the entire crowd could hear. "Have you found Vidar?"

Trygvi kept his eyes leveled on his uncle's face. "No, lord. He is gone."

"Very well. Since Vidar and those who fled with him are not here to defend themselves, I am left with no choice. I sentence them all to three years as outlaws. They are nithing, cowards worthy of no more protection under the law than a slave. Their property I take as my own, as wergeld for the death of my guest. I will rethink my decision should they come in person to convince me of their innocence."

Behind their leader, Trygvi's remaining men looked at each other and cursed aloud. Trygvi did nothing to stop them.

Hakon turned his attention back to the crowd. "My brother may have tolerated lawlessness, but I will not. Justice will be served in all cases. No man will exist outside the law. Is that clear?"

The crowd mumbled its assent.

"Is that clear?" Hakon yelled again, his anger spilling over.

The crowd's affirmation rippled across the field.

Hakon stepped from the bench and the assembly dispersed. He watched them in silence until they had reached the bottom of the hill, wondering silently what they thought of the decision he had just laid before them. Most of the townsfolk knew nothing of Vidar and his men, though Hakon was certain that word of the dead hanging from the trees had had more than enough time to work its way from ear to ear. Those things mattered little. What mattered was how Hakon responded to them — they needed to know that Hakon would uphold the law, whatever the circumstances.

With a final deep breath, he walked over to his former tutor. "I am sorry for your loss, Father Otker. Though my words to the townsfolk won't bring Wulfstan back, I hope they will at least protect you."

Father Otker patted Hakon's shoulder, looking suddenly very weary. "I thought it would work. God spoke to me, and I followed His word." He shook his head as his eyes studied the sodden earth.

His uncertainty unnerved Hakon. "Your strategy can still work, Father. Your men just need to stay vigilant. Everything happens for a reason; perchance —"

Father Otker held up his thin hand to stop Hakon. "Forgive me. It has been a long two days. I must pray." With a final, tired pat on Hakon's shoulder, Father Otker walked over to Wulfstan's grave and fell to his knees.

Chapter 16

Hakon awoke in the dead of night to the stentorian blast of a war horn.

He rushed out into the dark with the other warriors, his seax and shield in hand and his eyes scanning the darkness for trouble. All was quiet save for the horn, which filled the air yet again with a long, melancholy warning.

"There!" called someone, pointing south at a distant flame that licked at the sky.

It was the fort on the headland that overlooked the mouth of the Viksfjord. The garrison had seen something, or worse, had been attacked. Gudrod looked north, toward Skiringssal. Hakon followed his gaze and saw nothing but darkness, which was good.

"Trygvi," Gudrod said. "Grab your gear and make haste for the headlands. Take arrows. I will take half my men north to Skiringssal. Geir, remain here and protect the town."

Hakon gathered his men and together they shrugged into their byrnies, donned their helmets, cinched their belts, and grabbed their shields. Hakon also grabbed Quern-biter and his smaller seax. Others grabbed spears and if they had them, bows and quivers. They followed Trygvi and his own hirdmen down the hill.

"Follow closely," Trygvi called over his shoulder at Hakon. "I don't want you getting lost."

"What's he take us for," grumbled Didrik as he jogged beside his king, "a bunch of fledglings?"

"Keep quiet and be ready," said Egil. "Trygvi knows this place better than us."

The night was clear and cold, the wind gentle. A half moon sat high in the southern sky, its light glinting off shield rims and clouds of breath as the warriors trotted past the town to the headlands about a mile distant. It had been two weeks since Wulfstan and some of their own had perished on the nearby hill — two weeks marred by oppressive fog and the silent specter of fear that the sacrifices evoked. Though the fog had finally lifted, the people's trepidation had not. It resided now in their faces as they stood like silent sentinels outside their dwellings, watching the small army pass.

As Kaupang faded into the darkness behind them, Trygvi directed the warriors to fan out into a long, loose shield wall. He raised his fingers to his lips to signal that they should advance in silence. Five hundred paces before them a tree-studded slope climbed to the rocky hilltop upon which the flame danced. Hakon kept his eyes averted from the fire lest it blind him to the darkness. He was not sure what they would find, but if an enemy waited, they'd certainly be waiting among the trees, not on the hilltop. The thought made him lift his shield a little higher.

Trygvi began to jog. The men followed, their gear rattling as they trotted over the uneven ground. Three hundred paces. Hakon's blood began to rush in his ears. Two hundred and fifty paces. He drew his seax from its sheath and tightened his fingers on its leather grip. Two hundred paces. They were now in range of arrows. Trygvi waved his sword again and his warriors broke into an all-out sprint. Hakon braced himself for the hiss of flying steel and the cry of dying men, but it never came.

The warriors rushed into the woods at the base of the slope and wove around thick trunks and low limbs. Here and there men stumbled on hidden roots and muddy patches. Hakon's eyes darted left and right in search of a moving shadow or glint of steel, but the only enemy he found was darkness. At one point, Hakon's feet slipped beneath him and he fell to his knees, but Didrik was behind him and yanked him to his feet.

Quickly they climbed to the summit and emerged to find guards at the ready, their blades out and their backs to the fire. When they saw Trygvi, they lowered their weapons.

"You lit the beacon fire," Trygvi huffed. "What's the matter?"

The guards pointed out into the fjord. "Ragnvald is here."

Trygvi and Hakon walked to the far side of the hilltop and gazed down at the water. Two large dragon ships bobbed in the moonlit current, their outlines sitting just out of arrow range.

"Ragnvald!" roared Trygvi. His voice echoed across the water.

A few heartbeats later came the reply. "Trygvi Olavsson! Is that you?"

"Aye."

"Is Hakon with you?"

"I am here," yelled Hakon.

"That is good, for I have a message to deliver to both of you," called Ragnvald.

"Then come deliver it face to face, like a man, rather than skulking in the dark like a common thief," shouted Trygvi.

"You flatter me, Trygvi. For I am a thief, but no common one. I rob your shores and grow rich off your lands. But I do not just rob defenseless steadings — I even steal your oath-sworn who grow tired of your young king and his priests!"

"Vidar!" roared Trygvi, calling for his former hirdman.

"You can bellow until your voice is gone, Trygvi, but you will get no response from Vidar or his shield-brothers. They are not here."

"Where are they?"

"He is off to do my bidding and to prove his loyalty."

"Which is?"

"To kill your priests, of course. And if the night goes the way of the true gods, he has already succeeded." The ships began to row from the fjord. "I bid you both a good night."

Hakon spun in alarm at Ragnvald's words and peered back at Kaupang. There, flickering in the distance, was another flame, only this one was on the hill where the new hall — and the priests — were located.

"No!" Hakon howled and darted off toward the hall.

Out on the fjord, Ragnvald and his crew roared their delight.

Back down the hill and across the field Hakon ran, outpacing the others in his desperation to reach the monks. He arrived in Kaupang, lungs bursting and limbs tingling from exertion, to find his worst fears realized. Though the town itself was unscathed, up on the hill flames engulfed the guest hall.

Hakon ran to Geir, who stood at the base of the hill directing a water train. "Where are the priests?" he called over the din of shouts and crackling flames.

Geir turned to Hakon. "I don't know," he yelled back.

Hakon climbed the hill, dodging men and flying ashes until he reached the plateau on which the hall sat. Fire and smoke clogged the air and seared his lungs as he peered upon the heat-quivering chaos. Flames engulfed the guest hall, sending fiery ash high into the air. It was clearly lost, so men and women focused on the other structures. Some pulled animals, food, and other valuables to safety. Others doused the thatching on the rooftops to protect them from the swirling ash.

Hakon ran to the abandoned guest hall, his only thought to save the priests. Holding his arm to his mouth, he forced his way into the inferno, pushing toward the flaming hall. There, lying dead on the ground just outside the door of the hall, were four priests. He could not see who they were, only that their habits and hair smoldered in the heat. Hakon tried desperately to get closer to pull the bodies clear, but the flames were too intense.

Backing away, he circled the hall, searching for signs of Father Otker and Egbert and the others. As he rounded the back corner of the hall, something smacked into his left thigh just below the lower edge of his byrnie. The force of it spun Hakon around and knocked him to the ground. He lay there, stunned, until an arrow smacked into the dirt beside his head. It was only then that he realized his peril. He looked down to see an arrow shaft protruding from his leg. Instinctively, he rolled away and raised his shield to cover his head. A second arrow bit into the dirt where he had just been. A third arrow smacked into his shield, and in that instant, Hakon pushed himself to his feet and dove around the flaming corner of the hall.

Hakon limped back toward the water train as fast as his wounded leg would allow. He braced himself for the bite of another arrow in his back, but it never came. In the smoke, Hakon saw Toralv's massive outline and limped toward him.

Toralv's eye scanned his friend and came to rest on the arrow poking from his thigh. "What happened?"

He had not felt anything until that moment, but now the wound began to throb. There was warmth running down his trousers. Blood. "Behind the hall," he managed to say. "Bowmen."

Toralv grabbed Hakon's arm and placed it over his shoulder. "Come. We need to get you to safety." Toralv lifted Hakon in his arms and carried him to Egil, who did not conceal the shock of seeing his wounded king. "Egil," Toralv yelled. "There are still enemy behind the hall."

Egil called to Didrik and Ottar, and together they ran off in the direction of the trouble.

Toralv adjusted Hakon in his arms. The movement forced an involuntary moan from Hakon's mouth as first dizziness, then nausea, took hold of him.

"What happened?" It was Trygvi's voice, though it sounded far away.

"Is it not obvious?" said Toralv. "Your man Vidar came to claim his prize."

Hakon lost track of what happened next, for a fresh wave of agony rolled over him and he slipped into darkness.

Chapter 17

"Hakon."

The voice came from far away, as distant as a whisper in a vast tunnel.

"Hakon," came the voice again. Closer now. Near him. "Can you hear me?"

Hakon's eyes fluttered open to see a face — Egbert's face — over his, though Hakon couldn't keep it in focus. "Hakon, it's me." Like his face, Egbert's voice ebbed and flowed, as if carried on a fickle wind. "It's Egbert. Can you hear me?"

Hakon tried to speak but his voice would not come. He nodded weakly. The young monk lifted Hakon's head and brought a wooden cup to his lips. "Drink," he urged.

Cool water filled his mouth, bringing with it memories of violence and bloodshed. A burning hall. Dead priests. The bite of an arrow. Blackness and fire. He remembered too being sucked from consciousness into a bog of strange and frightening dreams. Dreams of Father Otker, and Wulfstan, and doves that would mutate into ravens, and men who slaughtered other men with glee on their faces. He saw Aelfwin too, her tanned skin pasty in death despite the smile on her face.

"Hakon?"

"What is wrong with me?" Hakon's voice sounded distant to his own ears.

"You have been asleep and feverish, and I have given you an herbal drink to calm the pain."

"How long have I been asleep?"

"Many days, my lord."

"And the wound?"

"The arrow went deep. I removed it, but it was barbed and did much damage." There was a long pause.

"Will it heal?"

Hakon slipped from consciousness before he heard the response.

Egbert appeared sometime later with a steaming pot. He placed the pot on a bedside table and helped Hakon work his body into a sitting position — an effort that left Hakon's forehead glistening with sweat. The monk then reached into the pot and extracted a sopping rag from which he wrung the excess water. It splattered on the wood floor beside the bed. He then pulled the bed covers aside to reveal a swollen, bruised leg that Hakon could scarce believe was his. High up on the side of the leg was a large bandage held in place by twine.

"Where am I?"

Egbert began untying the twine. "Avaldsnes."

"Avaldsnes?"

"This may hurt a little." Egbert delicately peeled back the bandage. The pus had dried in many places and the bandage clung jealously to Hakon's bruised thigh. Hakon sucked in his breath as his tender skin pulled and stretched with the folding bandage to reveal a long, jagged wound held in place by thin sutures. The edges of the wound had scabbed, but the middle was yet deep and leaked a yellow fluid.

It stank.

The wound was not the only thing that troubled Hakon. "Why are we not in Kaupang?"

Egbert sniffed at the wound. "Your nephews and Egil felt it would be safer here for you ...and for me, I suppose."

"Me? Where are the others? Where's Father Otker?"

Egbert looked up at Hakon, his freckled face a mask of grief, his eyes full of welling tears. Hakon's heart sank, for in that look he understood there were no others. Hakon's head fell back on his pillow and his eyes stared up at the rafters above his head, though he saw only the burning hall and the bodies of the dead monks in the flames.

"I am sorry, Egbert."

"We knew the dangers, lord," he said.

"Did you?"

Egbert looked up briefly, then went back to cleaning the wound. "No. Not really. We were full of hope."

"How did you alone survive?"

"I was not in the hall when the men came, my lord. I was...indisposed. Dinner that night didn't agree with my stomach. When the hall started to burn, I ran for help, but by the time I returned, it was too late." The anguish in his voice tore at Hakon. A single tear dropped onto Hakon's skin. Egbert wiped it away. "I could hear them screaming, lord. They were burning alive." The tears streamed down his cheeks. "I tried to help. I ran for the door and removed the bar. Those that lived stumbled out coughing, but the assassins were waiting. I dove for cover when the arrows came. The others didn't make it." He wiped his sleeve across his eyes. Hakon recalled the monks' bodies lying before the door. "Father Otker never came out. He must have died from the smoke."

"I am sorry, Egbert," Hakon said again.

"God spared me." He wiped at his tears. "Why, lord? Why was I alone spared?"

Hakon had no answer.

Egbert shook his head and turned his attention back to the wound, dabbing at it gently. The silence stretched.

"Do you wish to leave the North?" Hakon asked.

"I don't know, lord. For now, I stay to heal you. But once that is done..." He shrugged and let the sentiment hang like a wet cloak between them.

The words struck deeply, for in Egbert's simple statement, Hakon heard the death knell of his own mission to Christianize the Northmen, as a dying warrior hears the call of ravens coming to feast. Though painful, they weren't unexpected. Hakon had failed to protect the monks and could not ask Egbert to stand alone, armed with nothing more than his holy books and his faith, if either still existed.

"Are you moving in your sleep?"

The question took Hakon by surprise. "What? No. I don't think so."

Egbert dropped his rag into his pot and made ready to leave. "The wound isn't healing as quickly as I had hoped. It is tearing inside. I will strengthen your sleeping herbs."

"No. I must regain my strength."

Egbert was mild mannered, but in the realm of healing, he was all earnestness. "Would you rather feel groggy or lose your leg to wound rot?" He didn't wait for an answer. "If I return tomorrow and the wound looks the same, I will increase your dose."

Toralv arrived some time later. It was late. The wall sconces hissed and spewed their smoky flames as Hakon pushed himself up in his bed to receive his friend. A stab of pain shot through Hakon's leg and he winced.

Toralv pulled up a stool and sat his hulking body upon it by Hakon's bed. He was yet young but the shifting light of the candles made him look twice his age. It must have been raining outside, for Toralv's black hair and wet cloak clung to him. "How is your leg?" he asked.

"Egbert says I'll be back on my feet before the new moon."

Toralv's expression was sullen. "You are a bad liar. Will it heal?"

Hakon's smile evaporated. "It will heal...in time."

"I should have been there. You ran off. I couldn't find you in all of the smoke."

"Stop sulking, Toralv. You said it yourself — I ran off. I would have been wiser to wait for you, but I did not think that enemy would still be there. It was stupid of me."

Toralv grunted and a smile stretched across his face. "It *was* stupid of you."

Hakon smiled. "How are the men?"

"Settling in. Egil has us busy preparing for the winter. There is much to do."

"How many are here?"

"All of us." Which meant roughly one hundred boys and men.

"Egbert tells me that Gudrod and Trygvi felt I'd be safer here. Is that what you think?"

It took Toralv a long time to answer. "Aye. We had more warriors in Kaupang, but the allegiance of your nephews' men was...questionable."

"And what of our men? Think you that their allegiance might be faltering?"

"There is some talk among the men about your luck. They say it changed when the priests came. If we linger here too long, hiding or playing nursemaid to Egbert...aye — it will falter. You must get healthy."

"Is Egbert at risk?"

Toralv chewed on his response for some time.

"Out with it. It is a simple 'yes' or 'no,' Toralv."

"Then the simple response is 'yes.' He keeps to himself mostly, but I know the men well enough to see that there is resentment there."

Hakon nodded at the bitter truth in Toralv's words. A wrong look or a misspoken word and Egbert's life would end. It might not even take that much.

How quickly things had changed. Just a few months before, Hakon had sailed onto this estate as a victorious king, and men flocked to his side. Now he crept into his hall roughly two moons later, battered and luckless. The kingdom he had fought so hard to gain was no closer to uniting; indeed, it felt more like it was unraveling. If his men believed his luck was gone, they would abandon him and his kingship would crumble, for men followed lords who fed them and made them rich, and would not hesitate to leave if they sensed that their leader had lost his ability to provide for them. Oath or no oath. Hakon swallowed the bitter truth of that like bile.

"I need you to look to Egbert's safety, Toralv."

Toralv frowned. "He would be better off disappearing."

"I agree, but for now, I need him to help me heal. When that is done, we can find somewhere else for him to be."

Toralv nodded. "I will see to it."

Hakon reached up a weak arm and grabbed Toralv's wrist. "You are a good friend, Toralv. I shall not forget this."

"You better not," he responded with a wide grin. He pushed his body from the stool and stood. "Rest, lord," he called as he neared the door. "We need you well."

His friend left Hakon to his thoughts and his aching leg. He was tired. Tired of being a king. Tired of chasing a dream no one else seemed to embrace. Even his body had turned against him, stabbing him with every wrong movement, forcing a grimace to his face and sweat to his brow. He needed time to think and to plan and to heal. Winter's darkness would come soon enough, and so he would hide and take advantage of the time.

Chapter 18

Trondelag, Spring, AD 936

Dragon dove into a sea trough and bit into the next wave, pushed along by a gusting southerly that carried with it the last vestiges of winter's fury. White foam poured over the prow and splashed across the deck, pelting Hakon and his men with icy spray.

Hakon's warriors bellowed with delight, for they had lived elbow to elbow in Hakon's smoke-thick hall at Avaldsnes for the better part of five moons, biding their time as the gales and winter storms blew in from the sea and battered the wooden structures. It had not been easy. Most of Hakon's men were yet young and unused to close-quartered idleness. And even though Egil trained them constantly, or put them to work fixing the estate's various structures, the men grew restless. Arguments were commonplace, and more than a few fistfights had broken out. Some had even vanished, presumably to find another lord to whom to offer their sword. Now, finally, they had a new adventure into which to pour their energy.

Hakon did not share in their revelry. They traveled north at the request of Sigurd, whose messenger had brought with him grave news about the state of affairs in the realm. As his comrades had warned, and as the Upland traders had suggested, Thorgil had allied himself to the Swedish family of his former hostage, Gudmund, by marrying his mother to the young Swede. The choice of Holmfrid amused Hakon.

She might never give him children but she was still a better option than the foul Groa. It was a desperate move and a dangerous one for Thorgil, for the Swedes and the Uplanders had fought each other for generations over the rich forested land of the northern interior. Now Thorgil had invited his enemies into his kingdom, and the Swedes had come gladly. They would use Thorgil for as long as they could to carve out greater and greater swathes of land to their west, then rid themselves of the Upland prince and take possession of what he had so hastily given them.

The wheels were already in motion. The combined army had harried south with the thawing snow, moving toward Kaupang. According to Sigurd's messenger, Thorgil had used the excursions to reassert his claim to his grandfather's former territories, making bold proclamations that Hakon and the Yngling line no longer held sway in that region. With little choice left to them, the people had sworn fealty to Thorgil and his Swedish allies.

Farther south, Ragnvald the Dane had reappeared with winter's retreat, only now he came with the support of his king, Gorm, who had heard of his successes and given him ships and warriors to rob the land of even more wealth. But booty was not all they sought. They also came for land. Long ago, the Vestfold and Ostfold had belonged to the Danes, and more precisely, to Gorm's forebears. Now Gorm had sent Ragnvald to reclaim those territories.

Stuck between them, like a deer's leg in the closing jaws of a wolf, sat Trygvi and Gudrod. If they committed too many men to finding Ragnvald, Thorgil could attack them from the north. Likewise, if they committed too many men to defending themselves against Thorgil, they would expose themselves to Ragnvald and his attacks from the south. So instead, they stayed close to home and built their defenses in anticipation of a war that now seemed imminent.

And all of this was happening because of Hakon. His rashness with Groa had led to Thorgil's dangerous alliance, and the blind pursuit of his religion had ratcheted up the tension in an already volatile environment. His wound bore witness to his mistakes and had created the vacuum into which his enemies now crept like wolves seeking their bleeding prey.

The wound had not only been to his leg, but also to his soul. Gone was the notion that all would be well if he just clung to his dream. His dream had perished in part with the loss of Aelfwin. The killing of Father Otker, Wulfstan, and the other monks had taken more, leaving in its place a bitter desire to avenge their deaths and prove to his people that even as a Christian, he deserved to be king.

And then there was Egbert, whom Toralv had hidden as soon as the danger to Hakon's leg had passed. It was necessary to keep him safe, but his hiding ate on Hakon's mood like a flea-ridden cloak. If all went well, Hakon would return to retrieve Egbert and give him the option to sail home or stay. But if Hakon perished, so too would the red-haired priest.

All of these thoughts swirled in Hakon's mind like the froth that danced around *Dragon's* hull. Which was why the men now shouted their delight at the waves and Hakon brooded by the steer board.

"We're here," Egil said, meaning they had reached the wide bay that marked the mouth of the Trondheimsfjord, where Sigurd's estate at Lade lay.

Hakon pushed his concerns aside and focused on the task at hand. Gradually, he angled *Dragon* toward the mouth of the fjord, which lay unseen in the distance. They finally reached it at dusk, and Hakon called his men to oar, for the wind here was blustery and directionless, and a sail would only get in their way. North and south, the shoreline rose in mounds of white snow punctuated with brown and evergreen where spring's thaw had taken hold. Far to the west, shafts of fading light broke through the billowing clouds, illuminating points in the wintery sea. His mother used to call those beams the fingers of Sunna, the sun goddess.

"We will need to find a place to make camp," called Egil above the wind.

"We can camp at Halla," Hakon said distantly, thinking of the trading town where one of his half-brothers had once lived. It was the closest settlement known to Hakon.

"Halla? Have you so quickly forgotten? The soil there is soured by blood." Egil was referring to a night battle they had fought against Erik shortly after Hakon had arrived in the North. That had been Hakon's first battle, and though it had been but a skirmish, the blood had run thickly.

"Nevertheless," said Hakon, "it will be good to see if any life has come back to that place, and to rest if it has."

Hakon received his answer soon enough. The charred remains of Halla lay in the shadow of the trees that surrounded it, unchanged from the night it had been left in ruins. A thin mist crept along the beach, casting a bleak pall over the decaying structures that languished there. Off the coast, the skeletons of two charred warships poked out of the surf like the fingers of drowning men. The place raised the hair on Hakon's arms.

Egil spat at the sight. Hakon did not need to look at him to see the scowl on his face.

"We row for Sigurd's estate at Lade," said Hakon. "The men can take turns at the oars. Get some rest, Egil — it will be a long night. I will handle the steer board for a time."

They reached Lade just as the stars began to fade to morning's soft light. Sigurd was on the beach waiting for them, apparently alerted to their arrival by one of the warriors keeping watch over the Trondheimsfjord. Rather than hail the ship and approach the water with open arms as he had done when Hakon first arrived in the North, he stood rock-still upon the strand, his arms crossed and his gaze hostile. Assembled about him were his household warriors, each with an expression as stern as their leader's. As Hakon turned *Dragon* toward the shore, two of his crewmen rushed to remove the serpent head so as not to anger the spirits of the land. Hakon hailed Sigurd with a wave as the prow came about. Sigurd did not return the gesture, nor did his warriors.

"You'd best conjure up your father's talent for words, boy," Egil grumbled. "They look ready for a fight."

Hakon barked a command and *Dragon* came to an abrupt halt. He climbed up onto the gunwale and leaned on the prow for balance as his men stretched their backs and weary arms. Cupping his hands around his mouth, he called to his friend and counselor, "You summoned me, Sigurd. Now I am here."

"Have you any priests with you, Hakon?" Sigurd called back.

Hakon thought to explain that most had perished, but changed his mind. "No," he responded simply.

"That is a good thing, for I would flay them all before your eyes."

Hakon ignored the gruesome comment. "I come as an invited guest, so I ask again — are my men and I welcome here as guests under your roof?" It was an important distinction, for custom dictated that the host must treat an invited guest as a member of his or her own family.

There was a long pause. "Aye. Come ashore."

Hakon leaped from the gunwale as soon as the prow bit into sand, determined to appear as fit as ever. But despite his good landing, his healing leg protested and he grimaced. Sigurd lumbered forward, his gaze set squarely on Hakon's face. Hakon had seen Sigurd's anger before and knew instinctively that something was yet amiss. He braced himself, though for what he could not tell.

As Sigurd came within striking distance, his right leg swung up toward Hakon's hurt thigh. Hakon stepped back to evade the blow and brought his own fists up in anticipation for the next attack. It came in the form of a right hook aimed at Hakon's jaw. Hakon barely drew his head back in time as the fist sailed past his nose, but the move had forced Hakon backward toward the water, and off balance.

Sigurd stepped back and held up his arms to the warriors around them, many of whom had drawn a weapon. "This is between Hakon and me. No one intervenes. And if any of you fight each other, I swear by the gods I'll kill you myself!"

So this was how Sigurd would repay Hakon for the failed marriage to Groa, for the priests and the chaos they had unleashed, for the alliance between the Uplanders and their Swedish enemies — for the unraveling of his intricate plan. *Let him come,* thought Hakon as he moved to his right onto firmer ground. Sigurd knew only what served him best.

"Are there no words we can say to settle this matter, Sigurd?"

Sigurd guffawed. "Words cannot repair the damage that you have done! Words will not keep the Uplanders from our threshold or keep more blood from spilling."

"Yet you would see one of us beaten here today instead of discussing how best to protect ourselves. So be it then." Hakon unbuckled his sword belt and let it fall to the sand. He held out his arms in the manner of Christ upon the cross and looked his friend full in the face. "If you think you were the only man wronged, do as you wish. Prove your point and beat me into the sand. But know this first: I will not fight you. And besting me will not change the past; it will only harm the future."

Sigurd scowled at Hakon, but something in the older man's eyes told him he'd cracked through the wall of Sigurd's fury. Slowly the jarl's fists dropped. "Odin's balls! Pick up your damned sword. Once you've unloaded your ship, join me in the hall. We have much to discuss." Sigurd stalked away with his retinue of warriors in tow.

Hakon dropped his arms and retrieved his sword from the sand. He then looked at his men, who had not expected so cold a greeting from Hakon's friend and counselor. Hakon did not wish to explain. "Stop your gawking and start unloading."

Together with Egil and Toralv, Hakon walked up the short grassy slope from the beach while the crew unloaded the ship and made camp. Before them loomed the earthen rampart surrounding Sigurd's estate, a poignant reminder of the uncertainty of these times. Two armed warriors stood by the open gate, silently eyeing Hakon and his comrades from under the brim of their helms.

Beyond the gates lay an estate to rival a king's. In the middle of the compound sat Sigurd's huge hall, which in turn was surrounded by a large barn, a smithy, storehouses, a woodshed, a guest hall, and various huts. It had been built from the wealth Sigurd's father had amassed trading with the Halogalanders and Sami to the north — a trading empire that Sigurd had inherited and expanded. That is, until Erik came to power. His favoritism, his greed, and his fratricide threatened to dismantle all Sigurd had built. And so Sigurd had called on Hakon, the sole remaining son of Harald. It was hard to believe that had been less than two summers ago.

"We should have brought the whole crew," mumbled Toralv as they stepped into the empty courtyard. He was referring to the men Hakon had decided to leave in Avaldsnes under the care of Didrik to protect it. Though it was only twenty men, it was twenty more swords than they had now. "Even Ivar gave us a warmer reception, and he was dying."

"For once would you keep your lips tight, Toralv?" Egil hissed. "By the gods, man, you curse our luck with your ill-timed words."

"Shut up, both of you," Hakon said as they reached the door to Sigurd's hall and stepped inside.

Like its owner, the interior exuded an aura of warmth, with just a touch of crudeness. Cod oil lanterns cast a soft glow on the aging bear and wolf skins that hung on the pine walls and draped across the earthen platform encircling the room. Between the furs hung dented shields whose faded colors glinted in the firelight like unpolished gems. A fire crackled in the stone hearth that ran up the middle of the room, its smoke billowing in the rafters overhead.

Across the hall, near the dais, stood a sour-faced Sigurd and his very pregnant wife, Bergliot, whose ochre-dyed cloak could not hide her distended belly. A step behind them stood Astrid, her tight auburn curls even more wild so early in the morning. Sigurd's warriors had taken their seats on the platforms lining the walls and to a man eyed Hakon coldly.

Hakon approached Bergliot and kissed her cheek lightly. "It is good to see you again, Bergliot. I congratulate you on your pregnancy."

"Thank you, Hakon. It is good to see you again too."

Hakon moved past her to Astrid, who bowed. "I did not expect to see you again so soon, Hakon."

Her frankness brought a smile to Hakon's face. "Nor I you, though it is a welcome meeting."

The meal that followed was paltry and subdued, a far cry from the last time they had all seen each other. Then, the men celebrated their victory over Erik and Hakon's rise to power, and held none of their emotions back. Now, they spoke in hushed tones, if they spoke at all. Sigurd kept his tongue, letting his wife and daughter engage Hakon about the weather, the crops, and the upcoming feast to celebrate spring, which the Northmen called Ostara and which bore a striking resemblance to the Christian Easter in name and timing.

"When is your child due?" Hakon asked Bergliot between bites of bread in an effort to get him to speak.

"My boy," Sigurd interrupted, "should come this month, the gods willing."

Hakon turned to his host. "You are sure it is a boy?"

Sigurd gave Hakon a hard look. "My godi has consulted the runes. I am certain."

"I see," Hakon acquiesced. "Then I shall pray for his health and safe arrival."

Sigurd grunted. "We don't need your Christian prayers, Hakon."

"Sigurd!" Bergliot said. "Mind your tongue. Hakon is our guest."

Sigurd cursed under his breath. "Bergliot has more patience than I do." He bit into his bread and chewed for a bit. "We shall see if the nobles also share her patience."

"The nobles?"

"Aye. Now that you are here, they will want an audience with you. They know of developments in the south, and many are aggrieved. They want to speak with you."

Hakon had expected this, but even so, the prospect of facing the Trond nobility, many of whom had not supported him initially, tightened a knot in his stomach. "The last time we spoke to your nobles, you had a plan," Hakon said, thinking back to that time. "Do you remember?"

Sigurd wiped his mouth on the back of his sleeve. "I remember."

"Do you have a plan now?"

Sigurd took a gulp of ale and belched. "A plan. Do *I* have a plan?" Hakon could hear the malice rising in his voice. "You destroyed the road I set before you and now you turn to me for another?" Bergliot placed a calming hand on his shoulder, but he shrugged it off. "This time, you are on your own, Hakon." Sigurd drained his cup and rose. "Tell your men not to drink all my ale." And with that, he disappeared into his bedchamber.

Bergliot smiled apologetically. "We have prepared a guest hall for you, though you may prefer to sleep with your men. I will leave it up to you. Come Astrid." She grabbed her daughter's arm for support, stood with difficulty, and waddled from the hall.

Hakon pushed his plate away and rose. "Set a watch," Hakon said to Egil and Toralv as they exited the hall and strode back to the ship.

"With the coldness of that greeting, I'd rather cast off and find a friendlier place to camp."

"A watch should suffice...for now."

Hakon climbed aboard *Dragon* without speaking to a soul. His crew had stretched the sail from the port to starboard rail to fashion a crude tent over the deck. He ducked underneath and lay down on the furs that served as a makeshift bed near the aft platform. In short order, his fatigue overwhelmed him and he slipped into a dreamless sleep.

What seemed like moments later, Toralv shook Hakon awake. "You have a visitor," he said.

Hakon peered out at the night from under the canopy. Streaks of red cloud striped the dusk sky. He stretched, then rose and walked to the foredeck with sleep still clinging to him.

On the beach below stood Astrid, clad in a fine, red-dyed dress that accentuated her auburn curls — which, Hakon noticed, had been tamed by water. Over her shoulders was a fur-lined cloak held in place by a beautiful copper pin. She was alone save for Toralv, who towered over her. Beyond them, Hakon's men were just settling down to their cooking fires. "I would have a word with you, Hakon," she called up to him.

"Has your father sent you to speak for him?" That was harsh, he realized, but he found her appearance there strange.

She ignored his brusqueness. "Please."

"Come aboard. We can speak in private. Toralv was just leaving."

Hakon ignored the impish glances of his warriors as he extended a hand to Astrid. She ignored the proffered assistance, pulled her skirt up to her knees, and pranced up the gangplank to the ship's deck. He smiled at her agility and gestured to the furs where he had just been sleeping. "We can talk there."

"You think that wise, with so many eyes watching? We can talk here, in plain view."

Hakon laughed at the suggestion. "I suppose I've angered your father enough already. So be it, we can talk here. What have you to tell me?"

She looked into his eyes and the sadness he saw in hers alarmed him. The smile vanished from his face. Several years before, his boyhood love Aelfwin had come to him and taken him to the shores of the River Itchen where, with a similar look on her face, she had told him that she was to be married. His heart had sunk then, just as he found it inexplicably sinking now. "What is it?" he whispered with barely concealed concern.

"Do you know why my father has sent for you?"

Hakon wasn't sure whether to feel relief or panic. "He wishes to discuss this land's future with me and his nobles."

Her look of sadness only deepened. "If you truly believe that, then you are a fool. He wishes to make an example of you, Hakon."

So it wasn't sadness but pity he marked on her face. "To make an example of me? Why?"

"Why? To show that he, like them, no longer trusts you. He rules with their support. He supported you when they would not. With your recent follies, he can no longer afford to show that support publicly."

"How do you know this?"

"You've seen his anger, Hakon. Your escapades have not gone unnoticed. He and his nobles have already been meeting, and I've heard their words. They fear you and the things you've done. They see the realm falling apart and their sacrifices coming to naught."

"Their sacrifices?" Hakon whispered fiercely. "Their sacrifices have been no worse than my own, and truth be told, they've profited off the convenience of my existence. At first, I thought they truly rallied in support of me. Now I understand that they rallied for their own gain only when the opportunity was right."

Though her voice remained calm, Hakon could see the color rising in her cheeks. "Do not be so naïve. The nobles are doing what they have always done. I have said what I have come to say. Soon you will face my father and his nobles. You have been warned."

"It sounds like a trial, not an assembly. Is that what I am to face?"

She turned to go, but Hakon grabbed her arm. "Why do you warn me? What have you to gain?" He regretted it the moment the words left his mouth.

Astrid's eyes flashed. "Have you become so jaded? I want nothing more than to see this land united and peaceful. You and my father are friends, and allies. Not enemies. If you can't find a way forward, the tenuous peace we cling to — that you and he created — will dissolve. But I think you know that or you would not be here." She pulled her arm free of Hakon's grip and descended the gangplank.

On the beach, the men stared, first at her, then at Hakon. He ignored them and turned his mind to the days to come, when he would stand before the Tronds and face their questions. In his mind, he could already see the displeasure on their faces, but just how far that displeasure would go was anyone's guess.

Chapter 19

"Half the men stay on board," Hakon told Egil as they neared the traditional meeting place of the Tronds, known as Frosta, which was nothing more than a flat finger of land that poked into the Trondsheimsfjord, a morning's sail from Lade.

For as long as men could remember, Tronds from the eight areas of the Trondelag had come to this place annually to shake off the winter's chill, to reconnect, to trade, and to pass laws. But this gathering was different. Gathered here, at this moment, were the most powerful men among the Tronds, those who would be called upon should war come to the land. No women or trading goods or animals came with them. Custom dictated that Frosta assemblies remain peaceful, but this was no ordinary assembly, and Hakon was under no illusion that his presence here wouldn't be without unrest.

Hakon glanced over at Sigurd's ship, which sailed beside his. Sigurd wore a white tunic and a dyed, fur-lined cloak. From his thick neck hung a polished torque of twisted silver. Hakon wore no such fineries and silently cursed his jarl for so openly displaying more wealth than his own king. He would remember the affront.

When they beached at Frosta, the eight chieftains gathered on the shingle to greet Sigurd's ship. They made no such effort to greet their new king or his crew. The slight was purposeful, and pointed.

"Some welcome," Egil grumbled.

"Toralv," Hakon called to his friend. "Stay with the men and the ship. Egil — come with me."

"There's no amount of running that will save us now, Hakon," commented Egil. "Let the men come. At least they can greet some friends and stretch their legs."

Egil had the right of it. If it really came to a fight, there would be little chance of escape. Nevertheless, Hakon had made his decision and would stick by it. "The men will stay. Our ship is all we have." Hakon ignored their grumbles. "Stay alert!" Hakon called as he jumped to the beach, gritting his teeth against the pain in this thigh. "We will need our wits about us this day."

Sigurd did not bother to come to Hakon's ship. Rather, he strode toward the Frosta-field surrounded by his nobles. Hakon followed with Egil. Some Tronds nodded to Hakon as he passed, but only a handful engaged him in anything more than a quick greeting. Outwardly, Hakon did his best to appear unfazed. Inwardly, the cold reception infuriated him.

The Tronds assembled on Frosta's flat field before the massive Speaking Stone that, if the legends were true, had been lodged in the earth by giants before the time of man. Shortly after arriving in the North, Hakon had spoken from this very spot with Sigurd by his side. Then, the Trond nobles had openly expressed their distrust for his age and religion. Now, he was here again, without Sigurd's support. What words would they have for him now?

As jarl of the Trondelag, Sigurd stepped up to the Speaking Stone and turned to face his people. A hush rippled across the assembly like a gentle wave. "Men of the Trondelag," he called with his deep, booming voice. "Welcome and thank you for coming here at such short notice. Know that I would not have called you here if this matter was not of utmost import. I will get straight to the point. We are here because of troubling reports we're receiving from various fylker — reports that involve our king." He gestured to Hakon with his big paw.

"As you all know, Hakon was to be wed to Groa Ivarsdottir from the Uplands. As distasteful as that bond to the Uplands was for us, it was that very bond that helped us win the day against Erik. Our king," he growled, "has recently broken off the wedding." Sigurd paused to let the curses and grumbles of the gathered Tronds diffuse in the air. "With the alliance broken, the Uplanders have now allied themselves with their ancient enemy, the Swedes, and are at this very moment pushing south into the Vestfold." The grumbles exploded into shouts of fury.

Sigurd held up his hands for silence and the uproar slowly died down. "Unfortunately, there is more. For those of you who have not heard, Hakon has now brought priests into the land and is allowing them to spread their Christian spells in Kaupang. Of course," Sigurd called above the din, "let us not forget the Danes, who have returned to the Vik with the support of the Danish king and harry the area unimpeded. How quickly we have gone from bad to worse," Sigurd roared, "when a peaceful realm was so close at hand." Sigurd closed his fist as if crushing an egg in his palm, his face flushed with emotion.

"The last time we came here, I tried to convince you that Hakon Haraldsson was the rightful king; you argued against me. Perchance you were right. But —" Sigurd held up a finger and the frenzied crowd hung on that word "— there are always two sides to a story, which is why I have called upon our king to come. And come he has. So let us hear from him. Mayhap he can shed some light on recent developments and help us understand how all of this could have happened so swiftly."

As Sigurd reclaimed his place in the crowd, Hakon stepped up to the Speaking Stone and looked out on the sea of hard eyes and stony faces. He had wronged them, and the depth of that wrong stared back him now. Pushing his fear aside, he lifted his chin and spoke. "Men of the Trondelag," Hakon called, his teenage voice sounding shrill to his ears. "Sigurd summoned me here, and despite knowing how hostile my reception would be, I came. Why? Because as Sigurd explained, I have my side of the story, and I wish for you to hear it."

Hakon shifted on his feet to relieve his shaking knees. "Sigurd has spoken the truth. I only hope that my words provide you with a better understanding of what has transpired these past months. So let us begin with the Uplanders. This may not mean much to some of you, but Sigurd invited the Uplanders to join us without my consent. I am not so naïve that I cannot see the wisdom in that action, but I ask: which of you would want that decision foisted upon you?"

The people grumbled at that, though one man called out, "You are king! Is that not one of your obligations to your people?"

"I am a king, but I am also a man, with my own mind. Just like you," Hakon pointed at the man, then picked out others at random, "and you, and you! Yet unlike most men, I swallowed my pride and agreed to meet Ivar and Groa, and to consider the union of our two realms in our fight against Erik." Hakon contemplated speaking of Aelfwin but knew it would be of little consequence to the Tronds. "From the outset, I knew in my heart that marrying Groa was wrong for me. Jarl Sigurd also knew how opposed I was to the union. Yet what did I do? I agreed to the marriage. Why? For the betterment of the kingdom."

The crowd stood silent. Hakon barely noticed, for the swell of his emotions was carrying him forward, and his words came effortlessly now. "It is true that many brave warriors perished in our struggle. But let me remind you that Erik would have sent men to their graves regardless, as he did when he attacked this very fjord. As he did to my brothers in battle after battle. And so we fought with Erik — you, me, Sigurd, Tore, my nephews, our warriors. And in doing so, we lifted Erik's yoke from our neck and the specter of his threat from our minds. We now have a foundation from which to build!

"But let me return to the Uplands. Sigurd believes the Swedes entered into alliance with the Uplanders after I broke off the wedding. Mayhap they did, but know you this — the Swedes were already speaking to the Uplanders. They had already exchanged hostages. I saw with my very eyes a Swedish hostage in Ivar's hall at my wedding." Hakon paused to let that fact sink in. "Had I married Groa, Thorgil might still have allied himself with the Swedes. We will never know. Though I do find it strange that that same hostage is now marrying Ivar's widow. How quickly that happened and how convenient for Thorgil." The men looked at each other, for that was another fact unknown to them.

"Now we are faced with their alliance, which is dangerous, to be sure. If we do nothing, they will grow in strength. They are already pressing south. How long before they press northward to your borders? They must be stopped, with or without your help.

"So that brings us to the Danes. Actually, one Dane in particular. Ragnvald. He was once the ally of Erik, and escaped after the battle. Before he fled, he burned Kaupang to the ground and slaughtered its people. He harries the Vik as we speak to fatten himself on defenseless towns before slipping away like a cowardly nithing. And now he comes with the support of King Gorm to take what Gorm believes to be his. Well, it is *not* his. It is ours!"

Hakon paused for a moment to gather his thoughts, and as he did, a chieftain named Asbjorn of Medalhus spoke into the silence. "Think you it possible for the Danes to join Thorgil and his army?" He was a barrel-chested man with a kindly face grooved by wrinkles and a large, square beard streaked with gray that hid his round chest. He was known as an eloquent speaker, made more so by his deep, resonant voice and his thoughtful choice of words.

Hakon had indeed thought of that possibility. "It is possible, Asbjorn, though I think it unlikely. The Danes and Swedes have fought each other since the time of our grandfather's grandfathers. If they did unite, it would be a tenuous alliance at best. But it's possible, which is why we need to move quickly."

"And what of the priests and the threat they present to us?" he asked.

"And what threat is that?"

Men parted to give Asbjorn room to speak and to hear his words more clearly. "We Tronds thought, King Hakon, when we took you as our king here in Trondelag, and in return you gave us our odal rights, that we had struck a fine bargain. But now we know not whether we have received our freedom, or whether you plan to enslave us anew with your religion. Why must we forgo the faith that has been passed from fathers to sons since the burning age? We followed you in your fight against Erik and have bled for this cause. And as long as there is blood in our bodies, we will continue to follow you as we have sworn to do. But if you pursue your religion with zeal, and force us to adopt it, you will leave us with little choice but to break our oath and protect our ways."

"Your words, as always, are wise, Asbjorn," said Hakon. "But you will see that the choice is yours, not mine, to make." Hakon wanted to smile at the confusion on Asbjorn's face but thought better of it. "I did bring priests to this land, but I did not allow them to leave Kaupang. They were to build a church there and hold their sermons there. That is all. People were free to come and hear their words, but they were never forced to do so. Of course, it is my wish that all men and women and children in this realm be baptized and become Christians, but I will not force them to do so. Still, men — some of my own nephews' warriors — saw their very existence in this land as a threat. So you need worry no more — only one priest remains, and he may soon leave. The rest have been murdered. If the remaining priest stays and preaches to the people, you are free to listen or to walk away. The choice is yours as it has always been."

Asbjorn nodded, seemingly satisfied. "So you have spoken, King Hakon," Asbjorn said. "What is it you would now have us do?"

"Here is what I wish: follow me once more. Let us send out the war arrow, assemble an army, and together put an end to the Uplanders. Then let us turn our attention to the Danes."

"Wait!" called a voice. They turned to see Thorberg of Varnes standing before them. He was the youngest of the chieftains and possessed of broad shoulders and wild curls of blond. "Do not be blinded by Hakon's smooth words! This boy has risen to power with the sacrifice of many men and many families. Mostly Tronds, in fact. Families like mine who lost loved ones on that forsaken hill in the Uplands. I would not lament the loss of my father if I knew he had not died in vain. But now I wonder. I see what has happened since that victory and the new perils we all face." Mumbles of assent met his words. "Hakon has dug a grave for himself and now comes to us to keep himself from falling in. How much more Trond blood needs to be spilled to correct his mistakes?"

"Perchance you forget, Thorberg, that the Tronds who fought by my side did so willingly, including your father," Hakon said, trying but failing to keep the edge from his voice. "I ask now for men to do so again. If you wish to remain here, that is up to you. You are free to decide as your father did. But know that if I fail to subdue the Uplanders and their Swedish allies, or the Danes, they will come here next, sure as the snow falls in winter. They will come for you and your land, as they did in the time of our ancestors."

As Hakon spoke, Thorberg's cheeks were growing ever more crimson and his body more rigid. Sigurd must have seen it too, for he stepped between the king and the young chieftain. "Right. It is time for us Tronds to make some decisions." He turned to Hakon. "We will come to your ship as the sun sets."

Hakon nodded and left the Frosta-field with Egil by his side. Behind him, the chieftains and their men broke into a heated debate.

"So what now?" Egil asked.

"Now we wait for the Tronds to respond," said Hakon.

"And if that decision doesn't favor us?"

Hakon shrugged. "There are always men ready to seek fame, Egil. If we don't find them here, we will find them elsewhere."

For the rest of the day, Hakon and his crew busied themselves with work around the ship while they listened to the far-off shouts of the debating Tronds. The uncertainty of the outcome weighed on Hakon's mood, as did the question Egil had posed. If the Tronds refused to follow him against the Uplanders, he would be forced to petition the other fylker one by one — a task that could take months he did not have. Every day, the weather got warmer and the Uplanders got stronger. And every day, Ragnvald took more booty and slaughtered more people. Time was not Hakon's friend.

As the sky's light began to soften, Sigurd came to Hakon's ship with the eight chieftains. The rest of the warriors stopped in the distance, watching. A wind had picked up and Sigurd's auburn mane blew about his stern face.

"We have reached a decision," Sigurd called up to Hakon, who gazed down at them from his ship's deck.

His own cloak snapped behind him in the growing wind. "Let me hear it."

Hakon's warriors formed a semicircle around Sigurd and his nobles. Sigurd glanced at them, then turned his eyes back to Hakon. "What is done is done. We cannot change the past. And so, the Tronds have decided to remain oath-bound to you and heed your call to war. But in return, they ask that you sacrifice to our gods. We have consulted the runes and the gods have revealed to us that only through the hlaut blood will you enjoy their favor and so, ours."

"And if I don't accept the hlaut?"

"Only the foolhardy would follow a king to war who is not favored by the gods."

"Yet the men have followed me before."

Sigurd shrugged. "It is different now, Hakon. The runes have shown us this. The gods have spoken." Sigurd turned to someone behind him and brought forth a crude wooden bowl filled with the blood of sacrifice. Hakon wondered briefly who or what had been killed to fill it. Had Wulfstan's blood been used to fill a similar bowl? The thought sickened him. "I invite you to drink of the sacrifice," Sigurd continued, "and pay homage to our gods."

Sigurd lifted the bowl toward Hakon, but Hakon did not move to accept it. "Please," Sigurd implored. "For the sake of friendship and peace. For the sake of the realm."

Hakon reached down and took the bowl from Sigurd's hands. He sniffed at the coagulating blood. How easy it would be to sip the offering and put this whole affair behind him, and yet, how deceitful to himself and how contrary to everything he believed. His heart pounded as he swirled the bowl and watched the fresh blood ripple beneath the hardening top layer. Every eye was upon him at that moment. *Were God's?* And with that final thought, he knew what he must do.

Hakon held the bowl aloft and slowly poured its contents over the side of the ship. He then cast the bowl down to Sigurd.

The Jarl of Lade gazed at the bowl, then nodded curtly at Hakon. Behind him, the Tronds stood silent, though in their eyes their fury burned. "I was afraid you would answer thusly."

Unable to contain himself, Thorberg burst forth. "How dare you insult the gods so!" he yelled. The other chieftains tried to calm him, but he would not be mollified. Only when Hakon's warriors drew their swords did Thorberg stop himself.

Hakon kept his emotions in check. "Do you presume to understand the will of the gods, Thorberg? Do you, Sigurd? How about you, Asbjorn?"

The chieftains held their tongues.

"I am glad you did not respond. For in truth, none of us truly knows what the gods have in store for us. You say that only through the hlaut blood will I receive the favor of the gods. But what if I could prove to you that your gods favor me regardless? Would you follow me then?"

"What do you propose?" This question came from Sigurd.

"Tomorrow, I will duel whichever champion you choose for me to fight. If I win, I shall prove their favor of me. Your champion's death will be my sacrifice to your gods. And with that favor, I will ask that each of you send a ship full of men to fight the Uplanders. Of course, you are free to send more, but at the minimum, I ask for a ship. If your champion wins, well, then I will be dead and you will be free to choose another king, and you will have proven that your gods had the right of it."

"You weigh your kingship on a duel?" Sigurd blustered.

"Aye, Sigurd. I do."

"You are mad!"

"Yes. I have been told that before. What say you?"

Sigurd turned to his chieftains and in hushed but ardent tones, they discussed Hakon's proposal.

"You are a fool," Egil said under his breath.

Hakon kept his eyes on the bickering Tronds. "Only if I die, and if that happens, I won't care what you think of me. If I live, who then will be the fools?"

Egil snorted, though whether derisively or in humor, Hakon had no time to discern, for Sigurd had turned back to him.

"It is decided, Hakon," he called. "My people agree to your folly. We will assemble on the Frosta-field when the sun reaches its highest point tomorrow. Until then."

And so it was settled.

Chapter 20

For the duel, the Tronds chose a warrior of medium height and muscular build. He wore his brown hair in a tight ponytail, revealing a long scar that disfigured his left cheek. He carried neither shield nor helm, and wore only leather trousers to protect his legs. The inked designs of serpents and animals snaked across his muscled chest and arms.

"Who is he?" Hakon asked Toralv.

"They call him Ketil Widowmaker. He was a professional dueler before joining Thorberg's hird."

Ketil's dark eyes studied Hakon intently from across the dueling ground as he tossed his seax from hand to hand. A spear stood beside him, its butt planted firmly in the soft ground.

"I am glad I'm not married," said Hakon with a smile as he handed his cloak to Toralv.

"Where is your weapon and armor?" asked Toralv, for Hakon wore only trousers and a rough shirt.

"I left them on the ship."

"You did what?"

Hakon patted his giant friend's shoulder and turned to his opponent. A biting wind blew across the field, though Hakon barely felt it, for his skin glistened with the sweat of growing apprehension.

Ketil straightened and called to Hakon, "Arm yourself!"

Hakon wanted to say something grandiose for the crowd. A boast, perchance, to frighten his opponent; something to stick in the memory of those who looked on. Something about his God being his weapon and his armor. But his mind could think of nothing more than surviving, and so he settled for a simple, "I am armed." If nothing else, it was true.

Ketil looked to Sigurd, who frowned at Hakon, as if waiting for a further explanation. Seeing that none was coming, the disgusted jarl waved a hand at his king and turned back to Ketil. "There are no rules against fighting without a weapon or armor. If King Hakon wishes to fight thusly, he is free to do so."

Around the dueling field rang the shouts of men placing their bets. Hakon fought the sudden urge to piss. His legs felt as if they'd buckle beneath him. His arrow wound throbbed.

Ketil shrugged and cast his seax aside. His entire being exuded nonchalance, and with growing apprehension, Hakon wondered about the sanity of his plan. "I have never killed a king, but I will not have people saying I killed you unfairly."

The crowd erupted with a fresh wave of betting.

Hakon pulled the cross from his shirt and kissed it. "Give me strength," he prayed aloud, for this would be no ordinary fight. Hakon had wrestled frequently as a boy, but this one was to the death, and men did not die easily in such fights. This would be up close, and it would be ugly.

Sigurd raised his hands and the crowd fell silent. Hakon tensed.

"Begin!" bellowed the jarl.

The two opponents inched to the center of the dueling ring, each crouched and ready to spring. Hakon circled to the right, his left leg pulsing where the arrow had struck, his arms up in anticipation of the attack he knew would come. Quick as an adder, Ketil darted low and lifted Hakon's weaker left leg from the ground. As he did, he drove forward with his body. Suddenly Hakon was in the air and falling backward. In desperation, he tried to spin so that he wouldn't land flat on his back. It was a mistake. As Hakon landed, Ketil's shoulder drove into Hakon's ribs and forced the wind from his gut. Ketil rolled away and onto his feet as Hakon sucked desperately for air. It would have been so easy for the dueler to finish Hakon then, but instead he stood aside and waited.

"Get up," he called to Hakon. "At least make this a fight before I kill you."

Hakon rolled to his hands and knees, gasping for breath. His mind raced, but without air, his body refused to do his bidding. Just then, Ketil's boot connected with Hakon's belly, and Hakon collapsed again, this time curling into a ball to protect his stomach from more assaults.

Vaguely, he could hear the shouts and laughter of men as he coughed. Through squinting eyes he saw Ketil parading around the dueling ring, arms raised in victory. Hakon stayed on the ground. His limbs tingled from lack of oxygen. His head spun.

Suddenly Ketil turned and, in two quick steps, launched his right foot at Hakon's face. Using what strength he could muster, Hakon blocked the kick with his right hand as his left caught Ketil's heel. Ketil yanked his leg in an effort to free it, but Hakon slid his right hand down until he had a better hold and twisted viciously. Ketil rolled sideways to keep his ankle from snapping but Hakon held on, using the momentum of his opponent's falling body to pull himself upward. Ketil kicked futilely with his loose foot as Hakon wrenched harder. The ankle snapped and still Hakon twisted. Ketil yelled and bucked his body, coming up hard with his healthy foot at Hakon's arms. It was a glancing blow, but it was enough to shake free.

Ketil rolled away and pushed himself up, his right foot bent at a hideous angle. Hakon gave him no quarter. Before Ketil was fully balanced, Hakon lowered his shoulder and rammed Ketil's waist. The dueler wrapped his arms around Hakon even as he fell backward, using Hakon's momentum to flip him over and onto his back. Hakon rolled away and rose quickly to his feet.

Ketil too had risen, but instead of attacking Hakon, he hobbled to his spear and pried it from the turf, using it to gain his balance before leveling the point at his opponent. Hakon backed away and circled. The spear point followed him. Gone were the shouts of the crowd and the nagging aches in his body. All Hakon could see was his opponent. All he could hear was the rush of blood in his ears.

"Come on, Hakon," Ketil hissed through his pain.

Hakon would not be baited. He continued to circle, first right, then left, like a wolf looking for a weakness in its prey. Suddenly he jumped within the spear's range and feigned an attack. Ketil poked at him, quick as a snake but lacking in power, for he could only plant one foot. Hakon dodged and danced away.

Twice more Hakon came, and twice more he eluded Ketil's thrust. On the fourth such attack, Hakon jumped to his left and inside the dueler's defenses. Ketil swung his spear away to keep it from Hakon's grasp. As he did, he hopped backward and brought the spear up over his head in an arc. The spear came down hard toward Hakon's head, but Hakon had anticipated the move and ducked, letting the momentum of the swing unbalance Ketil. As the dueler fought for equilibrium, Hakon slammed his foot down onto his wounded ankle. Ketil collapsed with an anguished yell, his grip loosening on the spear as he fell. Hakon leaped for the shaft and ripped it from Ketil's grasp. Realizing his peril, Ketil tried to roll away toward his seax, but Hakon spun the spear with force and cracked it against Ketil's skull.

The crowd stared in stunned silence as Hakon lowered the spear point to the throat of his unconscious opponent. When Ketil awoke moments later, he rolled slowly onto his side and blinked through the mud that caked his face, the spear point inches from his throat. "My seax," he croaked. Like most warriors, he wished to die with his blade in hand so he could carry it with him to the mead hall of the gods.

Hakon contemplated his victim's request. "I am sorry."

Ketil's eyes went wide an instant before Hakon rammed the spear into his neck. The thrust ripped through his windpipe and severed his spine, killing him instantly. His body twitched for a moment and then lay still.

"The gods have spoken," Hakon said as he handed the bloodied spear to Sigurd.

Sigurd nodded, his expression solemn. "So they have."

"You made an oath to me, and now you must keep it."

Sigurd nodded and stepped to the center of the dueling ground. "We have witnessed the duel and seen with our own eyes the outcome," Sigurd called to the silent crowd. "Now we must honor the bargain we collectively struck. No more questions. No more challenges. Hakon has shown that our gods favor him as much as any man. Let us put this matter behind us and focus on the future."

Hakon walked over to his waiting comrades, most of whom grinned stupidly at their king. Even Egil could not conceal his mirth.

"What is so funny?" Hakon asked no one in particular. His pain had returned, and he was in no mood for jokes.

Egil brandished a heavy sack filled with coins and hack silver. The betting proceeds. "It seems the gods have favored us in more ways than one."

Hakon smiled despite himself. "Come. It is time to leave."

Chapter 21

They returned to Lade on the first day of Ostara, when the Northern people celebrated the retreat of winter's darkness and the renewal of the land's fertility. Though Bergliot was abed with child and no one felt much like celebrating, Sigurd insisted they feast, for the past few days had been trying, and he was anxious to rid himself of his foul mood.

Families began to arrive within two days of Sigurd's return. It was early spring, and though the flowers had started to bloom, Sigurd's stores had not yet recovered from winter. For that reason, each family brought with them whatever morsel of food they could spare: hard cheese, a duck, a loaf of bread. Most also arrived with a rabbit or two, for rabbits were the symbol of fertility and thus the symbol of Ostara.

Sigurd's thralls quickly set to work and, by evening, had prepared a smorgasbord of food and drink, with rabbit stew as the main course. Sigurd blessed the stew in the name of Freya, the goddess of fertility, whose favor brought crops to the fields and a fresh stock of animals to the barns. To conclude the prayer, he pried off the tops of two ale barrels, dipped a wooden cup into the dark liquid, and promptly guzzled it to the cheers of his people.

From that moment forward, the night dissolved into a whirling celebration marked by heavy drinking and a stark departure from normal decorum. Husbands flirted and grabbed at young ladies and thralls. Wives discarded headdresses and moved freely to the benches of single men. Under normal circumstances that would be cause for fighting, but on this evening no one seemed to notice or to care.

Hakon turned to question Sigurd about it.

"Oh come," said Sigurd, elbowing Hakon as a grand smile spread across his face. "Do not look so alarmed. It is Ostara. It would be rude of us not to honor Freya with a little flirting, eh?"

Off in the shadows of the hall, several couples were doing more than flirting. Hakon's mind turned to Wessex, where he knew his foster-father would be celebrating Easter with a lengthy Mass and a far more subdued feast. "The Christians have a celebration called Easter at about this time. It is to celebrate Christ's defeat of death and his ascension to the heavens. But the celebration looks nothing like this."

Sigurd snorted and slapped Hakon on the back. "I am sure of it! It's probably filled with a bunch of sober, sniveling priests. Your Christ is a strange god, Hakon, with the things he requires of his followers." Sigurd beckoned to one of his thrall women, a pretty thing with golden hair and a warm smile. "If my feast makes you uncomfortable, you are free to go. I will not keep you here. Though you more than any man deserve to bask in the attention of my lovely thralls after what you've been through. Besides, we will be heading for the speardin soon enough. Best take advantage of life's gifts as they present themselves, eh?"

Hakon laughed as Sigurd grabbed the thrall woman around the waist and sat her on his lap. She smacked his chest in mock alarm. It was good to see Sigurd is high spirits again.

Just then, Hakon caught sight of Astrid weaving her way through the crowd and his mouth fell open. She wore a long gown dyed a green that mirrored her eyes and complemented her auburn curls, strands of which had been braided and twined with small white flowers. Under her gown, she wore the traditional white frock, though this one was cut low to reveal the fair, freckled skin at the base of her neck where a pendant of Freya hung. She looked stunning.

"Ah, daughter. You've arrived. Come. Join us."

Astrid smiled at her father, then stepped up onto the dais and presented Hakon with a cup. "I brought you some ale. I thought you might need it after your recent exploits."

Hakon took it awkwardly, for his eyes were on the beauty that stood before him. "Thank you," he said when he regained his tongue.

The amused look had returned to her face. "May I sit?"

"Please."

She pulled a chair up beside him. It was so close, their knees touched. Hakon glanced at Sigurd to see if he minded, but the thrall women was now pouring ale into his open mouth from a cup, and his full attention was on making sure he swallowed every drop. Hakon turned back to Astrid, who smiled and shrugged. "This is Ostara," she said, as if that explained everything.

"I heard about your duel with Ketil," she said after a moment.

"What did you hear?"

"That you bested him without weapon or shield or armor. That Egil thinks you a fool for taking that risk."

As usual, her directness amused him, and he found it hard not to grin. She grinned back at him. "That sounds like Egil," he said. "Though I don't see why he has any cause for complaint. He profited nicely from my fight. Do you think me a fool as well?"

"I think I am glad you are sitting here now." She smiled and rubbed his leg gently.

Hakon's stomach fluttered at her touch. "And I, you." He lifted his cup to her and together they drank.

"I wanted to apologize about my behavior at the ship the other day," he started after swallowing the ale. "I had no right to —"

She stayed him with a hand to the lips. "It is over," she said, then leaned toward him and whispered in his ear, "Come. I have a surprise for you. Unless, of course, you would rather finish your ale."

The flutter became an all-out dance. "Will you not be missed?" he whispered.

"By whom?" She motioned with her chin to her father, who was still fully engaged with his thrall woman. Astrid drained her cup and stood. "Come."

Hakon followed her through the crowded hall, where couples danced and jostled and groped each other among the tables, and out into the darkness. In the crisp evening, Hakon's excited breath rose in clouds about his head. He felt as if fire coursed through his veins.

Astrid stopped at a small shed and pulled the latch. The door creaked open to reveal a steaming tub surrounded by sputtering candles. Hakon's surprise was complete and his expression must have shown it, for Astrid chuckled as she pulled him into the bathhouse. The smell of lavender enveloped him as he stepped into the candlelit space. She latched the door behind them.

"Are you sure?" Hakon whispered, feeling his excitement grow.

Astrid grabbed his cheeks and looked up at him. "Yes," she whispered. "I am sure."

He could feel her breath warm upon his mouth as she pulled him ever closer. Their lips touched and his blood surged. For a long time they embraced, pressing their bodies close as their hands and mouths sought each other. Then, suddenly, she pulled away, her cheeks flushed.

"The water will stay hot for only so long," she said, as if in answer to his uncertain gaze.

Then, without word, she undressed before him, revealing bit by bit her long body with its slender limbs and small round breasts. He followed her lead, stripping himself until he stood, like her, fully naked and fully alive. Without a word, they climbed into the water and came together with all of the impatience and awkwardness of youth.

It was only afterward that Astrid spoke. They lay in each other's arms, becalmed by exertion and the water's warm embrace, she gently running her fingers over the bruises left on his ribs from his duel while he caressed the goose-pimpled skin of her back.

"Tell me of Aelfwin," she said softly.

"I have told you that story already."

"You told me what happened to her. But you have never told me *about* her. What was she like?"

He sighed. "I'm not sure I can."

"Try."

Hakon closed his eyes and tried to picture her as she was on that day beside the Itchen, the last time he had seen her as she truly was. He could still see her bright smile and olive skin, and the charming gap between her teeth. He grinned. "She had a different sort of beauty. A beauty that glowed from within, like a furnace. She was strong, like you. I don't mean physically, I mean emotionally. In here." He tapped his chest. "When I found her here in the North, that inner light was gone, but I could still see that strength." His mind flashed to Aelfwin on the night of her death — knowing she must die, and having the courage to face it.

"She sounds remarkable."

"She was," he affirmed.

"I am sorry she is gone."

"I am too." He kissed Astrid's head and switched the subject. "We should probably get back to the hall. Your father will be missing us."

Astrid reached up and kissed his neck in the warm curve where it met his furry jaw. "Aye, that would be wise," she responded as her hand slid beneath the water. "Though the feast continues and my father is occupied elsewhere. Just a few more minutes…"

Hakon returned to his ship at some point during the night, using the glowing embers of dying campfires to chart a course down to the beach. Here and there, blanketed forms nursed cups of ale, or snored, or fornicated, heedless to Hakon's intrusion.

Egil's nephew, Ottar, stood guard, and greeted Hakon with a devilish smile when he reached the ship. "You smell pretty." He winked.

Hakon remembered the lavender-infused water and smiled at Ottar's joke. It would be days before the smell left him. "You don't."

"I might if Egil allowed me to attend the feast."

Hakon patted his shoulder. "There's always tomorrow." And that was true, for the feast would last several days.

Hakon tiptoed past the sleeping forms of his men to his bed of furs near the aft platform. There he lay for a long time, his body relaxed as his mind replayed every moment he and Astrid had shared together. He knew not whether he would ever lie with her again, but he made a pact with himself that he would try. And with that pledge settling in his mind, he slipped into a sound sleep.

The feasting continued for several more days. For Hakon, it was a time of bliss. While Hakon's crew slaked their thirst on Sigurd's ale and mead, he stole every opportunity to spend time with Astrid. Each evening, they waited for the feasting to turn raucous before stealing away to a quieter spot, free from official duties and prying eyes. There, they would make love long into the night, until one or both of them began to panic that their disappearance would be noticed.

But their time together was slipping away. The ships of Sigurd's chieftains were beginning to arrive, and with their arrival, the local families dismantled their tents and headed for their homes. Soon the air hummed with the grind of whetstones along blades, the rhythmic pounding of the smith's hammer on the anvil, and the call of men making repairs to their wave-riders that would take them southward.

On the eve of their departure, as the men gathered to witness the sacrifice of one of Sigurd's thralls, Hakon and Astrid snuck away to a storage shed and made love for the final time, their frenetic whimpers and moans drowned by Sigurd's booming invocations to the gods and the cheers of warriors witnessing the death of his slave. Afterwards, they lay in each other's arms, she caressing his sweating chest as he played with her auburn ringlets.

"The feast will begin soon," she whispered in the shed's darkness. The sacrifice had ended, and they could hear men trudging to Sigurd's mead hall. What she meant, however, was that it was time for them to part. The last time. For Astrid's duties at the final feast would not allow her to sneak away again.

"I know," Hakon responded, his heart heavy with the thought.

She kissed his jaw, then his lips. "I will miss you, Hakon Haraldsson."

He kissed her back. "And I, you."

She rose and fumbled in the darkness with her clothing, her long shadow backlit by the torchlight seeping through the shed's wall planks. Once dressed, she knelt beside the now sitting Hakon and kissed him again. "Come back to me," she said, then slid to the door and disappeared.

Hakon dressed quickly, cursing as he tripped over a bucket in the darkness. He then slipped outside and joined the men headed to the final night of feasting.

"You'd be wise to let her go now," Egil grumbled from the side of his mouth as he moved to his lord's side. "Sigurd would flay you alive if he knew you were bedding his daughter. And in a storage shed of all places. At least have the decency to find a bed."

It was Egil's job to keep an eye on Hakon. He should have known that the crafty hirdman would be watching his moves. "Do others know?"

Egil shrugged. "If they do, they aren't talking. Not yet, anyway. You better pray to your Christ that word of your fling never reaches Sigurd's ears, or you'll be dueling him next." He shook his head. "By the gods, boy, you have a nose for trouble." They reached the door of the hall and stopped. "Let this be the end of it, eh?" Egil gave his lord a smile filled with rotten teeth, then led the way into the crowd of men gathered under the high beams of Sigurd's hall.

The following morning, Astrid guided the uncomfortable Bergliot down to the shore to see the men off. Hakon watched them from the prow of his ship where he coiled a line, his head pounding from Sigurd's ale. The family stopped to let Sigurd rub his wife's belly, then lean over to speak some words to the unborn child. Even from a distance he could see Bergliot blush, and that made Hakon smile.

"You watch out for my husband, lord," Bergliot commanded gently when Hakon had reached them, his stomach aflutter at the prospect of having to say such a public farewell to Astrid. "He now has one more reason to return." Bergliot patted her belly. "Besides, he's not a spry young warrior any longer."

Hakon smiled fondly at her despite the weight of her words. "Worry not. One look at this fearsome man and his enemies will flee in terror."

Bergliot chuckled, her round cheeks aglow with her pregnancy. "I wish that were so."

Sigurd looked offended. "By the gods, women! Truer words have never been spoken."

Bergliot rolled her eyes, and Hakon felt himself smile. That is, until his eyes landed on Astrid, whose own eyes were filled with tears. A lump caught in his throat and his smile faded.

"Be safe," she managed through her tears.

Hakon nodded, wishing he could find something witty to say to lighten her mood, but it was as if his thoughts were mired in a bog. Bergliot's brows arched as she looked from Hakon to Astrid, then over at her husband, who just shrugged dumbly. "I will," he finally managed, blushing at his lack of cleverness.

A long horn blast interrupted the awkward farewell. The wind was up and it was time to leave. "Goodbye, Astrid," Hakon said hastily, then turned and strode to *Dragon*, glad to be on with the journey.

Part III

Blows battered the shield,
Blades clashed,
My hard hand
Hurled the steel-flash.
Egil's *saga*

Chapter 22

The sail snapped as Hakon's crew lowered the yard. Those men not scrambling to secure the heavy sail ran their oars through the oarlocks and pulled to Egil's shouted cadence. They would row the rest of the way, for they were entering the narrow Karmsund Strait, where the wind blew erratically.

Hakon gazed behind him and smiled at the forest of masts. In one month they had amassed one of the largest fleets the North had ever seen — a fleet to rival his father's at Stavanger, or so the elders among them said. While they feasted the arrival of spring, the war arrow made its rounds to the mead halls of chieftains and jarls far beyond Sigurd's Trondelag. Up and down the coast went the official summons, accompanied by the promise of battle, riches, and fame earned in the ranks of the god-favored boy king. Men from Halogaland, from North and South More, from the Sogn and Fjord fylker, and others besides joined the Tronds as they passed, so that by the time the fleet reached the strait, it numbered nearly fifty ships, or two thousand spear-warriors in all.

Nine more ships lay at anchor in the bay below Avaldsnes and a sea of tents dotted the hill to the west. Hakon guided Dragon into the throng and slid his ship onto an empty spot on the strand, where Didrik met him. Beside him stood one of Gudrod's older and more experienced hirdmen — a black-haired fellow named Bjorn.

"They have come to join in the fun," said Didrik with a sweep of his arm in response to the question that must have been visible in Hakon's face. Didrik's scar stretched with his smile.

Hakon grabbed his hirdman's wrist in greeting. "It is good to see you, Didrik." It was then that Hakon caught sight of the crude metal cross hanging from Didrik's thick neck, partially concealed by his blond beard. Hakon grabbed it in his fingers. "What's this?"

Didrik shrugged his shoulders. "If the nailed god is good enough for you..." He left the rest unsaid.

Hakon smiled at his warrior. There was much he wanted to say, but now was not the time, for Bjorn stood beside them, his face grave as he waited his turn to speak. "What news from the Vik?" Hakon asked him.

"Grim news, lord." He had lost one of his front teeth to rot and spoke with a slight lisp.

"Save it until the others are here."

By dusk, most of the ships lay at anchor, and the chieftains had gathered in the hall. A fire crackled in the long central hearth to warm the sea-soaked men. They greeted each other amicably as they feasted on steaming broth, warm bread, and ale. When the hall was sufficiently full, Hakon motioned for Bjorn to speak.

"I bring tidings from the Vik," he called with his lisp. "Our fears have been realized. Thorgil and the Swede, Gudmund, have joined forces with Ragnvald."

Bjorn's words ruffled the gathered nobles. Some cursed aloud, others grumbled under their breath. Still others turned their eyes on Hakon, who raised his hand for silence. "When did this happen, Bjorn? And where? Silence!" Hakon called to some of the nobles who continued to grumble. "Let Bjorn speak!"

"Thorgil and Gudmund took their armies down through Vingulmark to the mouth of the Glomma half a moon ago. There they joined forces with Ragnvald, who brought ships with him from the land of the Danes. Many ships."

"How many ships?" asked Hakon, dreading the response but having to know.

"We counted seventy ships from Ragnvald alone. The Uplanders and Swedes came with a few more, though most of their army is afoot. Mayhap a thousand more warriors. More ships come daily."

Cold dread seeped into Hakon's veins as he did the calculation. The combined army could easily number four thousand men or more — twice the size of Hakon's army.

Thorberg of Varnes stepped forward, his wild curls of blond still wet from a day at sea. "By the gods! I warned you all of this! You," he pointed at Hakon, "have lead us into this folly!"

The hall went silent at Thorberg's outburst. It was one thing to voice your displeasure, but quite another to publicly accuse your king of witlessness — something he had now done more than once. Even for those who had not been at Frosta, his eruption was troubling.

Hakon regarded the young Trond coldly, yet calmly. After a long, tense pause, he spoke. "I have said this before, but I will say it again for you. You are a free man, Thorberg. No one is keeping you here. You can come with us, or you can slink back to your lands and wait for the enemy to come to you. I do not care one way or the other."

The entire hall turned their eyes to the young noble with his wet curls. His face had gone crimson and his fists had coiled at his sides, but there was nowhere for him to go. If he left, he would forever be branded a coward. If he attacked Hakon further, he would die. Ultimately, he chose the wisest path left to him and muttered a dull curse, then sat back down, defeated.

Hakon stood and looked around at the others. "Any man in this room is a fool who thought this journey would be easy. But I know you, and I know you are no fools. You do not seek a fool's death. You came because you seek glory and riches." Hakon paused and scanned the hard faces in the room. "If that is not what you seek, then I beg you to reconsider. Go back to your warm beds and wives and mistresses and livestock. I will not judge you, nor will I have your blood on my hands. Go." Hakon pointed to the hall's door and waited. Some men looked away and cursed, but not one man left the hall. "Alright then. Let us end our worries and put our minds to a plan."

"That bastard's been planning this for a while," Sigurd grumbled. It was not a particularly useful thing to say, but it turned everyone's mind back to the mission at hand. "They may have taken Kaupang already."

Bjorn nodded his assent.

"How many men do Gudrod and Trygvi have?" asked Hakon.

"A few hundred warriors between them, though when I left, they were recruiting local men."

"Old men and boys," grumbled Egil. Bjorn grimaced at the truth in Egil's words. They would last minutes under the sword blows of Ragnvald's men.

"Then we have no options," said Hakon matter-of-factly. "We must sail as soon as possible, either to save Gudrod and Trygvi, or to prevent Ragnvald and Thorgil from recruiting more men to them."

"We take only our biggest and fastest ships — the remainder should stay here," put in Sigurd. This received some grumbles, for no man wanted to leave his ship behind. But Sigurd had the right of it — if they wanted to reach the Vik in a hurry, it was the only way.

"So it shall be," concluded Hakon. "We leave on the morrow at first light and sail with all haste for Kaupang. Ready your crews."

Hakon went in search of Egbert after the assembly. The monk had been on Hakon's mind of late, and Hakon wished to speak with him before heading off again, especially in light of the new danger that faced them all. Hakon found him packing thatch into the rafters of a newly built structure that stood just to the west of the palisade surrounding Hakon's estate.

"I thought you were in hiding," called Hakon as he neared.

Egbert straightened and smiled when he recognized his king. "I was, but I got tired of talking to myself. I am no hermit."

Hakon laughed as he approached, then studied the structure on which Egbert stood. "What is it?" In truth, he knew full well what Egbert was building, but felt like teasing the monk.

"It's a church, lord," he said. A few twigs of thatch stuck in his orange shock of hair. "What else would I build?"

"You did all of this yourself?"

"I had a little help from your thralls."

"The thralls? Truly?"

"Aye." He climbed down a rickety ladder and stood beside Hakon. "Of course, they were just following Didrik's orders."

"I saw his cross."

"The Lord is working His magic."

Hakon grinned. "As are you."

Egbert laughed, pleased with Hakon's compliment.

Hakon studied the workmanship. It was a solid structure, built to last. "That looks permanent."

Egbert nodded. "Indeed. It should last several winters, anyway."

Hakon lifted his eyebrows. "So that means you stay? Here, in the North?"

Egbert shrugged his thin shoulders and grinned. "For a time."

"That is great news, Egbert, though you know I can't protect you here. I leave again on the morrow."

Egbert's grin faded. "I know."

"Come with us. You have considerable skills in healing. Skills some will need. And you will be safer in my company."

"You have a strange notion of safety, lord. A battle is no place for a monk. I would just get in the way. Besides, I was no safer in your company the last time we were together." He nudged Hakon to show he was jesting. "No, you are better served with me here, praying for your victory."

Hakon liked the idea of Egbert praying on his behalf. Perchance there was hope for his dream yet.

"Come back tomorrow morning. We will pray together before your departure."

Hakon nodded. "That would be good."

The next morning, Hakon awoke in his bedchamber to the frenzied shouts and sounds of an army on the move. He rose quickly and splashed water on his face, then dressed himself and draped his thick war cloak over his shoulders, for the room's hearth fire had long since died with the night's chill. Hakon walked through his empty hall and paused at the doors to peer down through the receding darkness at the bay. There, crews packed supplies and readied their ships under the watchful eyes of tired lords and circling gulls.

A shout from the beach caught Hakon's attention. There stood Sigurd with a blade in one hand and the reins of a frightened horse in the other. The men stopped their toil long enough the see Sigurd slash the horse's neck. But rather than collect the hlaut into bowls to splash on the hulls of ships, Sigurd let the poor beast collapse in the water, where its blood mixed with the gray currents that carried it out to Njord, god of the sea and wind. On the ships, the men looked on in reverent silence.

Hakon tightened his cloak over his shoulders and marched to the small church. He found Egbert kneeling on the packed dirt floor and joined him there. Before them stood a small stone altar shaped like a crude cross. On it burned a single candle that cast its waving glow on the dark walls of the interior.

Egbert nodded a good morrow to his lord, then bowed his tonsured head again. Hakon followed his lead. "We shall say the prayer of Saint Patrick. I think it is more fitting for your undertaking, lord." Egbert spoke softly in the holy space. "Do you remember it?"

"Aye."

"Let us begin then."

They began to pray. The words came easily to Hakon from the recesses of his memory, from a time and place that were gone and yet would always be with him. From his thoughts to the lips they came. And to God's ear, or so he hoped, they went.

"I bind unto myself today the power of God to hold and lead, His eye to watch, His might to stay, His ear to harken to my need. The wisdom of my God to teach, His hand to guide, His shield to ward, the word of God to give me speech, His heavenly host to be my guard..."

The prayer ended and Hakon's voice trailed off. He opened his eyes and brought his focus to the single candle before him. Gradually, the prayer's words receded in his mind, replaced instead by the shouts of his army down at the beach. He glanced at Egbert. "I should go."

Egbert nodded. He climbed to his feet and blessed Hakon with the sign of the cross, not attempting to conceal the sadness in his face as he did so. "Go with God, my lord."

"And you, my friend."

Chapter 23

A strong northerly gusted down the Skaggerak and churned the sea into a seething onslaught of whitecaps. Unable to use their sails, the men rowed, though the angry ocean made it tough for them to find their rhythm. They were close. Hakon could see the island and the headlands that guarded the entrance to the Viksfjord, within which Kaupang lay.

"Put your backs into it!" Egil called above the wind, as if reading Hakon's mind. It had been five days since they had left Avaldsnes, and though they had made good time, Hakon was anxious to reach his nephews to make sure they were safe. The men grunted at the oars and pushed on through their pain.

As they reached the headland, they smelled the smoke. It lingered on the wind, too heavy to be campfires or beacons. Hakon glanced at Egil, who had stopped his yelling and stared ahead at the waterway. He too had smelled it.

They rowed onward with the sun overhead, slower now in their caution. Not far into the fjord they found the source of the smell — a thick cloud of smoke billowing into the sky. It lay off the port side, drifting toward them on the northerly wind.

Kaupang burned.

When they reached the town, Hakon's heart sank at the sight of the destruction. Bodies littered the shorelines on either side of the inlet. Ravens and seagulls fought over the corpses and flapped their wings jealously at the new intruders. Hakon's warriors looked on silently, some grabbing at their charms, others clutching their weapons tighter. Hakon crossed himself.

The battle had been recent. On the beach, several scuttled ships smoked, while just inland, the town's newly built structures burned. All about, the dead lay in heaps, their shields and blades and severed limbs strewn about them. So fresh was the clash that the bodies had not yet begun to bloat nor the flies to swarm, nor the blood and shit, which ran in rivulets to the sea, to harden. Some of the younger men vomited over the gunwales. Hakon covered his nose with his sleeve. Even Egil, who had witnessed more carnage in his life than most, gazed slack-jawed at the scene. This was the aftermath of war never glorified by the skalds.

Hakon ordered Sigurd and Tore to take most of the ships and guard the entrance to the inlet, for the enemy could still be present in the nearby waters. "Toralv. Ottar. Take some men and look for survivors," ordered Hakon as the prow of *Dragon* slid onto the sand. "Egil. Didrik. Grab the rest of the men and come with me. Bring my standard."

Hakon and his men jogged up the beach and skirted the town. When they reached the base of the hill on which Gudrod's hall sat, they stopped and eyed the network of boulders and logs that crossed the slope like the rungs of a ladder. A second battle had been fought here, for more dead warriors littered the ground — though the numbers tapered the higher up the slope one's eyes traveled. At the crest, Gudrod's hall still stood, looking for all the world like a wounded boar with spears and arrows protruding from its sides.

Hakon motioned to his standard bearer to unfurl his colors. The golden boar danced on its black field in the wind. "I am King Hakon. If you serve Gudrod or Trygvi, I come in peace."

Several warriors slowly raised their helmeted heads from behind the last line of logs, far up the hill. There couldn't have been more than a dozen. One of their number worked his way down the hill and stopped a few paces distant. Soot and caked blood covered his skin and armor.

His sweat-soaked hair fell limply from beneath his battered helmet. It was Gudrod's hirdman, Geir.

"You come too late, King Hakon."

Hakon knew not what to say, nor could he bear the man's bloodshot eyes upon him. He turned his face away and pretended to study the hillside. Over his head, his standard snapped in the wind. "Where are Gudrod and Trygvi, Geir?"

"Come."

Hakon and his men followed Geir up the hill to the damaged hall, where the wounded lay in rows above the bloodstained rushes. The place smelled of sweat, and smoke, and death. Several thrall women worked their way among the bodies, cleaning wounds and offering water and comfort where they could. Hakon thought briefly of Egbert and was suddenly glad the monk had not come to this place.

Gudrod lay in the sleeping chamber off the main hall, his body stripped to his trousers, a semi-clean bandage coiled about his head. A polished stone — a charm of some sort — lay upon his chest. His sword rested in his grip.

"He took a blow to the head," explained Geir. "We carried him here and cleaned the wound as best we could."

"Will he survive?"

Geir shrugged. "If the gods allow it. We've done what we can."

"What happened?" Hakon asked Geir when they had exited the hall. They were gazing out over the inlet to the sea beyond, where the water twinkled between the wind-swept whitecaps, oblivious to the struggle that had befallen this place.

"The enemy attacked early in the morning. Thorgil and Ragnvald and the Swedes. Thousands of them. They came by ship, in the gray morning. The sentries lit their fires, which gave us just enough time to arm ourselves and get the townsfolk to safety." Geir stared off into the middle distance as he spoke, his mind clearly reliving the morning. "By the time we formed our shield wall, the ships were in the inlet and coming fast. There was no parlay. They came to kill. We held them for a time on the beach, but then Thorgil appeared on our left. He had come overland, and his men streamed down through those trees." Geir pointed at the hill to the north with its copse of trees — the same spot where Wulfstan had been buried. "Our lines broke, and we ran for the hill. The enemy tried three times to take it, but we held. Eventually they gave up and retreated to their ships, but not before setting torches to the town."

"Did you see where the ships went?"

"North, lord."

Hakon dreaded the question, but had to ask. "And Trygvi?"

"He lives, I think. When they left, he gathered what men he could and went after them."

"To fight them?"

"To trail them."

That made sense. The Danes had been evading him since the previous fall. This was Trygvi's chance to discover their lair, unless they discovered him first. If that happened, Trygvi and his men were as good as dead.

Hakon glanced at Egil, whose eyes studied the battlefield. "The dead need a burial," the old warrior said. "But we could use their armor and weapons."

"You can take the enemy's," Geir retorted sourly. "Our men will take theirs to their graves."

Egil scowled at Geir but otherwise held his tongue.

"Didrik," called Hakon. "Start building pyres and collecting weapons, armor, and shields."

"We should prepare," responded Egil. "Tie our ships together just beyond the mouth of Kaupangskilen and sleep aboard ship. If Thorgil returns, we need to be ready."

Hakon doubted Ragnvald would come again so soon. He'd lost many men and would be licking his wounds. Nevertheless, one couldn't be too cautious with that snake nearby. Hakon accepted Egil's suggestion with a nod. "Spread the word, Egil."

But Egil didn't move.

"You have more to say?"

Egil pursed his lips. "It's a hard thing sailing as far as we have and rowing through that chop today. The men need rest before setting off again. The fight we sail into is no place for tired arms."

Hakon considered Egil's words. "It is true what you say, Egil. The trip to Kaupang has been taxing, and the men are tired and sore. But Ragnvald and Thorgil will be licking their wounds too this night. To tarry would be to give the bastards more time to recover and re-organize. We can't allow that."

Egil grunted.

"I wish we had more time, Egil, but we don't. I will speak to Sigurd and Tore and the others, and tell them to have their men fed and rested. We leave at first light, wind or no wind."

"And us? What would you have us do?" Geir asked when Egil had gone.

"Stay here with Gudrod and protect the hall."

"Have you any men to help us?"

"No," Hakon responded flatly. "I know not what we'll find, but I fear we'll need every man we have. Besides, I don't think Thorgil will return. He will want to, but Ragnvald is too sly to attack the same place twice, especially one with an impregnable hilltop like this one. You have done well here, Geir," he offered. "The enemy will be sore from their beating this night."

Geir accepted Hakon's compliment in silence, then left Hakon alone with his worries. Worry that he had guessed incorrectly about Ragnvald and that the bastard would return with Thorgil and Gudmund. Worry for his nephews. Worry that his decisions had led to the slaughter on these shores and that more men would soon perish. Worry about the battle his army would soon fight. For if the carnage in Kaupang was any indication of how things would go, then Egil had the right of it — they would need their strength.

I see battles. Storms of blood. Christian crosses and bodies lying in piles upon the ground. A feast for ravens, lord. Hakon shuddered at the memory of the ship captain's words — words that had now become prophecy.

The raven's feast was upon them.

Chapter 24

The next morning, Hakon's army was up before dawn. Under the orange glow of the funeral pyres they unpacked their armor and found what food they could to break their fast. The air was thick with ash and alive with shouted commands, uneasy laughter, and the rhythmic grating of whetstones on blades. As the first hint of light stretched across the fjord, the army launched their ships, leaving Geir in command of the ruin that was now Kaupang. Above them, a solid sheet of steel-colored clouds stretched to the horizon. An omen of the battle to come.

They rowed until they reached the open seas of the Skaggerak, then pointed their prows northward, but luck was not with them this day, for the air was calm and windless and the sea tame beneath their hulls. Hakon's men would have to pull, a hard enough task in normal clothing, but even more strenuous in full battle gear. Egil cursed their luck, and Hakon knew his mind — this was not what they needed. Still, no man complained, despite their grunts and the sweat that gathered on their brows.

Overhead, gulls hovered and called, looking for scraps of food among the ships. A scruffy, freckled boy skewered a bird's chest with an arrow, sending the creature plummeting into the sea. His young comrades cheered his skill, but Egil cuffed the back of his head. "Save your arrows, you idiot!"

They rowed on, keeping a keen eye on the port shoreline and the many coves and fjords and islands that defined it. But they detected none of the telltale signs of a concealed army camp. No ships' masts. No smoke or smells of wood fires. No flock of birds encircling the dying. For if the combined army of Thorgil and Ragnvald was truly as large as Bjorn reported, then surely they'd seen some signs of their encampment. Then again, Ragnvald had evaded them this long. Could he do it now, with so large a force? It was possible, which may have explained why the crews kept their eyes fixed on the land rather than on the sea ahead.

Near mid-morning, Ottar suddenly called out, "Ship to port!" He stood on the foredeck, pointing due west at a single warship that had suddenly appeared from behind the cover of the rocky islands. The fleet slowed, sensing danger, and Hakon worked his way to Ottar.

"It's Trygvi." Ottar said.

The ship was still some way off, with no sail or markings to distinguish it. "Are you certain?" Hakon asked.

"Aye. I can see its prow-best."

Which was remarkable, because to Hakon it looked like any other prow bobbing in the waves. Hakon called to Egil and *Dragon* peeled off to port. Seeing what Hakon was about, the other ships lifted their oars to wait.

The new arrival drew nearer and up to its prow stepped Trygvi's hulking frame. Hakon smiled as Ottar ribbed him. "You see? These eyes never fail me."

Trygvi and his men looked as though they'd walked through the fires of Hell. They had not yet washed, and the blood and ash and dirt of battle clung to them like a second skin. They neither smiled nor offered greeting when their ship pulled alongside Hakon's — they just stared flatly at Hakon and his crew.

"You are well met, Trygvi," Hakon called to him, which was true. Despite their recent strife, Hakon was genuinely glad to see his nephew hale.

Trygvi did not waste his breath on cordiality. "You are late to the feast, uncle. Many men died yesterday for your delay."

Hakon understood his nephew's anger and did not try to placate him. Instead, he answered as truthfully and as calmly as he could. "Had you not shipped me off, I would have been here all along to share in your struggle. Still, things are as they are. We came as fast as circumstances would allow. What news of Thorgil?"

"We trailed his army to a bay just north of the Glomma River, which lies on the eastern shore. There is an island that hides the bay, so it is hard to find unless you approach it from the south. Between the island and the mainland is a narrow channel that leads into the bay. If we sail due east, then stick to the coast and come through the channel quickly, there's a chance we can surprise them." Trygvi looked up at the sun. "We could be there by midday, if the weather holds."

"They will be waiting for us."

Trygvi shrugged. "If they saw us trailing them, then it is possible. But does it matter? You are here with a fleet and spear-warriors who have come to fight. So let us do so."

Hakon considered his nephew's words. Though Hakon expected Thorgil's army would be guarding the channel, would he be expecting so large a force to come against him so soon? Would he be recovered from his fight with Gudrod and Trygvi? If he looked anything like Trygvi, he and his men would be resting, or at least that is what Hakon hoped.

"Will you lead the way?" Hakon asked.

Trygvi smiled, though there was no humor in it. Rather, it reminded Hakon of the way a dog might show his teeth to protect his bone from another dog. The only thing missing was the growl.

"Consider carefully, Hakon," grumbled Egil as Trygvi's crew pushed his ship away from *Dragon* with their oars. "You know as well as I that Trygvi acts before thinking. Our men are lathered from rowing, and it looks like Thor is about to piss on us. We might do well to slow our pace."

Hakon cast his eyes to the sky. The morning's gray was now dark and angry, and Hakon couldn't help but wonder whether Thor sensed the looming slaughter.

"I have never heard you sound hesitant, Egil. Why now?"

It was the wrong thing to say. Egil scowled, and the edge in his words was as leaden as the clouds above. "There's a difference between hesitation and common sense, boy," he growled, drawing the men's eyes to him so that he lowered his voice. "I have no fear of death, but I am oath-sworn to protect you, and I will not have you slipping on slick decks in the sword-song because you were in a hurry to fight."

Hakon acquiesced with the nod. "You have more battle wisdom than the fleet combined, Egil. But I feel in my gut that to wait will only bring more bloodshed, not less. Besides, if the heavens open up, the rain might just provide us with the concealment we need." Hakon clasped his shoulder, for his excitement was beginning to grow. "Get ready for a fight, Egil. This will be one for the skalds to remember."

Egil studied Hakon's eyes for a long moment, then finally spat as if to say that he saw something there that gave him hope. "Let us hope we're the heroes of that tale," he said, then turned to the crew. "Back to your oars!"

Hakon relayed the news to his jarls and the fleet turned, following Trygvi's ship eastward. As they moved, the rain began to fall and the wind picked up, which in turn coaxed the sea to dance beneath the ships. The crew hoisted the yard and fastened the sheets. Egil adjusted the steer board and found the wind and *Dragon* leaped forward like a stallion given its reins. The crew cheered and hauled in their oars. More than a few men stretched their aching backs.

Egil pointed Hakon to a barrel of ale and a crate of salted fish near the mast. "Everyone eats!" he called to his lord. "No man fights on an empty stomach!"

Hakon wiped the rain from his face and moved to the barrels, yelling for the crew to join him. "You heard the old man!" he called as he tossed stiff pieces of salted cod to his gathered crew. For his part, Hakon did not feel much like eating, but he refused to let that show. So instead, he ripped a piece of dried cod with his teeth and downed it with his rain-soured swig of ale.

By noon, they reached the eastern coast and turned their prows northward. They were now north of the Glomma River, which meant that they were close to the channel Trygvi had described. The rain fell harder now, coming down in sheets that pooled in the holds and drenched the men.

"Lower the sail and secure it tightly!" Egil shouted. "And secure those damn lines! I won't have you fumbling over coils and strands in the thick of battle! You men," he called to the younger boys, who knew little of warships. "Make yourselves useful and either start rowing or start bailing!"

The enemy was close. Every man could sense it in the urgency of Egil's voice and the shouts that rang out across the fleet. Some fondled the charms at their necks or murmured silent prayers to their gods. Others mindlessly caressed the grips of their weapons as their eyes squinted into the rain ahead. Hakon crossed himself as Toralv, Didrik, and Ottar stepped to the prow.

Ottar, as usual, was the first to see the channel and pointed ahead with a shout. A large island formed the western flank of the channel, its southern tip climbing out of the sea in the gray day like the hump of a whale's back. To the east lay the rocky coastline of the Ostfold with its many bays and islands and waterways. The entire channel stretched several arrow flights across.

As they drew nearer, a long, low horn howled, its sonorous notes barely perceptible through the patter of rain and the splash of oars. Thorgil's scouts were watching. The horn sounded again. Hakon would have liked to stop and organize his fleet, but the alarm erased that possibility. Speed was their only advantage now. The others knew it too, for up and down the fleet shouts rang out and the ships surged forward. On his ship, Hakon's warriors yelled their excitement and Egil called for the rowers to pull. A few of the boys craned their necks to see what lay behind him. Egil cursed them for their carelessness. "Don't look, you louts! Row!"

The rest of the fleet fell into their places behind their respective leaders. Trygvi and Hakon held the middle. Sigurd veered off to take the right flank, while Tore took the left. Their ships fanned out behind them so that the entire fleet hit the channel in two successive waves. To their left, on the island, the horn continued to send its grim tidings to Thorgil and his army.

"There they are!" called Ottar from the bow.

Thorgil's massive army had camped on the lee side of the western island rather than in the bay. Hakon had never seen so many ships amassed in one place, and the sight gave him pause. Yet a closer inspection exposed their disarray. Most of the ships had yet to cast off from the beach where the army camped. Only a handful of ships — mayhap a dozen — bobbed in the channel. These were lashing themselves together to form a defensive island that, if nothing else, might give the rest of the fleet just enough time to organize and join the fight. A number of Hakon's ships would need to engage that island of wave-riders to keep them occupied, but the remainder could skirt them and attack the others before they rallied. If they did that, they just might emerge from the day victorious.

Being in the center of the fleet, it would fall to Hakon and those ships around him to take on the floating defenders in the channel. He'd have to hope that the other jarls on the edges would focus their attack on the rest of the enemy fleet. He signaled with his hands to Trygvi, who sailed to his left, to stay the course; then he motioned the same to the ships on his right. The captains waved their understanding, and Hakon turned back to his crew.

"Row!" he yelled from the steer board. "Faster!"

The rain continued to fall, obscuring details of the defenders until Hakon's ships were but an arrow's flight away. Slowly, those details materialized and Hakon's heart leaped in his chest, for dead ahead, in the center of the floating island, lay Thorgil's ship. Though his sail was furled, Hakon recognized the prow-beast. Ottar recognized it too and yelled his fury. Those of Hakon's warriors not at oar took up Ottar's call — a call that quickly rippled across the fleet. The defenders roared back, adding their voices to a din that sounded to Hakon like thunder.

This was the part of battle that tore at Hakon's nerves. It always had. It was the moment between life and death, when his emotions swirled and his bowels loosened and the dark cloak of doubt ate at his thoughts. The moment when the two armies had committed and the anticipation was at its highest; and yet, there was still time to wonder whether a sword would spill his guts or he would drown in the gray sea or, by God's grace, he would live to see another dawn.

And then the arrows flew and the air darkened with their shafts and his doubts transformed into a dark thrill that coursed through his veins. A thrill he would feed on to face the cold steel that came for him. He could see the missiles streaking darkly against the gray day. Yet they were useless at this distance and in this weather, for the rain dampened their fletching and altered their flight. Most dropped harmlessly into the sea, though a few plunked onto the deck. One of the arrows struck a warrior's foot and pinned him to the strakes. The hapless warrior cursed and fell to the deck, grabbing at the missile in an effort to dislodge it.

The next volley was slightly more accurate. It sprayed the decks as the vessels drew closer. Those in the bows hid beneath their shields as the missiles landed, but the oarsmen weren't so lucky. Unprotected, they took the brunt of the attack on their backs. Two rowers rolled to the deck, wounded and yelling in pain and fury. A third died without a sound. Hakon's own archers loosed in return, though what damage they did was impossible to say with the rain coming down as it was.

Off on the flanks, ships peeled away. Hakon hadn't directed this — his jarls just knew what to do. They'd pour arrows into the flanks of the defenders and then, with luck, engage the remainder of the enemy fleet before they could put up a stout defense.

Hakon's ship drew closer. Egil roared for the oarsmen to ship oars and grab their weapons. An arrow slammed into Hakon's shield. He cut it away. Two more streaked over his head. Before him, Toralv heaved his spear at an enemy berserker preparing to leap onto their deck. The man saw the spear coming and knocked it away with his shield. He then leaped, but slipped on the rain-slick gunwale as he pushed off and smacked into *Dragon's* siding. For a moment, he clung desperately to *Dragon*, until Ottar's sword shattered the man's skull and he fell away.

"Brace!" yelled Egil.

The air rippled with the sound of splintering wood as Hakon's hull scraped into the gap to the left of Thorgil's vessel. The crews of both sides pitched and stumbled with the impact. More than a few fell backwards to their deck. Grappling hooks arced through the air and bit into the wet wood. To Hakon's right, an enemy hook scraped across the deck and pinned the leg of the freckled boy who had killed the gull that morning. Didrik cut the rope away, but as the boy worked his leg free, a spear pierced his stomach. The boy gazed in shock at the weapon, then slumped down to the deck.

In the foredeck, warriors jabbed with their spears and tried with little success to clear a spot for boarding. It was not easy. Even though *Dragon* was taller than Thorgil's ship, the decks bobbed in the churning sea, throwing off every thrust and parry. Hakon had never been in a sea battle but instantly understood the difficulties of fighting in such a crowded, awkward space — difficulties compounded by the rain that clouded their vision and slickened the deck beneath their feet. Here and there, bare-chested berserkers leaped across the gap and smashed into Hakon's shield-men in an attempt to open a space for others to follow. Like crazed animals, they thrashed with their weapons at the shields blocking their path and died from their wounds before breaking through.

Looking across the gap, Hakon saw Thorgil. He stood behind his men, yelling furiously for them to attack. Before him stood Vidar, his face a mask of savagery as he awaited his chance to join the crowded fray. Though just how he came to be in Thorgil's ship rather than Ragnvald's was a mystery.

A cheer rose up and Hakon glanced to his left. Trygvi and a handful of his hirdmen had boarded the enemy's ship there and were forcing their opponents backward. As the enemy retreated, Didrik took several men and moved to join that fight. If they could overpower that deck, they could flank Thorgil and come at him from behind. But Didrik never made it. A random arrow caught him in the neck in mid-leap, and he fell away like a sack of stones into the gap between the ships. His men hesitated behind him, but Trygvi waved them forward and they leaped.

On Hakon's ships the battle raged, but neither side could press an advantage. The stalemate benefited Hakon, for if Trygvi could flank him, Thorgil would be forced to fight in two directions. Thorgil must have sensed it too, for he yelled at his men to cut the ropes.

Just then, Toralv picked up a barrel and heaved it at Thorgil's warriors. It sailed over the heads of Hakon's men and into the enemy. Some men saw it coming and ducked. Others tried to block the barrel with their shields and collapsed under its weight. Toralv pushed his way forward and leaped across the gap, landing on the enemy deck where the barrel had cut its swath. Toralv's axe killed one of the fallen warriors instantly and forced two more back. Ottar and Egil joined the fray, followed by Asger and one of his friends.

With a yell, Hakon leaped and joined the fight. Before him, Egil, Toralv, and Ottar held their line, their shields locked as they fought. Ottar jabbed his sword into a warrior's throat, while Toralv swung his axe in a menacing arc, taking the head of a man too slow to duck. Egil smashed his shield edge into a man's chin, then gutted him with his seax. To Ottar's left, the young Asger thrust his sword at a warrior but dropped his own shield as he did so. He took an axe to the head for his mistake and dropped dead, leaving Ottar's left side exposed. Ottar lifted his shield to take the burly enemy's next blow but underestimated the force behind it. The blade tore through the wood and smashed into his armored shoulder. Ottar staggered back and Hakon filled the gap, screaming his rage as he jabbed with his seax into the axe man's exposed gut.

As Hakon pulled his blade free from the dying man, he caught movement to his right. He brought his shield up and across just as something slammed into it. The force of the blow rippled through his arm and staggered him. Before he could regain his balance, the blow came again, only harder this time, and Hakon collapsed to the deck. Vidar sneered down at him as he raised a two-handed axe above his head for the final strike. All Hakon had time to do was lift his damaged shield.

But the blow never came. Instead, Vidar's body fell atop Hakon's shield, his face inches from Hakon's own. His eyes were wide, and blood and spit trickled from a mouth that reeked of ale. Hakon rolled Vidar aside to find a spear protruding from his back. Jumping to his feet, Hakon looked for his savior. Trygvi stood on the deck of the ship to his left, looking at Hakon.

"We're even!" he called, then turned back to the battle.

In that brief pause, Hakon took stock of the situation. Up and down the line of ships, all was chaos. Blades hacked and came away crimson. Screams of fury and pain shattered the air. Farther up the channel, Hakon's fleet rained arrows and spears into the enemy ships coming from the shore. Some of those ships fled. Others returned the volleys and pressed forward into the mayhem. To his left, Trygvi and his men had nearly cleared the ship. The last of the enemy warriors had mounted a defense, but they were quickly falling to Trygvi's blades.

"Back!" roared Thorgil at his men. His dark hair fell in sweating rivulets from beneath his helmet and framed a face etched with pain. As he retreated to the aft deck with his men, Hakon could see that he was limping. His old wound.

"Thorgil!" Hakon yelled.

Thorgil's eyes turned to Hakon. Seeing his enemy before him, Thorgil did not hesitate, nor did he waste his breath on any fine boasts or taunts. Instead, he simply rushed forward. He moved with surprising dexterity, smashing his blade into Hakon's tattered shield, then blocking a sidelong swing from Hakon with ease. Again, he brought his blade down at Hakon's head and Hakon raised his shield to meet it. But at the last minute, Thorgil twisted his wrist so that his blade now angled toward Hakon's exposed side. Hakon dropped his shield, catching Thorgil's blade just as it licked the ringlets of his byrnie.

To the left, a cheer rang out as Trygvi's men celebrated their victory. The shouts distracted Thorgil, who knew he was now in danger of being flanked. "Back!" he yelled to his men, and just as he spoke, Hakon attacked. He jabbed at Thorgil's face, then blocked a counterattack to his left. Hakon slammed what was left of his shield into Thorgil's own, driving him backwards. Thorgil tried to resist the charge but slipped on the drenched deck. As he struggled to regain his balance, his left heel caught on a coil of rope. Hakon pressed his advantage and brought his blade down hard toward his foe's head. The sword blades sang as Thorgil parried the swing, even as he fell.

The Uplanders tried to help their chieftain, but Hakon's men were now too many and blocked their path. A better man would have allowed Thorgil to rise, but Hakon's fury overpowered any sense of honor he might have felt. He wanted only to finish the bastard, to send him to the death he so deserved.

Thorgil thrust with his sword to give himself some space to rise, but Hakon parried the strike easily, knocking Thorgil's arm aside and opening his defenses. In that brief opening, Hakon stroked backward at Thorgil's neck. It was not a hard blow, but it was enough. The seax sliced across Thorgil's throat, through skin, tendon, and vein. Thorgil grabbed at the wound, as if trying to force the life that poured crimson through his fingers back into his body. Realizing that death had come to him, he fumbled for the sword he had dropped, wanting to take it with him to the afterlife, but Hakon kicked it away.

Thorgil stared at Hakon, his fury burning in his gaze until death took his soul.

Hakon spat on his corpse and turned to what was left of the Uplanders. They huddled, silent and miserable, in the aft deck, peering out from behind battered shields. Their will had died with their leader, but Hakon was in no mood to show them mercy. Hakon's own men gazed at him, waiting. He knew their minds — they wondered why he'd shown no charity for Thorgil when he'd shown it to so many others. But the dark anger hung on him, and he felt no compulsion to explain. Instead, he turned to Egil.

"Kill them all," he said.

Egil grinned wolfishly at his king, then turned back to the enemy.

Later, when the slaughter was done, Hakon took in the scene around him. In the bay, small skirmishes continued, the shouts of men and the clash of arms echoing across the water. But with no more than a glance, it was clear the enemy's resolve had broken and the fighting was close to an end. On the beach, the wounded remnants of Thorgil's army stood to face Hakon's approaching ships, whose prows bristled with the spear points of warriors eager for more bloodshed. In minutes, those wounded warriors would be cut down, their possessions taken, their followers raped or enslaved.

Something landed on the deck near Hakon, interrupting his cruel thoughts. He looked down to see the head of Gudmund at his feet. A blade had taken it clean off his shoulders, leaving it almost unmarred. Even in death, the Swede was strangely handsome.

"A gift for you," Sigurd called from his ship, which bobbed a short distance away.

Hakon pulled his eyes from the bodiless head to face Sigurd. Blood streaked the jarl's cheeks and clung to his beard, but he was otherwise hale. Farther off, on his own ship, stood Tore, his left forearm wrapped in a bloody cloth. It was good to see them both.

"Thorgil?" called Sigurd.

"Dead."

A brief smile broke on Sigurd's face. "Any word of Ragnvald?"

Hakon shook his head.

"Dislodge yourself and see to your wounded. We will search for him." And with that, Sigurd's ship rowed away.

In the end, they learned that Ragnvald had escaped. As the battle raged in the bay and men died to slake his ambition, the cowardly Dane had run, leaving his men to their doom.

Egil cursed. "I wonder what the gods think of him now, running like a whipped dog from the raven's feast."

Hakon spat a glob of blood and bile from his mouth. Half of his crew had died in the fighting, including Didrik, Asger, and most of the other boys. Ottar's shoulder was badly damaged and probably broken, though thankfully the axe had not bitten through his byrnie. Above them, seagulls circled, their shrill calls filling the air as they eyed the bounty beneath them. On the beach, Hakon's army was finishing its slaughter. The blood had run thickly this day, but it was not yet over, for Ragnvald could not be allowed to live after all he had done.

Hakon sighed. The battle lust was slipping from his veins, leaving in its wake a deep hollowness that sucked at his energy. "We will take our wounded to Kaupang. If there are enemy survivors, we'll take them with us."

"What of Ragnvald?"

"We must find him," said Hakon, resigned now to what he knew must be done. "But first we must take care of our own."

Egil nodded. "So be it."

Chapter 25

The next day, the fleet glided into Kaupangskilen and beached along the shore. Just inland, the town still smoldered, as did the funeral pyres that hastened Gudrod and Trygvi's fallen warriors to Valhall. A thick ash pall hung over the area, searing Hakon's eyes and chilling his already somber mood.

Geir met Hakon and his army on the strand with the remnants of his men — a band of nearly two dozen bandaged and filthy warriors. They cheered the sight of Hakon's ships, though their cheers were hollow and dispassionate. They were battle-worn and bone-tired — Hakon could see it in their faces.

"You are a welcome sight, my lord," Geir commented as Hakon approached. "For a moment, when we saw the masts approaching, we thought Ragnvald had returned to finish us."

After he'd spent a sleepless night on his ship surrounded by the wreckage of battle, Hakon's battle-bruised muscles felt as if a dozen horses had trampled upon them. He too was tired. "We destroyed Ragnvald's fleet, but the bastard escaped," he muttered. "You're more likely to see him rowing back to his hovel than looking for another fight."

Geir chewed his lip as he considered Hakon's news. "What of Thorgil?"

"He and the Swede are dead."

Geir smiled — or mayhap it was a sneer; Hakon couldn't tell. "Well, that's something, I suppose."

Trygvi cut Geir's next words short. He was marching toward them from his ship and called out to Gudrod's hirdman as soon as he saw him. "Where's Gudrod?"

"He rests, lord," answered Geir, pointing vaguely toward the hall.

"Is he awake?"

Geir shook his head. "No, lord."

Trygvi cursed at the news and marched away toward his cousin's hall on the hillside. Hakon and Geir watched him for a moment.

"We have wounded that need care," Hakon finally said.

Geir sighed. "Have them brought to the hall. The thralls will do what they can, which isn't much. If you have any healers among you, bring them."

Hakon called to Egil, "Spread the word among the captains. All wounded are to be taken to the hall. If they're too wounded to move, we'll tend to them on the beach. Toralv!" Hakon called to his giant friend, who was coiling one of the lines on the ship. "Leave that. Find a spot for our prisoners."

By nightfall, the army had settled itself south of the razed town and away from the stench of the bloated enemy dead still littering the landscape. Hakon's warriors had done what they could for their wounded comrades and now rested beside their campfires, eating smoked meats, stale bread, and ale. No one had the energy to forage for other food, nor did Hakon wish to rob the locals of it. So they settled for what they had on them, eating in hushed groups around small fires as they discussed the battle, fallen comrades, and the exploits of certain warriors that deserved to be lauded. Tomorrow, thought Hakon as he watched them, they would feast their victory. Tonight, they would rest.

"How do you suppose Vidar ended up in Thorgil's ship? Was he not Ragnvald's man?" This question came from Trygvi.

"Mayhap Ragnvald didn't trust him," answered Egil. "It takes a snake to know a snake, eh?"

Hakon pictured Vidar's dead face with its one blackened eye and shuddered. "It no longer matters. He is gone and we have you to thank for that, Trygvi."

Trygvi grunted, his mind obviously conflicted by killing one of his former hirdmen.

"He deserved his death, Trygvi. Don't give it another thought," said Egil as he shifted his butt against the rock that served as his seat.

"He deserved it more than Didrik, that's for certain," put in Toralv. His gaze was lost in the flames of the small fire that crackled before him.

"Aye," confirmed Egil. "Though it is good to think that he and Gunnar are reunited again. I bet they're toasting their exploits in Valhall just about now, eh, Toralv?"

Toralv scratched at his beard. "That is my hope, though I wonder how the Alfather will feel about that Christian cross about his neck."

The men looked at Hakon as if expecting him to have another opinion on the matter. In truth, Hakon felt Toralv had the right of it. He too wondered whether Odin would welcome the stout Didrik to the Hall of the Slain. He hoped so, for it seemed a lonely afterlife to sit in one hall while your brother feasted in another. But in his heart he doubted Odin would be so welcoming. Didrik had turned his back on old Flaming Eye, and the valkyrie, if they existed, had probably passed him by. All these thoughts ran through Hakon's head as the men looked at him, but he had not the energy to speak them, so he simply raised his cup. "To Didrik. May his memory live with us always."

The men seemed satisfied by that response and hoisted their own cups. "To Didrik!"

They sat in companionable silence for a long time, each lost in his thoughts. The past several days had been rough, but Hakon was glad to be alive and glad to be sitting next to his comrades. In the back of his mind, though, was a thought that would not release its grip. Ragnvald still lived, and as long as he lived, there would be trouble in the North. They needed to find him and put an end to him. And they needed to do it quickly, while he was still licking his wounds and Hakon had warriors at his disposal. With that thought lodged in his head, Hakon broke into the silence with a question: "Where are the prisoners?"

"They're in the holding shed up on the hill," responded Toralv. He was referring to the shed in which Hakon had discovered the priests. The shed that had been cramped for twelve men. It was hard to imagine more than double that number — all the prisoners they'd managed to take — finding space in those quarters. As if divining Hakon's thoughts, Toralv added, "They'll have to stand tonight. The shed is too small for all of them, but I could find no other place to quarter them."

"It's more than they deserve," grumbled Trygvi, who had visited with his cousin for most of the afternoon and been despondent ever since. According to Trygvi, Gudrod had mumbled and drooled like a madman in his feverish sleep. That somber news had weighed on all of their spirits.

"They won't be there long," Hakon countered.

"Why?" This question came from Sigurd, who held a cup of ale in his paw-like hands and was too tired to do anything but stare into it.

"We need them to tell us where Ragnvald is."

Tore snorted. "You expect them to talk?"

Hakon shook his head. "No. I expect it to be difficult, but we must try."

Trygvi grinned wolfishly through his bushy beard. "That is unlike you, lord."

"And what do you intend to do when you have your answer?" This question came from Egil. He was staring at Hakon intently now.

"I have not yet decided, Egil," responded Hakon as he rose and stretched his aching limbs. "The only thing that is certain right now is my need for sleep." And with that, Hakon strode into the darkness in search of a place to rest, leaving his comrades to their ale and their fire.

Hakon found Egil in the pale light of the following morning. The older man was awake and sitting on the strand, watching the bay as he ran a whetstone methodically along the blade of his seax. His back rested on the charred remains of a funeral pyre as he focused on his work.

Hakon knelt beside his friend and took in the scene. Before them, lined up along the length of the beach, were the ships of Hakon's fleet. They had lost nearly a dozen ships in the battle, and the vast number that remained stretched from one end of the beach to the other. Those that could find no space on the crowded strand floated on Kaupangskilen. A gentle breeze blew northward and the inlet waters rippled with its gentle touch. Here and there, a gull floated on the wind, searching the waters for fish to break its fast.

"Peaceful," commented Hakon.

Egil glanced at his charge, then turned his eyes to the scene before him. "Aye. A peace of sorts, I suppose. Or a moment's pause, for us at least." Egil's whetstone continued to scrape along the blade. Out in the bay, a gull spotted its prey and dove into the sea to kill it. The morning's peace slipped away.

"I need your help, Egil."

The older man nodded. "What scheme have you concocted now?"

Hakon ignored the jibe. "Come. Bring your blade."

Egil sighed and pocketed his whetstone. "Lead the way."

Hakon led Egil south along the beach to Halldor's hall. As they neared, Egil said from the corner of his mouth, "What are we doing here?"

"You'll see."

The two comrades found Halldor chopping wood outside his modest home. He stopped his labor when he saw them approaching and wiped the sweat from his forehead with the soiled sleeve of his tunic.

"I am glad to see that you yet live, Halldor," Hakon called by way of greeting. "The fighting in Kaupang was fierce."

"Thankfully, your nephews gave us fair warning before those bastards came, otherwise I would not be standing here," Halldor said, his weathered face moving from Hakon to Egil. Dark crescents still underlined his bloodshot eyes, and Hakon wondered briefly if the Night Mare still visited him at night, plaguing his mind with images of bloodshed and terror. "But I do not think you came to speak to me of that,"

Halldor continued, bringing Hakon's thoughts back to the present. "Did you?"

"No, I did not. I came to collect what is owed to me."

Halldor hefted his axe and brought it down into a log, where it lodged. "And what would that be?"

"A trip to the land of the Danes." Hakon could sense Egil's eyes turning toward him, for this was news to him as well.

Halldor grinned, deepening the lines in his face. "Pardon my manners, lord, but what business does a Northern king have in the land of the Danes?" He lifted the axe and log together and slammed them onto the stump he was using as a chopping surface. The log split in two with a crack and fell away.

"That is for us to know."

The grin vanished. "You are serious."

"I am serious." Hakon's eyes shifted to the beach, where Halldor's boat normally lay, but found no vessel there. "Where is your knarr?"

"Gone, lord. Taken by Ragnvald and his army when they retreated. You will need to find someone else to take you."

"We shall find another."

For the first time, Hakon saw genuine concern seep into the ship captain's face. "My lord. I am no warrior. Surely, there is a sword arm among your army who knows the land of the Danes as well as I."

Hakon ignored Halldor's pleas. "I would not be here if I thought someone in my army knew it better."

At that moment, the door to Halldor's home opened and a portly woman appeared in the doorway with her hands on her hips. "Halldor! I can't cook without a fire. Oh!" She bowed hastily. "I thought...I beg your pardon, my lord."

Hakon nodded to her, then shifted his gaze back to Halldor. "Gather your things and meet us on the beach tomorrow morning. Do not try to run, or I will catch you and flay you alive."

Halldor's concern had transformed to a red anger that glowed on his cheeks. It was clear he wanted to say something — mayhap curse Hakon — but he wisely held his tongue. "Aye, lord."

As they marched back to camp, Egil stroked his white beard, his mind obviously chewing on some thought. "How many ships do you plan to take on this expedition of yours?" he finally asked.

"One ship."

Egil stopped and rounded on his lord. He was scowling. "One ship?"

"Aye. A knarr."

Egil barked a laugh that dripped with incredulity. "A knarr. So we pretend to be traders, then?" He was shaking his head. "You've got some balls, boy. And how do you know Ragnvald will be there?"

Hakon said nothing for a time. "I don't. But I know he will be nursing his wounds. Chances are, he's doing that close to home. I intend to find him. But I don't want to do that with a fleet that will attract every Dane who can carry a weapon."

"And what happens when you find Ragnvald with all his men? We will have — what? — mayhap twenty men in all to fight them. That is, if we manage to make it that far. Those are some poor odds, boy."

"I know."

At midday, Toralv brought the prisoners to the beach and knelt them in a line facing Hakon and his lords. Hakon's own men surrounded them, watching the scene unfold in silence. Each prisoner had his arms tied behind his back and had been stripped of everything save his tunic and trousers. Before them was a charred log. They eyed Hakon, some defiantly, some nervously. All, it seemed, understood what fate lay before them.

"I will get straight to it," Hakon called to them. "You are my prisoners and I need information. If you provide it to me, you shall live. If you refuse, you shall die. Each of you is the master of your fate. Do you understand?"

There was no response from the prisoners; but then, Hakon had not expected one.

"We will start with you." Hakon pointed at the man on the right end of the line. The man was older and one of those who stared truculently at his executioner. "Are you Ragnvald's man?"

"Aye."

"Where is his hall?"

The man did not speak. Hakon nodded and Trygvi stepped forward. In his hands was a large, two-handed battle-axe. Trygvi moved over to the man and stared down at him. Behind the prisoner, Toralv stepped out of the crowd and leveled a spear at the man's spine.

"What is your answer?" Trygvi asked, his voice full of menace.

"Make it clean, you bastard," the man growled. He then placed his forehead on the log and started to pray. Trygvi swung his blade down and severed the man's head from his neck. The head rolled away as his body crumpled to the sand and a plume of red shot forth from his neck.

Hakon winced at the sight. It was one thing to kill a man who was trying to kill you but quite another to watch a defenseless man be executed. He absently folded his hand over the cross hanging from his neck as he asked the next man the same questions.

Fifteen men died before someone finally spoke: a boy of mayhap seventeen or eighteen winters, not much older than Hakon himself. He had tears in his eyes as he recounted what he knew — that he had never been to Ragnvald's hall but knew it to be on the eastern coast of Jutland in the land of the Danes.

"Could you find it?"

The young man nodded through his tears.

Hakon motioned to Toralv. "Unbind him."

Toralv did his lord's bidding and pulled the boy to his feet. "What is your name?"

"Harald," said the teen, wiping away his tears.

Hakon smiled at his father's name. "You have done well, to tell me what you know."

"What is to become of me?"

"You shall come with me," Hakon said. "We will see whether you speak the truth about Ragnvald's hall. If you cannot find it, you will die."

The boy looked uncertain. "And when we find Ragnvald's hall? What then?"

Hakon was in no mood for bargains or more killing. "If you live, mayhap I'll keep you. Or mayhap I shall sell you as a slave. Who knows?" Hakon took no pleasure in saying the words, but he also saw no reason to lie. Fate could be cruel.

"What of the others?" This came from Trygvi, who straddled the log, axe in hand, his blood-soaked tunic sticking to his muscular chest.

"Spare them. We need slaves to bury the dead and to help us rebuild."

Hakon turned from the grisly scene and wove his way through the blackened town and the bloated bodies, waving away seagulls and crows that protested his intrusion on their feasting. Climbing the hill to the crest, he looked about. The entire hillside was littered with wounded men. Most seemed coherent enough, though some rested quietly in the shade of the hall.

Inside the hall, moaning bodies lay upon the wall-platforms and floor, and the stench of death hung heavy in the air. Thrall women moved among the men, dressing wounds and wiping sweat-beaded, bloodless faces. One woman swept the crimson rushes toward the door while another tossed fresh pine needles onto the turf. It did little to curb the smell.

Hakon ignored the stares of the thralls and strode to the door of Gudrod's bedchamber. He entered as quietly as he could and sat on a stool beside Gudrod's bed. Small flames sputtered in their wall sconces, casting everything in a soft, quivering light. Gudrod shivered beneath his fur blanket. It seemed impossible that he could sleep with his teeth chattering as they did, yet he did not stir at Hakon's presence. Hakon rested his hand on his nephew's clammy forehead just below the line of the bandage that covered his head. It burned with fever.

"I do not know if you can hear me, Gudrod, but we are leaving to find Ragnvald. Thorgil and Gudmund, the Swede, are dead. I will not stop until Ragnvald is too. I shall pray for your strength and your recovery." He patted his nephew's hands. "Rest now."

Hakon retreated from the bedchamber and grabbed the first thrall he could find. He was an older fellow with a white shock of hair and barely a tooth in his mouth. "Go and fill a bucket with cold sea water, then bring it to your lord's bedside. Douse rags in it and lay them across your lord's forehead. Replace the rag every time you feel it warming. Do not rest in this until his fever breaks or he is dead. Do you understand me?"

"Aye, lord." The words slurred from his toothless mouth.

Hakon patted him on the shoulder and exited the hall.

That afternoon, he found Trygvi surveying the damage to his ship with his helmsmen and a bald fellow he did not recognize. The strakes to either side of the prow post had been cracked where the ship had rammed the enemy vessel in the sea battle.

"How bad is it?" Hakon asked.

Trygvi glanced at this uncle. "Not bad. We'll need to rove some new strakes onto her, but Orm here thinks he can get it done soon." He motioned to the bald man.

"That is good, for I need you to sail north as soon as you can."

"North? We just came from there."

Hakon pulled Trygvi aside, away from the prying ears of his men. "I need to you go farther north. To the Uplands."

Trygvi's bushy brows arched. "The Uplands?"

"Aye. Take your ship and what men you need, for I doubt they'll take kindly to a new jarl appearing in their midst so quickly."

"A new jarl? I am to see a new jarl placed over the Uplands?"

Hakon grinned at his dull-witted kinsman until understanding crept into the older man's brain.

"Oh! Me? I am to be jarl of the Uplands?"

Hakon's grin blossomed into a wide smile. "Aye. I give you the Uplands to rule for me. But," he cautioned, "you will need men and supplies. It may come to a fight. My guess is that there are still some men there who are oath-sworn to Thorgil and his family. And you will have the Swedes to contend with, who may wish to avenge Gudmund. Best to go as soon as you can to stake your claim."

"What about you? Will you not come to see the Uplands kneel to your rule?"

"I wish I could, but Ragnvald still lives. Once he is dead, I will come. In the meantime, take my standard as proof of my support."

Trygvi nodded. "I understand, and I thank you." He reached out and grabbed Hakon's wrist.

"There is nothing to thank me for. You have deserved it. I look forward to feasting in Ringsaker with you, Trygvi."

Hakon left his nephew then and went in search of Egil. It was time to prepare for his trip to Ragnvald's hall.

He found his hirdman down on the shingle, yelling at a bunch of warriors to make themselves useful. They scattered like rats before the broom as the old warrior berated them. "Damn coal-eaters," he growled as Hakon neared. "Here we are preparing to sail into the dragon's lair and your crew is resting like a bunch of dogs who've been fed too many scraps." He spat.

"So you've found a ship?"

"Aye." He waved a hand at the knarr resting at anchor near the shore. She was an old ship with side strakes that looked like they'd scraped many a jetty in her time. "She's a little loose in the strakes," he said, meaning she wasn't completely watertight. "But we'll have her ready in time. We'll be packing her with pitch and down as soon as those lazy fools return."

"What's she called?"

"*Sea horse*."

"Storage?"

"Plenty of room amidships, beneath the planking."

Hakon nodded appreciatively. They would need that for the weapons and supplies they planned to take. "Who is coming?"

"Well, now, that was a trick. It's a fool's errand we're on, so I sought out fools willing to go. Turns out, your army is full of them, all clamoring to get themselves killed, so I had to narrow it down. Chose only the best fighters and sailors, plus those we have to take, like Halldor and the boy, Harald. Toralv and I are coming. As is Ottar — he refused to stay even though his shoulder is useless. You. Gudrod's men Geir and Bjorn. Bard, Bjarke, Asmund, and Garth," he said, referring to some of the other men who had been with Hakon since the previous summer. "Several others. I'm leaving the younger boys here, or what's left of them anyway. They have no place on a crowded ship."

Hakon breathed a little easier. It was a formidable crew. "You have done well, Egil."

"We shall see about that, boy," he said, then growled at Toralv who was carrying a barrel of hot pitch by himself. "Stop your showing off, and get some help, you fool. You'll be worn before we even cast off. Not to mention burned to death by the pitch if you trip and fall."

Hakon smiled at his old hirdman and left him to the preparations.

Chapter 26

The night was dark, the moon's glow shielded by a solid layer of cloud. The only light came from the small fires crackling on the top of the earthen rampart that loomed before Hakon and his men — a rampart on which two guards strolled, keeping their tired eyes on the fjord that stretched eastward and on the horse track that meandered southwest to King Gorm's hall at Jelling.

Horsens. That was the name of this place, and it was formidable, though Hakon had expected nothing less. Beyond that rampart lay Ragnvald's hall and a maze of structures that supported it. Guest halls, storage sheds, a smithy, trading stalls, and more. Though Hakon had not seen them firsthand, he could picture them in his mind, for Harald had been thorough in his description of Ragnvald's lair. If they managed to get over the wall, they would then need to navigate the maze undetected.

And then there was the hall. Within it were at least fifty men, mayhap more, for two ships rocked against the jetty down by the harbor. Though it was late, Hakon could hear the distant murmur of the feasting and knew that if things did not go as planned, he and his men would be in for a fight — a thought that set his heart to thumping.

Hakon and his men had crossed the Skagerrak from West Agder three days before, leaving at nightfall to cover as much dark sea as possible before the sun's light came again. For two days, they traveled aboard the knarr, sometimes under sail, sometimes at oar. When the coast of Jutland revealed itself in the distance, Halldor turned the knarr's prow east until he found the middle of the channel known as Kattegat. There he turned south, keeping well away from land until he could avoid it no longer. It was risky to sail so far from the shore, as storms were common, but the coastline held its own set of dangers.

Only one ship stopped and questioned them on their southward journey, and in that moment Halldor stepped forward, explaining to the curious Danes that they came with goods to trade at Hedeby. He handled it with the ease of someone accustomed to such questioning, and Hakon silently thanked God that Halldor was with them. For their part, the Danes eyed the knarr dubiously, but ultimately had no stomach to dispute the claim. Whether it was the swords hanging at the sailors' hips or Halldor's offer of a keg of ale, Hakon knew not, but whatever it was, it softened their vigilance and they allowed Hakon and his men to pass.

It was Harald who guided them past Sams Island and into the fjord in which Horsens lay. There, they hid on a beach until the veil of darkness fell and they could press on up the fjord, sticking close to the north shore and away from the watchful eyes of the guards up on the rampart. When they could go no farther, Halldor guided the ship into a forested coastline where the shade of trees offered some protection from prying eyes.

Now they were here, staring silently at Ragnvald's lair in the deep silence of night. Hakon glanced over at Halldor, who knelt beside him in the tall grass of the field just to the north of the walls, his face a mask of concern. He was not a warrior and had not wanted to come this night. He would have much preferred to remain on the ship with the prisoner Harald. But Hakon could not risk it. How easy it would be for him to cast off and leave Hakon and his men stranded, just as he had the priests all those months ago. No, tonight Halldor would remain in Hakon's sight.

Hakon thought briefly of the boy, Harald, who was tied up, gagged, and guarded by Asmund to prevent him from escaping or warning anyone. The boy had served them well. As a reward, Hakon would give him his freedom when they returned to Kaupang. If they returned to Kaupang. The boy, he knew, would not wander far, for he had aided his lord's killer; if word of that spread, he would be hunted and killed. His safety lay with Hakon now.

Hakon's thoughts floated back to the present. To his hammering chest and the pumping blood in his temples and the breeze that whispered across the waters of the fjord where Ragnvald's ships floated. Hakon blinked his stinging eyes. He had not slept in over a day. There would be no rest this night, either.

Egil nudged him and looked up at the sky. The darkness was fading. Dawn would soon be upon them. Hakon listened. Within the walls, there was no sound. "It is time," Egil whispered.

Hakon nodded and sent out the signal: an owl hoot.

Toralv responded instantly and tossed a stone off to his right, away from their approach. It landed with a thud and a rustle of brush that in the still night sounded like a boar on the move. Up on the wall, the guards turned to the sound and approached with spears at the ready. At the same time, Hakon slipped forward, holding his breath as he picked his way through the knee-high grass and clawed up the muddy wall. For a long time, the guards stared out into the darkness, away from where Hakon lay. Somewhere across from him, Ottar lay in a similar position, waiting for the guards to draw closer.

Seeing nothing, the guards strolled back to their spots. One walked so close to Hakon's head he nearly stepped on it. But his eyes were trained on the field, not his feet, and so he passed within inches of Hakon's prone body and back toward the warmth of his fire.

Hakon slipped his knife — the knife that had been his mother's — from its sheath and crept onto the rampart, where he hopped to his feet. Sensing movement, the guard turned, but not in time. Hakon's blade winked in the firelight as it slashed the man's neck, opening his windpipe and shattering his vocal chords before he could scream. Hakon then pushed him from the top of the rampant and down toward the field where Hakon's men waited and where he would die in the mud. On the far rampart stood Ottar, who waved.

Hakon didn't hesitate. He grabbed a burning log from the guard's fire, careful to keep his eyes averted from the flames, and slid down the muddy wall toward Ragnvald's dwellings. Reaching the bottom, he sheathed his knife and pulled his seax. And there he waited as one by one his men appeared beside him with their weapons drawn and their shields up. Instinctively, they formed a shield wall as they waited for Ottar to join them and arm himself. In the light of the burning log, Hakon could see him grit his teeth as he hefted his shield and his damaged shoulder protested the added weight. Beside him, Halldor's eyes were as round as two full moons on a clear summer night.

Without a word, the warriors moved forward in single file, Egil in the lead. They scooted from shadow to shadow as they made their way through the maze of buildings to the mead hall. To conceal their movements, they wore no armor, but their belts and straps creaked nonetheless. Hakon cringed at the sound, and at every footfall, praying that Ragnvald's men were too drunk to notice and that none of his servants were about at this late hour.

And then, suddenly, Ragnvald's hall appeared in the darkness before them, its dark walls towering over the men. Egil motioned to Hakon, who turned with his flaming log to Toralv, Bjorn, Bjarke, and Geir, all of whom produced torches from their belts. Once lit, Toralv and Bjorn cast their torches up onto the thatched roofing at the rear of the hall. The men then moved left in the direction of the hall's entrance. Halfway there, they tossed the remaining torches up into the thatch. Hakon followed with his burning log.

Inside the hall, Ragnvald's hounds began to bark.

"Damn dogs," Egil hissed. "Hurry now."

But just as the group reached the main entrance and moved to secure the door, a man stumbled out into the darkness with a sword in his hand. He was obviously drunk and staggered a few steps before his mind grasped his danger. It was the last thought that crossed his mind, for Egil slashed his throat with his seax and his body crumpled wordlessly to the ground.

Two hounds came at his heels, their matted hair and gnashing teeth blurs of motion as they tore out of the door in search of prey. Ottar got his spear up just in time to puncture one of the beast's chests as it leaped for his throat. The momentum of the dog's attack knocked him on his ass even as it died on his blade. The second man — Garth — took the hound's attack on his shield, then slashed his blade down across the animal's back. The dog yelped and backed away, only to be killed by a stroke from Hakon's seax.

The entire attack had taken mere seconds, but it was enough to awaken everyone in the hall. The screams of women blended with the shouts of angry warriors as they scrambled for safety or for their weapons. On the roof, the flames grew and the smoke thickened.

"Axe!" Toralv yelled as he slammed the main door shut with his shoulder and slid the sliding handle into locking position. To prevent the men on the inside from sliding the bolt back, Garth drove his axe deep into the wooden door at the end of the slide.

"Spears!"

Ottar, Bjorn, and three others planted the butts of their weapons into the mud and jammed the points into the wood of the door. They held them firm as inside the hall, men smashed against their only escape. The force of their efforts drove the spear butts more deeply into the soil. Again they hammered on the door, and again the door held.

The roof was now a giant flame that licked high into the sky and sent its wicked ash and smoke down onto the heads of anyone near the inferno, its heat so intense that the men moved away to save themselves. In the hall, Ragnvald's warriors hacked desperately at the door with axes and swords. Toralv jabbed his own blade back into the holes at the men trying to escape, seemingly impervious to the heat that scorched his dark hair and the smoke that choked his breath.

"Shield wall!" It was Egil who shouted these words. He had been watching the buildings for signs of trouble, and the trouble had come. The men spun to face the new threat, and in that moment, Hakon knew that they were doomed.

Chapter 27

The men who approached came in order. Dozens of them, with shields and byrnies and helmets that reflected the glow of the climbing flames. They came in rows from the direction of the harbor, up a wide path that led straight to the door of Ragnvald's hall.

Hakon ran back to his friend. "Toralv! Come away! You'll burn, man!"

"But they'll escape!" he hollered.

"We have bigger problems!"

Hakon pulled him by the sleeve back to the shield wall to face the newly arrived threat — a threat that had stopped twenty paces away. Hakon looked left and right. There were smaller alleyways there that offered an escape, but Egil cut that notion short.

"Don't even think about it, Hakon," he called above the roar of the fire. "There is no way I'm letting you die with a blade in your back. Nor will I."

Hakon glanced at his men. Not one of them looked ready to run. Ottar even grinned as he studied the approaching spear-warriors. Hakon's pride in them soared even as his gut twisted, for as their leader, it was up to him to lead them to their fate — a fate that looked grimmer and grimmer by the moment.

"Lock shields!" Hakon called as he positioned himself in the center of the line. "Svinfylking!" Hakon yelled, calling for the boar's snout formation. As the head of the boar, it would be up to Hakon to smash

his way as deeply into the enemy line as possible. His men would follow, and with any luck, some would make it through to safety.

His men roared at the new foemen, cursing them as they brandished
their weapons and psyched themselves up for the bloodshed that
would soon follow. Before them, the byrnie-clad men stood silently,
which was strange. Hakon had never known warriors to make no
sound in the face of a fight. *Why do they not yell back? Do their hearts
not hammer in their chests? Does the blood not course in their veins?* In
the end, he decided it didn't matter. He would fight them regardless
and kill as many of the bastards as he could — a thought that made
him yell all the louder.

"Now!" he screamed, and charged.

Before him, the enemy parted and a warlord stepped forward. He
wore a polished byrnie that hung to his knees and a conical helmet
with a nosepiece that partially obscured his face. In his left hand was a
long sword. The warlord raised his left hand and shouted with a voice
that carried above the din, "Stop!"

Hakon felt his legs slow and the men behind him falter. The attack
ended not ten paces after it began.

"Who are you?" the warlord called.

Hakon stepped forward. "My name is King Hakon," he huffed. "I am
the son of Harald and the vanquisher of my brother Erik, whom men
call Bloodaxe."

The man's laughter filled the space between them. He removed his
helmet then, releasing a mane of strawberry blond hair that framed his
angular, mirth-filled face. He was mayhap in his late twenties, though
it was hard to say in the swirling smoke. "Hakon, you say? King of
the Northmen?"

That last comment made Hakon tighten the grip on his sword. "Aye.
You find that funny?" he asked as the man continued to smile at him.

"I find it funny that two kings should be in the same spot, at this time
of the night, with the same notion. The chances of that are as slim as
throwing a dart through a keyhole from across a mead hall." Which

was a long way of saying that he did not know that Hakon would be there, so he had not come to fight. "The gods surely had a hand in this."

Hakon relaxed a bit. "Who are you? And why are you here?"

"My men call me Gorm. I am king among the Danes, and I am here for the same reason as you — to end some unfinished business." He waved his sword at the burning hall.

As if on his command, Hakon heard the hall's roof collapse. He glanced behind him in time to see a plume of ash shoot into the sky and a rush of flame engulf the building and the people inside of it. The screams in the hall swelled, then ever so slowly died away. Somewhere in the inferno, Ragnvald burned. Hakon imagined the Dane roaring in impotent rage as the fire seared his eyes and filled his lungs and blistered his skin, bringing death slowly and painfully to him. It was gruesome, yes, and yet Hakon didn't care, for it was the death Ragnvald so deserved, his sentence for the destruction and misery he had brought to Kaupang and so many other settlements and homesteads besides.

Hakon turned back to the Danish king. "You came to kill Ragnvald?'

The mirth drained from his face. "I gave him warriors and ships — an entire army — and he lost them all to you. Worse, he abandoned them as they fought. And yet he still had the nerve to slink back to his holdings like a nithing and feast his survival." Gorm spat. "He deserves the death you have brought to him."

Hakon gripped his sword a little tighter, for in those words Gorm held Hakon accountable for the deaths of his men, and that thought put him on edge. "So what now?" Hakon ventured. He was in no mood to face the Danes if it could be avoided and thought better than to challenge the king directly. Best to leave his fate as an open question.

Gorm considered his answer carefully. More than once, his eyes scanned the burning hall and the group of Northmen standing before him before he finally issued a verdict. "The ways of the gods are strange, are they not? They must be laughing in their hall this night to see two kings — two enemies — come together like this. I suppose they would want us to fight. They would want me to avenge the death of my men. But I understand too that my men died well with their face to the enemy, an enemy who has far more courage than the coward to whom I entrusted my men. So rather than kill you now, I will thank you for finishing the job. There will be other days to fight, of that I am certain, Hakon."

Hakon bristled at Gorm's words but held his tongue lest he say something dim-witted and get his men killed.

Gorm stepped aside and his men cleared a path. Hesitantly at first, and then with more confidence, Hakon and his men strode past them and back to their ship. The Danes made no move to interfere.

Epilogue

An ungentle nudge woke Hakon with a start. He scrambled to his feet, his seax in his hand.

"Whoa!" Toralv backed away with surprising dexterity. "Easy, lord. It's me. Toralv."

Hakon was inside his tent, where all was shadow. The glow of Lade's summer twilight found its way through the tent flap, backlighting the towering form of Toralv and bedimming his features. Hakon rubbed at his face to remove the cobwebs of sleep. "What is it?" he asked.

"The child has arrived."

"The child?"

"The reason why we're here," Toralv explained in mock exasperation.

"I know why we're here, Toralv," Hakon grumbled as he pulled on his trousers. "Is he healthy? How fares Bergliot?"

Toralv shrugged. "I've only just heard that the child was born. I came straight away to tell you."

Hakon sheathed his blade and followed his friend out of the tent and into the sea of still-smoldering campfires, around which his men were beginning to stir. Hakon found the sleeping form of his nephew, Gudrod, and nudged him with his boot.

"Wake up," Hakon said. "Sigurd's had a child."

Gudrod grunted and sat up, rubbing the sleep from his one good eye. By the grace of God, he had recovered in full, though his left eye was now blind from the blow he had received to his head. Hakon had brought him to Lade in part to get him away from the ruin of Kaupang, and in part to put some spirit back into his soul, for the loss of his sight in that eye had depressed him greatly. "Couldn't Bergliot have waited for a more decent hour to give birth?" he muttered.

Hakon smiled at his surliness, for that was just the spirit he had hoped to rekindle. "Mayhap we should be blaming the child," he responded. "I don't think Bergliot had much choice in the matter."

Gudrod laughed as he rose and brushed the dirt from his clothes. "That is true. Let us hope he grows to be a bit more respectful of his elders' time...and sleep."

Around them, other guests were also beginning to stir. They too had been beckoned by Sigurd to witness the birth of his child. Hakon just hoped, as they wove their way through the guests to the entrance of Sigurd's estate, that the child had been born in good health, sparing Sigurd the embarrassment of an ill-born bairn.

Sigurd stood in the courtyard outside his hall, hugging those who stood about. Hakon forced his way to the jarl, who opened his arms when he saw his king.

"What's the news?" Hakon asked.

"Bergliot has given birth to a boy."

"Is he hale?"

"Aye!"

A healthy boy. So Sigurd had been right all along. The thought brought a wide smile to Hakon's face. He embraced the jarl, who crushed his king in a bear hug and lifted him from his feet.

"A boy!" Sigurd repeated, shaking Hakon now in his grip. "Did I not tell you?"

Hakon laughed. "I am happy for you, my friend. How fares Bergliot?"

"Tired but hale. She sleeps. Come!" he said suddenly, pulling Hakon by the arm. "We must name the child."

"Now?"

"Aye, now. The boy must have a name, and I can think of no better man to name him than the king. Come!" Sigurd bulled his way through the crowd with Hakon in tow. "Make way."

They entered the hall, which was now filled with bleary-eyed guests awakened by the commotion and the cries of a newborn. Sigurd pushed his way to the dais, where Astrid stood with a bundle of cloth bobbing gently in her arms. Hakon smiled at her as he stepped up onto the dais behind the jarl. She grinned at him in return, though it was plain to see that her cheer was muted by her fatigue. The dark rings under her eyes and the disarray of her auburn ringlets bespoke a sleepless night at her mother's side. Still, the sight of her brought a heat to Hakon's cheeks.

With his thick index finger, Sigurd delicately peeled back the wrap that partially covered the child's crimson, crying face. Sigurd smiled and took the bundle, ignoring the baby's shrill howls. He then held the screaming child aloft to the gathered guests, who cheered their jarl and his son. Hakon joined them.

Still holding the child in his arms, Sigurd spoke. "As you all know, my father's name was Hakon, the same name held by the king who stands beside me. And for good reason, for it was I who gave your king his name." He nodded to Hakon. "I knew not at the time how wise my choice would prove to be. But now I know. This Hakon is as earnest in his pursuits, as fair in his dealings, and as stout in his battles as my father ever was. And yes, he is also as strong in his beliefs as my father was in his. It is for these reasons that I shall call my son Hakon as well. May he enjoy the same success as his namesakes!"

Sigurd's words robbed Hakon of speech. While it was customary for a man to name his child after his ancestor, it was certainly not necessary to honor others by the same name or to laud their accomplishments as Sigurd had done. The fact that Sigurd had spoken the words made them all the more meaningful, for Sigurd always spoke from the heart, for better or worse. His speech touched Hakon deeply.

"Come, Hakon," Sigurd commanded.

Hakon dipped his fingers into the cup of water proffered to him by Astrid and sprinkled a few drops onto the baby's forehead. "Welcome to this world, Hakon Sigurdsson," Hakon proclaimed. "May you grow as strong and wise as your forebears."

Sigurd slowly handed the child to Hakon, who took the screaming bundle awkwardly and turned to the gathered crowd. They cheered the child again, and as they did, Hakon glanced at Astrid. Tears streamed down her cheeks despite the smile that graced her face. He smiled back at her. In his arms, the baby screamed and fought for release from his swaddle. Hakon laughed at his struggle and wondered if one day they might fight together in the shield wall as Sigurd and Hakon had done...and would surely do again.

For Erik's sons were out there somewhere. And when they came, there would be war.

Historical Notes

There is more fiction in this novel than in the previous novel, *God's Hammer*, due to the fact that less is known of this exact period in time. There is no real timeline citing when certain fights or political moves happened or how close in proximity to Erik's departure they happened. Hence, I chose those I thought might make the most sense and the best story.

We know, for instance, that Erik left his Norwegian realm circa AD 935 and appears again in the Orkney Islands and later, in Scotland and England, though we don't know any of the details surrounding his departure. We also know that Erik never returns to Norway, though why is not clear. In *Raven's Feast*, I've provided one explanation, though I freely admit there are no facts to back up that portion of the story.

After Erik's departure there is no mention of immediate challengers to Hakon, though the historical texts hint at unrest. Hakon spends more time in Erik's power base in the west, presumably to show his strength in that region and to thwart any return by Erik or Erik's sons. They also tell of Danes harrying the Vik and of Hakon giving control of the Vik to his nephew Gudrod. I used these historical clues to manufacture a plausible tale about opportunists — in this case Ragnvald, Thorgil, and Gudmund — seeking to capture land and fame in the power vacuum left by Erik.

Of the women in Hakon's life, nothing is known. History speaks of no brides or love interests, or of a daughter for Sigurd; yet it is likely that some love interests did exist. Thus, I created Aelfwin, Groa, and Astrid.

Sigurd, Tore, Gudrod, Trygvi, Toralv, and Egil are all mentioned in Hakon's history. In fact, Gudrod and Trygvi factor mightily into the ongoing story of ancient Norway, as does Sigurd's son, Hakon.

Old Norse and Old English are challenging languages for the modern reader, especially where character names and place names are concerned. That is further compounded by the fact that one name might appear in ancient texts with multiple spellings. For instance, the name Hakon appears as Hakon, Hacon, Haakon, Hákon, and so forth. Other Norse names just seemed too rigorous to use in their original form, such as Þrœndalǫg (Trondelag). Early on, I decided to adhere to names that were as historically accurate as possible but that would not tear the reader from the story. I realize that to some readers, close adherence to actual names and place names (where known) is important. My hope is that readers will accept the names I've chosen as decent replacements.

One of the main themes of both this book and the previous book, *God's Hammer*, is Christianity. In AD 935, it is known that Christianity was practiced in parts of Denmark and Sweden. However, nothing is known of Christianity in Norway, and it seems that *if* there were Christians there, they kept a very low profile. When Hakon arrives, he faces immediate skepticism from the nobles because of his religion. Hakon, however, seems undeterred, calling for a "bishop and teachers" to come from England, and for his close followers to be baptized. He eats only fish on Fridays and keeps his Sundays, and refuses in many instances to accept the sacrifice. He even changes the date of the Yule to more closely coincide with Christmas. These things only heighten the rift between his people and him — a rift that comes close to war with Sigurd's nobles at some point during his reign. That faith to which Hakon clings will prove to be a constant thorn in his side, yet there is no indication that he completely abandons it, despite the pressure he receives from his subjects to do so.

Hakon has now succeeded in becoming the dominant ruler in the North, yet his nephews and the Danes are still out there, waiting.

Dear reader,

We hope you enjoyed reading *Raven's Feast*. Please take a moment to leave a review in Amazon, even if it's a short one. Your opinion is important to us.

The story continues in *War King*.

Discover more books by Eric Schumacher at https://www.nextchapter.pub/authors/eric-schumacher-historical-fiction-author

Want to know when one of our books is free or discounted for Kindle? Join the newsletter at http://eepurl.com/bqqB3H

Best regards,

Eric Schumacher and the Next Chapter Team

About the Author

You might say that Eric Schumacher lives with one foot in the future and one in the past. By day, he runs his own award-winning PR agency, Neology, and shares stories with the press about the kind of future he believes his technology clients can deliver. By night (or frankly, whenever he can find the time), Eric wanders into his passion and unearths stories about people living in turbulent times.

Eric was born in Los Angeles in 1968. He is the author of two historical fiction novels, *God's Hammer* and its sequel, *Raven's Feast*. Both tell the story of the first Christian king of Viking Norway, Hakon Haraldsson, and his struggles to gain and hold the High Seat of his realm.

Eric's fascination with Vikings and medieval history began at a young age, though exactly why is not clear. While Los Angeles has its own unique history, there are no destroyed monasteries or Viking burial sites or hidden hoards buried in fields. Still, from the earliest age, he was drawn to books about Viking kings and warlords and was fascinated by their stories and the turbulent times in which they lived.

He began writing as a child, though never considered it as a career until he was in his second year of international business school and living in Germany. Poor timing given school loans but hey -- better late than never. It was there that Eric began researching and writing *God's Hammer*, his first novel.

Eric now resides in Santa Barbara with his wife, his two children, and his dog, Peanut.

He can be found here:
Website: ericschumacher.net
Facebook: www.facebook.com/EricSchumacherAuthor
Twitter: @DarkAgeScribe

Made in the USA
Coppell, TX
23 January 2020